THE RED

LABYRINTH

THE RED LABYRINTH

First Edition
First Printing, 2019

Book design by Jake Nordby
Cover design by Jake Nordby
Cover images by Sergey Nivens/Shutterstock, faestock/ Shutterstock

Flux, an imprint of North Star Editions, Inc.

This is a work of fiction. Names, characters, places, and incidents are either the product of the author's imagination or are used fictitiously, and any resemblance to actual persons living or dead, business establishments, events, or locales is entirely coincidental. Cover models used for illustrative purposes only and may not endorse or represent the book's subject.

Library of Congress Cataloging-in-Publication Data (pending)
978-1-63583-034-7 (paperback)
978-1-63583-047-7 (hardcover)

Flux
North Star Editions, Inc.
2297 Waters Drive
Mendota Heights, MN 55120
www.fluxnow.com

Printed in the United States of America

To all my wonderful friends, who always have my back—even when I write stories as bizarre as this one.

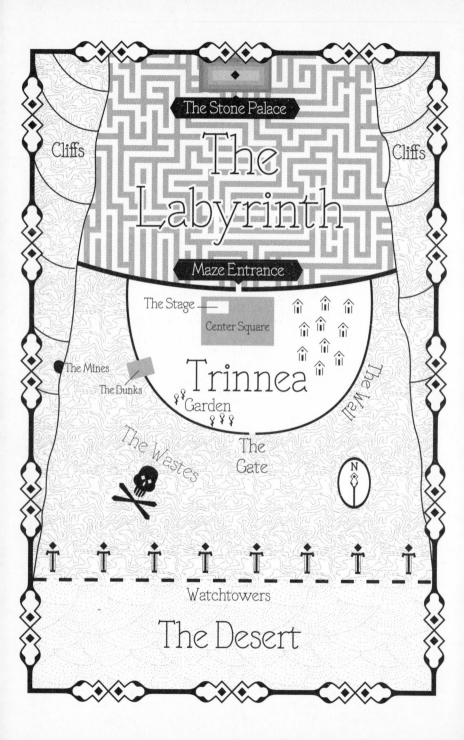

PART ONE
TRINNEA

I shouldn't have to be here. All week, I told Ma the same thing: I'd rather stick my face into a fire pit than go to the Waterday Festival. Yet here I am, weaving through the throng of people, my right hand latched onto the strap of Ma's shoulder bag to avoid losing her in the crowd. The sweet scent of sugar dough mixes with the savory aroma of warm spices in the air, but my stomach is too busy churning to eat.

"This is a mess," I mutter, shouldering past a guy pushing a honey-straw cart. A little girl holding an armful of overflowing water jugs skips past, and a few droplets slosh onto my sleeve. I wipe it off, but quickly slam my hand back to my pant leg so the passerby can't glimpse the brands on my palm.

"It's tradition," Ma replies, giving me a half-smile. She takes a bite from a sweet roll and offers it to me, but I shake my head. "You can't miss the celebration."

She says it lightheartedly, but the undertone is there; I *can't* miss the Waterday celebration, because it's mandatory for every Trinnean to attend. No one's allowed to leave the festival until the Leader gives his address. I have to scan my thumbprint again before I leave, so no one can say I skipped out early. I'm sure the city guards would love nothing more than an excuse to throw me in the stocks for a week.

"Besides," Ma adds, "we can't *not* get some of James's cactilixer—especially at the festival discount price. And we can't miss the Leader's address."

I'd love to miss all of it. I hate the Leader's address. They always bribe some poor little Blank kid from the wasteland or the bunks onto the stage in this humiliating water jug hat. The kid becomes the star of an awkward presentation about Trinnea's history and the drought, in exchange for a little cash. I always feel so bad for whoever they get. Probably because for years, it could've easily been me.

Someone knocks into my side, way too rough to be an accident. I grimace, keeping my head down. The woman glares at me, daring me to confront her. Of course, I can't—not unless I want a fist in my eye. "Just until the address," I say. "Then I'm going home."

Ma sighs. "Whatever you say, Zadie."

I follow her down the closest aisle, lined with stands. My pulse hasn't stopped ticking like a bomb since the second I got downtown. It's like I've been holding my breath for the past twenty minutes, waiting to go home and let it all out.

The normally vacant Center Square is jam-packed with wooden stalls selling spiced breads, fried dough balls, and stinky cheeses spider-webbed with blue mold. Other booths carry various elixirs and remedies, their stalls covered with glass bottles filled with colorful liquids. Little kids swarm around game booths, using their telekinesis and levitation Skills to knock over all the pins and win prizes. Excitement brims in their eyes. The only emotion I can muster is indifference.

My half-sister, Chantry, patrols the next aisle with a fellow guard. Their silver uniforms parade their authority to everyone in Trinnea. They just started their cycles of mandatory guard duty all Skilled must complete. That's something I'll never get to do. Not that people with zero Skills would be very useful guarding anything. Chantry whispers something to the other guard with her—her friend Nina, who's a total jerk. I duck lower, trying to stay out of their view.

"They're not talking about you," Ma whispers in my ear. Usually her super-hearing Skill is obnoxious, but sometimes it helps. "Chantry asked her friend about some attractive guy they met at the Tap Room. Don't worry."

"Thanks." I'm sure she's lying. Chantry isn't interested in guys, attractive or not.

I scan the crowd, searching for Landon. He's got to be here somewhere—he wouldn't leave me alone for this. Plus, I doubt his admirers would let him miss this festival even if he legally could. I shoot him a message on my comm: *Just got to the festival. You here?*

I rotate the device in my hands, my heart fluttering like hummingbird wings. But the screen stays black and quiet.

Ma shoots me a knowing smile. "Is Landon here?"

"I don't know."

A yellow banner stretches across the aisle above our heads, proclaiming *Happy Waterday: Celebrating 178 Years—Praise the Leader!* I follow Ma, snaking between people, all the way to the front of the Square by the giant wooden stage. The stage is used for everything from ceremonies to supply drops to executions. Today, it's decorated for the festival, covered in pink and yellow desert blossoms. Commissioned paintings on easels display pictures of noteworthy people and scenes of the old world before the drought. The largest portrait of the Great Leader himself hangs in the middle, old and wise and gazing down on us. I roll my eyes. If you ask me, he's not worth celebrating. Too bad no one ever asks me anything.

I do a double take at the smallest portrait on the end. Someone painted a picture of Landon, my best friend, with a sultry look on his face. I guess I shouldn't be surprised to see his face beaming down at me from the portraits of famous people, but still. He's got his arms crossed and a dangerous glint in his eyes. The words *All Hail Limitless Landon—Trinnea's Hero* are painted in swirly blue letters over his blond head. Those familiar butterflies churn to life in my stomach, and I look away.

Ma stops at a jewelry booth sporting dozens of shiny beads.

"What do you think of these crystals?" Ma cradles a string of shimmery blue gems in her hand.

The shopkeeper beams. "Those are one of a kind, from a supply drop last year."

"The Leader provides," Ma says proudly.

"The Leader provides," the man echoes.

I sigh, fiddling with my communicator. We can't afford real crystals, so I don't know why Ma's even looking.

A couple little Skilled kids tiptoe past me, heading toward the stage—and the labyrinth behind it. My skin prickles, and I can't look away. The rough, red clay walls tower high over everyone's heads.

"Dare you to run up to the entrance," the boy says. He's got dark brown skin, curly hair, and a gold pendant on his chest worth several times what Ma makes in a year.

"No way." The girl shudders, making the blonde pigtails framing her pale face quiver. "I dare you to get really close and say his name."

The boy puffs out his chest, but fear glimmers in his eyes. "I'll totally do it."

"You totally won't."

It's a common dare—to stand against the labyrinth wall and say Dex's name aloud. They say it summons him, and he'll grab the speaker immediately and drag them inside. I don't know if anyone's been brave enough to try it and find out.

The kids crouch by the corner of the stage and peek out. I roll my eyes; they think they're being sneaky, but it's so obvious they're trying to catch a glimpse inside the labyrinth. The foggy maze entrance behind the stage always draws at least a couple troublemakers who don't take the warnings seriously.

Our immortal Leader built this labyrinth centuries ago to protect his palace, at the other end of the maze. Legend has it, he wanted to ensure only those who truly deserved his consult, who were brave enough to weather the labyrinth's dangers, could complete the maze and reach him. It's the only way to see him face to face; he usually communicates with us through a giant screen. But no one's ever completed it—or even survived more than a couple minutes inside—so I'd say it's impossible. Especially when Dex lurks in its corridors.

I bite my lip. Drawing attention to myself isn't at the top of my list today, but I'm not about to let these kids wander inside and fall under permanent hypnosis. Time for a little intervention before they get any closer.

I take a deep breath and tiptoe toward the kids. "Psst. Hey."

They both jump, but turn their attention toward me. They're only about nine years old, but they're still Skilled, so I keep my branded palms out of sight.

"You've heard that Dex eats children so he can absorb their Skills, right?" I say, biting back a smile.

"Nuh-uh," the boy snipes back.

The girl stares.

"It's true." Actually, no one knows what's true about Dex, but I've heard these stories enough times that they're basically fact around here.

"My Pa says Dex was born in the maze," the little girl says, her eyes wide. "And absorbed some of its magic."

I shoot a glance at the too-close labyrinth, barely twenty feet away, trying to keep my heart from hammering. "That's one theory."

"That's not true." The boy whirls on her. "He was a Trinnean kid, abandoned at the labyrinth entrance."

The girl puts her hands on her hips. "You don't know that."

"Actually," I cut in before their raised voices attract any unwanted attention, "no one knows for sure." Anyone who gets close enough to learn the truth loses their mind before they can share. They usually end up in the asylum, if they aren't killed in the maze first. "You shouldn't stand so close to the entrance, though. Otherwise he might . . . jump out and grab you!"

They gasp.

"Delilah!" A woman with her lips pressed tightly together

marches toward them. "Delilah Anne, I swear to the Leader, if you're within ten feet of that maze . . ."

The kids both stiffen at once. "Go, go, go," Delilah whispers, pushing the boy back toward the crowd and away from the labyrinth.

I slink back into the shadows before the angry woman can see me. A slight smile twitches across my face. It's nice talking to people who don't immediately hurl insults at me, even if they are little kids. And really, they're lucky I was here. I'm not sure whose bright idea it was not to station guards outside the labyrinth entrance for the festival. If Dex was going to creep out of the maze and steal his next victim, this would be an opportune time, with everyone drinking too much grog and wandering around the Square.

I shiver thinking about it. With a quick glance left to right, I hustle back to where Ma stands, still examining the expensive crystals. "Can we keep walking?"

Ma puts the string of shiny beads back on their tray. "Where do you want to go?" She wraps a brown cloth around her head, protecting her neck and face from the desert sun burning in a sea of blue above us. Almost everyone around us wears either a scarf or a floppy hat, as the Leader picked the hottest hours of the day for this. My insides are practically boiling in my brown leather jacket, but it's better than frying my skin in the sun. Dry heat smothers my face like a blanket. "Want to check out Court Jentry's stand?" she continues, even though I'm only half listening. "Maybe he'll cut a bargain on that cured meat you love so much."

My fingers jitter against my thighs. "Maybe, yeah. Sure."

I click my communicator; the time flashes across the screen. The Leader's address should begin soon. Then I can go home. I wish I could get excited about Waterday like everyone else. But I'm *not* like everyone else, as they're always so quick to remind me. The burns on my palms make that super clear. In a few years, those two kids entranced by my stories probably won't even give me the time of day.

More and more people flood into the small space, elbowing through each other to gawk at the various stands. Stagnant heat floats between the tightly-packed bodies, tainting the sweet aroma of bread with the stench of body odor. I squirm, keeping my arms tight at my sides.

"They should let Blanks into town for this," a passing guy says to his friend. My ears perk. Blanks are so rarely allowed in Trinnea, they'd never guess one is standing right next to them. I'm here legally, but they won't care. As far as they know, I'm a Blank, and Blanks don't deserve to live within the city walls. I don't dare move a muscle.

"Why's that?" asks his friend.

He flicks a napkin to the ground. "To clean up the mess afterward. Not like anyone else is lining up to do it."

I press my palms harder against my legs. I wish I was allowed to wear my gloves. The two guys break into laughter and shoulder through the crowd. I hate this.

"I think I'm gonna go catch my breath for a moment," I say.

Ma's brow creases. "Are you all right?"

No. "Yeah. I'll be by my bike."

Before she can respond, I'm plowing away from Center Square, back to the edges where the crowd thins.

I reach the outskirts of the festival, all the way back by the apothecary. The orange clay building boasts a sign in the window: *Shop closed for Waterday Festival, visit our booth instead!* My silver airbike is parked in the rack by the door. I'm tempted to hop on it and speed away.

I check my comm; thirty-two minutes remaining, and no response from Landon.

I tiptoe behind the building, out of sight from the festival. The moment I'm away from the crowd, I relax. It's only for a minute. I just need to catch my breath. Then I'll go back to the party and wait for the Leader's address.

I scrub a hand down my face and lean against the side of the building.

"Ducking out of the festival early?"

The familiar voice sends a gust of frost through my veins.

Nina, the guard walking with Chantry earlier, saunters out from behind the next building in her silver uniform. My sister follows, a notepad clenched menacingly in her grip. Chantry's blonde hair is twisted into a tight knot on top of her head. While Nina's uniform is bare, my sister's uniform collar parades a gold *Guard Captain* pin. Of course the Leader appointed her the captain. He probably did it just to mess with me.

My heart pounds faster. "I was just checking on my bike." I keep my head down. "I swear."

"That's interesting." Poison taints Nina's words. "Because it *looks* like you were skipping out before the Leader's address." Nina's a Two; she can change her appearance at will and also use telekinesis. They're pretty useless Skills, but jealousy still revs to life inside me anyway, because I *wish* I had telekinesis, or the ability to morph, or *something*.

Chantry raises her brows and jots something in her notepad.

Nina continues. "And unless I am mistaken—which I'm not—that's illegal. Show me your ID."

I fight the urge to roll my eyes. She knows exactly who I am—she's just doing this to humiliate me. I fish around in my pocket and pull out my Trinnean identification. There's an incriminating black mark across the top, signifying that I'm a Blank who bought a pass to live here. She snatches it from my hand. Her eyes narrow as she reads, as if she's seeing my name for the first time.

I glance at my sister, hoping she'll stop Nina's wrath, but she stays focused on her clipboard, nothing but indifference in her eyes. The perfect guard's captain.

"I really didn't mean to leave early." I face my sister, desperation dripping from my words. "Please, Chantry—"

Nina's color-changing eyes blaze red, bright and dangerous against her pale skin. "She's the guard captain. You will address her as Guard or Sir." She thrusts the card back into my waiting hands. "Or you will suffer the consequences, Blank trash—"

"Hey!" Chantry whirls on Nina, emotion suddenly burning in her gaze. "Cut that name-calling shit. She broke a rule, she'll deal with the consequences. That's it."

I stiffen, darting my eyes to the ground.

Nina's face flushes. She bows her head. "Sorry, Captain."

Chantry nods, her face fading back into indifference.

Hells. Now Nina will be pissed at me for getting her in trouble, and I'll get it worse. I swallow hard, tapping my right fist to my left shoulder—the sign of respect. "I apologize for my lack of decorum, Sir." I just want them to leave. "Let me go back to the festival. I swear I'll stay and watch the address."

Chantry shoves her pen back into her pocket. "Wrap this up, Nina. I'm going to go see why the address is four minutes late." There's no sparkle of affection in her eyes when they coast over me. I've grown used to my sister's coldness over the past three years, but it still stings.

Nina salutes as my sister strides back into the crowd without giving me a second glance.

"May I return to the festival as well, Sir?" I ask.

Nina paces around me in a circle as if she didn't even hear me, so I take it as a no. "Living in Trinnea is a privilege for you, Blank tra—Zadie. You've been given the chance most Blanks dream of—a ticket out of the wastes—and you have the gall to be ungrateful and dodge our sacred festival?"

"I wasn't dodging."

Her eyes flash to mine. "Did I give you permission to speak?"

My ears burn. I never thought I'd say it, but I wish Chantry would come back. At least my sister won't deride me for my lack of Skills. "No."

"I could lock you in the stocks for this," Nina says. "Or sentence you to lashes in the Square at dusk."

My heart races. I don't dare avert my eyes from the red sand beneath my feet. I shouldn't have come over here. I should've stayed with Ma.

The air crackles around us. "If everyone would gather around the stage," Chantry's booming voice calls into a microphone, "we'll have the Leader's address shortly." Applause and cheers follow.

"But I have a better idea." Nina's face lights up. "You'll be the Leader's Waterday Representative."

My eyes grow wide. The water jug hat kid? That's the most humiliating, degrading role in the entire festival. "No, please, ask Chantry, she'll—"

"Would you prefer I revoke your Trinnean ID altogether? I could have you back in the wastes by nightfall."

"No, Sir." I cringe. The words ache as they come out. "I'll be the Waterday Representative."

"Of course you will." She smirks. "Let's go."

Before I can protest, Nina latches onto my wrist and yanks me back through the crowd. "Blank coming through!" she shouts. Laughter echoes around me. I stumble over some guy's foot I'm certain he stuck out just to trip me. "Waterday Rep, move aside! I've got a Blank volunteer for the water jug!"

My face burns hotter than the desert sun overhead, my hand growing clammy in Nina's grip. Gulping down the fear swirling inside me, I let her tug me through the masses of people, who scowl and hurl insults as I pass. A couple of kids snicker. My breaths come short and quick. I wish I had a Skill that made me shrink into the ground and vanish.

Ma stands by a spice stand. She tenses for a moment, panic flitting across her face when she sees me. I know my Ma. She'll freak out. I give her the slightest shake of my head; she can't cause a scene. They'll only take it out on me. "Oh,

Zadie." She catches my eyes as we pass, her fear contorting into sympathy. "I'm so sorry," she mouths, before disappearing from view among the hordes of people.

"Blank coming through! Make way for the Blank!"

"Blank trash," mutters a man as we pass. He spits a wad of saliva at me, striking my boot. Nina practically rips my arm out of my socket yanking me through.

My skin crawls when we reach the stage at the front of the crowd. Mist hangs in the dark labyrinth entrance, now a mere ten feet away. My heart rate quickens. I don't know what I'm more afraid of—the labyrinth's proximity, or being paraded in front of everyone like this. With a final shove, Nina pushes me toward the wooden stairs.

"Get up there," she snaps in my ear.

Chantry stands stoically by the stage, at attention. Part of me wishes she'd stand up for me, tell Nina to back off, but of course she doesn't. She doesn't even look at me.

A nearby woman in an official-looking uniform cocks her head. "We already have a Blank to do the onstage presentation." She indicates the dirty little girl beside her wearing the navy blue uniform I recognize all too well—she must be an indenture of the Warden. Her long brown hair hangs down her back in a single braid. My stomach twists. It's been three years, but it feels like yesterday I wore that same uniform. The child fidgets, and I'm all too aware of how old and awkward I look next to her. They probably bribed her into doing this with a handful of silvers; whatever they're paying her, it's not nearly enough.

"Well, now you've got two," Nina says. "Don't worry, Zadie is more than capable."

I fight back a groan. Of course I'm more than capable. It's a job meant for a six-year-old. I just have to stand there holding the jug and wearing the hat while everyone laughs at me. That's literally it.

The woman shoves a giant glass carton into my hand and slaps a water jug hat onto my head. It's way too small for me.

"Go on." Nina shoves me in the back.

Slogging through invisible molasses, I force myself up the stairs to boos, jeers, and roaring laughter from below. Thousands of eyes follow me, their attention searing into my skin like daggers. My boots press a path through the flowers scattered across the wood.

Landon's portrait greets me on stage, and I pretty much want to curl up and die. I scan the people in the crowd, but there's no sign of Landon's messy blond hair anywhere. I hope he's back by the stands or something. I don't want him to see me like this. The little girl volunteer plods after me in a matching hat, clearly just as thrilled as I am about this. At least her hat fits better than mine.

Crackling fills the air. I have to crane my neck to see the screen directly over my head. Where the Great Leader's portrait hung over the stage, a projection of his face now levitates instead, watching from the Stone Palace. In the distance, I can barely make out the black spires poking out over the red labyrinth walls. It's weird to think he lives there. He's so close to us, but still so far away. Funny how he built a whole labyrinth to isolate and protect himself from other people; right now, I wish I could do the same.

Every member of the crowd thumps their right fist to

their left shoulder in unison. I weakly mimic the gesture, my hands slick with sweat. My pulse pounds in my ears, drowning out the noise.

The Leader on the screen smiles. Gray hair puffs out on the sides of his wrinkly face. "Welcome, children of Trinnea, to our one hundred, seventy-eighth celebration of water. It's been 178 years since the Great Drought that ended life as we know it outside of Trinnea, and yet, here you stand—my people."

Everyone listens, enraptured by the Leader's words. Not a single whisper floats through the crowd.

"The Trinneans—the gifted, the Skilled—would not succumb to the plagues that took so many others. You are the survivors of the brave, new world."

Chantry yawns at the foot of the stage stairs. She absent-mindedly flicks her finger, making a pebble float a few inches off the stage and fall back down.

The stage feels about a hundred degrees hotter than the festival below. Sweat pours down my face, an oven beneath the hat propped on my head. Thousands of Trinneans stare up at me from the crowd, munching on snacks and giggling and being grateful they're not me. I close my eyes, focusing on breathing in and out. It'll all be over soon.

"Now, as is tradition to honor our proud history," the Leader says, "let's begin our presentation."

The woman in the suit takes the microphone. "On the final day of the drought, our Great Leader came to us and provided . . ."

The little girl and I raise our water jugs over our heads and wait. Giggles ripple through the crowd.

I scan faces, seeking someone to focus on. Something. Anything.

Unfortunately, the first person I see is the last person I want to. The Warden leans against a stall in the front of the nearest aisle, chewing tobacco. Her lip curls up when she catches me staring.

The moment her eyes lock with mine, my insides become jelly. The festival noises fade to silence in my ears. Just like that, I'm back in the bunks, cowering as she looms over me. My fingernails dig into my palms around the jug handles, leaving angry red crescents in my already scarred skin. I have to remind myself where I am. I'm not there. I don't work for her anymore.

"And the water was released from the air!" the woman's voice tears my attention, and at her cue, I quickly spin in a circle on the stage. A thin pipe stretches out from the Leader's screen and releases a steady flow of water, which I rush to capture in my jug. The light spray splashes against my hands as the water cascades into my container. Laughter fills my ears. I squeeze my eyes shut.

I'm not here. This isn't happening. In a few minutes, I can go home. I can go–

A sharp scream pierces the air. The Blank girl beside me drops her jug; it shatters against the stage, splattering water across the wood and soaking her dress. Shouts erupt from the crowd below me.

Following her fearful stare, I spin toward the maze. That's when I see it. Black smoke billows inside the labyrinth entrance. Gasps and shouts fill Center Square.

"It's him," the little girl whispers. "It's Dex."

No. It can't be. Not while I'm standing so close.

I scramble as far away as I can, toward the edge of the stage, shoving the little girl behind me.

The smoke floats out of the labyrinth, rolling thick and dark toward the crowd. Everyone screams, giving it a wide berth. People climb over each other to get away, but end up bottlenecking at the exits of Center Square. Goosebumps prickle across my skin.

Landon's fought him before, but I never thought I'd see Dex with my own two eyes.

The smoke swirls, blowing into a black tornado that materializes into a young man. Dex, the Devil of Trinnea himself, stands beside the stage, wisps of black smoke still whirling at his feet. His long black jacket hides his body in shadows. My blood turns to ice.

Everyone trips over each other, knocking over stands and scattering rice and trinkets across the red sand. I need to run, need to hide, something. But I can't move. Fear snakes itself through the soles of my boots, rooting me to the stage. It's him. It's really him. I throw my hands up in defense.

To my horror, the Devil of Trinnea looks right at me, his dark gaze coasting over my branded palms. Our eyes lock, filling me with dread.

Then he lunges toward me.

Chantry jumps between Dex and me, her eyes wide with fear. Before I can process, she swoops her hand; her telekinesis Skill throws me off my feet. I sail over the terrified spectators, away from Dex and the maze. The jug hat flies off my head and lands in the crowd somewhere.

My boots hit the sand back at the outskirts, where Chantry, Nina, and I stood mere minutes ago. My knees buckle and I crumble to the ground.

Chantry.

I rocket upward, my breath catching in my throat.

Dex seethes, rage radiating from him. He flicks his hand out, sending Chantry flying off the stage. She tumbles to the sand. I slap my hand over my mouth, but his attention's already turned to the crowd. Some people run out of the Square; others remain transfixed, frozen in fear.

I can't breathe. The Devil of Trinnea attacked me. He could've murdered me, or dragged me into the labyrinth, or . . . something worse.

If Dex is the one entrancing people within the labyrinth walls like everyone says, then I narrowly escaped that fate. His previous victims flash through my head, their vacant expressions and emptiness upon their return. A shiver ripples through my core. That was almost me.

Chantry–Chantry *saved me*. She hasn't spoken to me in three years, and she saved my life.

Ma barrels through the crowd and throws her arms around me. "You're safe–praise the Leader." She thrusts my bike helmet into my hands. "Go home. I'll meet you there. It's not safe here."

A terrifying thought jolts into me like lightning: Landon must be out here somewhere. He'll try and fight. I can't let him. I stand on my tiptoes to see over the crowd.

A chorus of shrieks rings out. The city guards bolt, shoving each other to get away–so much for defending Trinnea. Dex grabs the little Blank girl off the stage like she's weightless, tucking her under his arm. The little girl screams and kicks as he drags her down the steps.

Something ignites inside me. "Help her!" I shout.

In the pandemonium, someone trips over the projector box and the Great Leader's image fizzles out. We really are alone.

One of last year's guards takes a stand, blocking Dex's path. But Dex is too strong; he sends the guy flying with a flick of his hand. The guard's head smashes into the labyrinth wall.

"Go!" Ma shoves me toward my bike.

I jump on, swinging my leg over the side. I'm about to start the engine, but hesitate. That girl could have easily been me three years ago.

Dex slices his blade into another guard. He hoists the little girl over his shoulder and takes off, racing toward the laby-rinth entrance. A collective gasp rips through the suddenly still crowd. Everyone watches, enraptured.

No.

They disappear into the maze. The girl's screams fade into the distance until not even Ma can hear her anymore.

I clamp my eyes shut.

That was almost me. That was almost me. That was almost me.

Heavy silence descends over us like a shroud. One man near the back voices aloud what everyone's thinking: *The labyrinth will destroy her.* Other people mutter in agreement. I hate how casually they say it. As if I can't see the blatant relief written on all their faces that he didn't drag any of them into that horrible place; he only took a Blank.

Ma rests her hand on my shoulder. Guards rush to help their fallen comrades, their faces pink with shame. Not that there'll be any repercussions—no one's expected to risk their lives for an indentured Blank. I can't tell if it's bitterness or sadness whirling inside me, but I feel like a human sandstorm.

Among the many faces, I catch a mop of blond hair. Relief washes over me. Landon's safe. I haven't lost my best friend.

I wave to get his attention. "Hey! Landon!"

Landon's eyes lock with mine. His brows lower with determination.

I know what he's going to do before he does it.

"Don't!" My shout is lost in the stew of voices. "Landon!"

He charges after Dex, disappearing into the maze.

People shriek and yell, crowding around the slim gap in the labyrinth wall. They practically bowl each other over to peer into the maze and catch a glimpse of Landon's bravery.

Before my mind registers that someone with zero Skills shouldn't head *toward* the danger, I'm running. Ma makes a desperate grab for my arm, but I shirk out of her grip and bolt back into the crowd.

"Landon!" I frantically elbow past people, trying to hide my branded palms, but everyone recognizes me anyway. People glower as I shove by, muttering insults under their breath. I don't care. I can't lose him. He's all I have.

A little girl scowls at me. "Get lost, Blank."

"Get out of here, you'll make it worse." A man flicks his finger and my body is pushed a step backward.

I stumble, but stay on my feet. Sometimes I fantasize I'll wake up one day with Skills and teach these people a lesson. Right now, I imagine flicking this guy right back and sending him flying through the crowd. Of course, it doesn't happen.

I jump, trying to catch a glimpse, but can't see over their heads. People murmur and cry, their eyes dead set on the labyrinth entrance. No one dares to go in after him.

I shove further into the masses, knocking into bellies and tripping over feet until I'm close enough to see the front. My pulse races.

For half a second, I'm afraid for my own safety. Being a Blank, alone, in the middle of a horde of upset Skilled, never leads anywhere good.

A blonde-haired seventeen-year-old pops up in the crowd. Landon's sister, Valerie, levitates a foot in the air.

"Val," I call, pushing through people. "Valerie Everhart!"

Her cheeks flush at the sight of Blank me calling her name.

Valerie's body floats back down until her feet hit the earth. "This isn't a good time."

"We need to help your brother."

Valerie's a Two. She can levitate a couple feet and feel other people's emotions. As far as Skills go, they're not the most useful. Still, better than only having one—or being a Blank.

The people around us watch with disdain. At first I think Valerie won't answer me, regardless of what her brother made her promise. But her face scrunches up. "I'm so scared. I can't lose Landon, he can't become one of those . . . one of those . . . labyrinth victims."

"Don't say that. He won't." But I don't believe my own words. No one who enters the maze comes out the same. Landon's the only Trinnean who's survived in there, always rescuing Dex's victims in the dead of night. He rushes in and right back out before the labyrinth can claim him. He's either too heroic for his own good or too foolish.

"It's the first time Dex tried that in a while," a nearby woman mutters. "I can't believe Limitless Landon is risking his life for a Blank again. Should've just let her go."

I clench my jaw.

"That poor little Blank girl," another woman says. I want to punch her. The *poor little Blank girl* has a name. "Nothing good will come of this. Either the labyrinth will melt their minds, or Limitless and the girl will die in there."

I press the heels of my palms into my eyes, hating that she's probably right. If Landon's not back in a couple minutes, he's screwed. Hearing about Landon's rescues was always enough to make me wince, but seeing one is a thousand times worse.

The man beside her shakes his head. "Who knows if he'll even come out. Maybe he'll be the next Farrar Jensen."

"Don't say that!" The woman slaps his arm. "Last thing we need is more children lost to the maze."

A weathered poster of little Farrar's dimpled face flutters against the labyrinth wall. Farrar wandered into the labyrinth a few years ago, chasing his dog. The dog reemerged unscathed a few hours later, but Farrar never came out. Whatever horrors Dex and the labyrinth did to him, we'll probably never know. I don't know what's worse—vanishing inside those walls or coming back in a state of irreversible hypnosis.

"I wouldn't put it past Dex," the man continues. "He can crush organs with a snap of his fingers. Blank's probably already dead."

"I heard he's got Skills that turn his victims to stone. Stop their hearts and freeze them on the inside."

"I heard—"

My mind races for a solution. I'm so pissed at Landon. I open my mouth to scream, to shout how frustrating it is when your best friend constantly puts his life on the line, when everyone breaks into collective gasps and cheers.

Landon struts out of the maze, a red streak across his cheek, his sleeve torn. The Blank girl lies unconscious against his chest, wrapped in his arms.

He grins. "She's alive."

It's like a balloon inside my chest bursts open. Praise the Leader, the maze didn't take him.

"Limitless Landon!" A man thumps his right fist to his left shoulder. "Exalt!"

"Exalt." The crowd repeats in unison, mimicking the gesture of respect. My heart still hasn't managed to stop hammering.

Fire hells, Landon.

Valerie races toward her brother. Everyone parts, giving her a path to him.

Landon brushes aside the flowers on the stage and gently sets the Blank girl down. Her eyes are closed and her braid hangs limply over her shoulder. But she's alive. Thanks to Landon. She's barely left Landon's arms when spectators flock toward him, asking a million questions at once. The unconscious girl lies forgotten on the stage.

I fidget, watching her chest rise and fall with even breaths. She looks okay. For now.

"Whoa, everyone. Thank you. This is too much." Landon gives his admirers a shy grin. He takes the little girl's hands, not flinching at the marred skin on her palms.

"Steady pulse," Landon announces with a wink. "Someone get her to the infirmary. She should rest there until she wakes up. I'd say she's earned the afternoon off, wouldn't you?"

Applause explodes around me.

The Warden grimaces nearby. Clearly *she* doesn't think getting swept into the deadly maze by a criminal warrants a break. As far as the Warden's concerned, the Blank signed her soul away the moment she accepted shelter in the bunks. But the crowd has already lifted the unconscious Blank girl onto a stretcher, and she won't argue with Limitless Landon. She learned her lesson years ago.

"Zadie Lynn, don't ever do that to me again." Ma shoves

through the hordes of people and grabs my wrist. "I told you to leave and you did exactly the opposite."

"Sorry, Ma. I was gonna leave, but then Landon ran in there and—"

Crackling fills the air. The Great Leader's projection returns, his face flustered. Murmurs float through the crowd: *Will he scold us for not prioritizing him? Is he upset with us? Is he the only one who can stop Dex?*

"Children of Trinnea." The Leader's voice is low and calm, but still manages to quiet the crowd. "Would a volunteer please come forward to explain what just transpired?" Our all-powerful Leader has eyes and ears everywhere despite never leaving his palace. I'm guessing he already knows what happened; he wants to hear it from us.

"I can report, Great Leader." A middle-aged woman steps toward the stage, thudding her fist to her shoulder with a polite bow at the screen.

The woman regales the story with great vibrancy, depicting a tale of heroism and honor. How, as the Leader witnessed, the ceremony was underway. How Dex emerged from the maze and became black smoke, sweeping through the crowd and abducting the girl. How they'd barely disappeared beyond the wall before Landon took off after them, returning with the girl a mere two minutes later.

I can't help but smile. Limitless Landon, my Landon, is a hero. It's nothing new, but it never gets old.

I catch his eye, standing slightly off the stage with his arm around Valerie's shoulders. The corner of his mouth curls up in a half-smile. He holds out his communicator, indicating to me as he types.

I whip out my comm just as it vibrates in my pocket.

I think that's enough excitement for one day! Garden?

Something flutters in my chest. I type him a message back: *I have to work tonight, but maybe a quick visit first?*

Landon winks at me. I take that as a yes. Heat floods my face and I look away.

The Great Leader's forehead creases. "Is there any indication as to why Dex chose that particular girl?"

Is there reasoning behind anything Dex does?

"She was closest to the labyrinth, your greatness. And she was a Blank. He'd targeted another Blank first—where's that girl?" The woman squints.

I shrink down, avoiding her gaze.

Ma squeezes my hand extra tight. I can tell she's thinking the same thing I am: if the Devil of Trinnea wants Blanks, I need to be extra careful. If I'd been walking out here alone at night, Dex could've dragged me into the labyrinth and I'd be dead before anyone even knew I was gone.

"That is indeed disturbing," the Leader says. "It puzzles me."

"It puzzles me too, your greatness. I wish we knew . . ." The woman trails off. There are lots of things about Dex we wish we knew. Like where he came from. Or how he survives living in the maze without his brain turning to mush like everyone else. Or why he's so intent on killing and kidnapping and destroying anything in his path.

"It appears there has been an act of heroics today," the

Leader says. "Landon Everhart, you have brought honor to Trinnea."

Landon shakes his head. "Really. I was just doing my duty."

Several young women squeal.

"I love you, Landon!" some lady shouts from the crowd; I'm pretty sure it's Nina. A blush creeps across Landon's face.

"Nonsense." The Leader smiles. "As a reward for your bravery, and in recognition of Waterday, I have decided to pause the festival and bring up the springs for one additional hour. Please consider your duties met, and if you need to leave, feel free to do so. At the hour's end, we'll recommence with the festival for anyone who still wishes to celebrate. I will return at that time."

Cheers erupt. As the Leader's face fades off the screen, the ground rumbles to life. Two massive pipes grow from the earth like tree stumps, flanking the maze entrance. They sputter, choking out a dribble of mud that flows into clear gushing water.

Clean water. From the Leader's springs beyond the maze.

People of all genders and ages shove past each other, tripping over debris and abandoned festival carts, opening their mouths into the stream. Laughter and praises fill the air. I don't dare enter the fray, but I tilt my head back to enjoy the spray against my face.

"I'm going to go home and grab some buckets to fill." Ma's eyes light up, her anger toward me forgotten. "We can cook rice tonight!"

The Great Leader ensures we always have enough to drink, but water for cooking and bathing is scarce. Even on Waterday, he hardly ever releases the full springs. I nearly cry with joy at the thought of washing the grime and sweat off my skin tonight. I haven't bathed in a week.

"Okay. I'll help you."

"No. You should stay here." A mischievous grin stretches across her face. "Landon seems eager to speak with you. He just told his sister."

Of course Ma's hyper-hearing Skill caught that. But still, her comment makes my stomach do a somersault. "So much for privacy."

With a clap of her hands, Ma conjures a wave of red sand to carry her home. Show off.

I scan the crowd, bathing and laughing in the cool water. My best friend is nowhere to be found. Valerie stands by herself, typing on her communicator. Landon's probably already waiting for me at the garden.

Pushing against the current of people flooding toward the pipes, I snake away from the stage, scan my thumb onto the reader until it flashes green, and jump on my airbike. It hovers a foot off the ground. If I hurry, I can catch him for a good hour before the festival recommences and I have to go to work.

I rev the engine and kick off from the dirt. My bike growls as I speed away from Center Square, weaving between huts and shops.

I slow to a stop by the botany shop. I know the fastest way to get to the garden—take a right, pass the Warden's bunks, and it's a straight shot. I close my eyes and inhale deeply.

Pass the bunks. It sounds so, so simple.

I can do it. It's just a quick ride. I can already see the

Trinnean border in the distance. All I have to do is follow the wall for a couple kilometers, and the garden's there. And Landon. Weaving through downtown will take forever. Why can't I just get over this and take the shortcut?

My heart rate quickens. Sweat makes my hands go clammy around the handlebars. But I can't make myself take my hand off the brake.

I need to get over this. It's in the past.

I haven't been a part of the bunks for three years, but they'll never stop being a part of me. And I wish I could carve that part clean out of my body.

A six-foot brick wall surrounds Trinnea on the three non-labyrinth sides, with barbed wire curling across the top. It keeps out banished Skilled—like criminals or people who insulted the Leader—and Blanks. I've seen thinner walls on bank vaults. The Leader wants to make absolutely sure the people he locks out can't get back in. As far as Trinnea's concerned, Blanks could mean the end of the Skilled gene, and since un-Skilled people in the rest of the world didn't survive the drought, that could also mean the end of humanity; according to the Leader, the fewer of us in town, the better.

When I turned six and my blood test revealed my Blankness, the city guards branded zeroes on my palms and ripped me away from my mom and everything I had known.

The last thing Ma tearfully whispered to me before they wrenched me from her arms was this: "Find a job that'll put a roof over your head and stay alive. I'll get you back into Trinnea. Someday."

I didn't know what she meant until they drove me through the city gate and left me in the desert outside Trinnea, all alone.

My hands tighten around my handlebars, but I can't make myself move. From inside the Trinnean borders, the wastes might as well be a million miles away, rather than right behind that wall. That's the way everyone here likes it: out of sight, out of mind. But I can still picture it. All the way down to the musky, ashy smell that filled the air.

The wastes looked just like Trinnea, if all the buildings were layered with rust and one storm away from crumbling to the ground. When I first arrived, I could barely believe what I was seeing. Sickly looking beggars in dirty rags slept outside, wrapped in thin burlap blankets. An old man with leathery skin hobbled past me, coughing into his elbow. One child a few years older than me bludgeoned another with a stick before stealing the scrap of bread he'd been nibbling—and no one did a thing to stop him. The rancid stench of garbage permeated the air, tinged with smoke from the nearby mines.

I'd heard horror stories about the wasteland beyond Trinnea, but seeing it with my own eyes shook me to my marrow. This was the forsaken ground, the place not gifted with the Leader's resources and generosity, where starving people begged for scraps and turned to crime. I'd heard tales of people wandering into the desert to die rather than staying there.

The Leader didn't provide anything for us out there. Without Skills, we weren't deemed important enough to waste limited resources on.

Squinting at the wall in the distance, it's easy to forget

those Blanks—*people*—are just beyond the layers of rock and brick separating us. I guess it's easier for the Leader to banish people away if he doesn't have to look them in the eyes afterward.

Some Blanks make a livelihood out there in the wastes, bargaining resources and rising to power as crime lords, but as a little kid, I knew I stood no chance at that.

I remember that day so vividly, it's like it's happening now. I quivered, frozen in terror, as the gate clanked shut behind me, sealing me forever outside the town that had always been my home. My pulse kicks up a notch at the memory. I press the heels of my palms into my eyes. I hate that it still affects me this much.

There was only one rule in the wastes: don't try to re-enter Trinnea. Any person caught trying to scale the wall and get back in was executed. Some Trinneans were allowed to cross the gate into the wastes to recruit Blanks or banished Skilled for jobs, but otherwise, there was no contact allowed.

It was totally unfair. The only way for Blanks to re-enter town was to buy a special pass back into Trinnea, at a cost designed to ensure it rarely happened. People say the fact that the Leader offers that option to Blanks at all is a sign of his mercy and kindness. But I know it's not. It's about controlling us, giving us a bone so we're beholden to him. Blanks have to jump through expensive hoops just to access the same resources everyone else automatically gets. Trinnea has more than enough to go around, but they don't care. Leader's orders.

A couple of giggling little kids scurry past, their fingers clenched around bucket handles. For some reason, the sight makes something tug in my chest. I was never allowed to be a carefree child collecting water on a holiday. I had to survive.

That first night in the wastes, I ran from door to door, desperate to find someone to hire me before the sun went down, stranding me outside in this terrifying new place in the dark. I'd never survive until morning.

But not even the lowest jobs would hire a six-year-old. After begging at fourteen different shady-looking Skilled employers who trolled the wastes looking for new hires, I found her. The cranky middle-aged woman didn't tell me her name, just her title—the Warden. She was recruiting people of all ages to work in the mines in exchange for boarding in the bunks, a series of shacks cutting through the Trinnean border. Ideally, she wanted Skilled, but since most Skilled weren't interested in mine work, she sought Blanks. It didn't seem so bad. The bunks had doors on both sides of the wall, meaning even though I wasn't technically in Trinnea, it still would feel almost like being home. I'd be bunking with all her other employees—mostly Blanks, with the occasional Skilled. The Warden would give me three meals a day. It seemed too good to be true.

The thing about things that seem too good to be true is they usually are.

She said a word I didn't understand: *indenture.* When the Warden handed me the contract, I didn't think twice before scrawling my name across the bottom. My reading abilities were advanced for a six-year-old, but not perfect. Maybe I should've been more careful, but I was scared. I'd have done anything to avoid being stuck outside that awful place all night.

I often think back to that day, and wish I could've warned

little Zadie. Maybe life would've been easier if I'd tried making a life for myself in the wastes. Maybe not. I guess that's the problem with retrospect: you never really know.

I steady myself, gripping the handlebars so tight my knuckles are white. The familiar nausea percolates inside me, like it always does when I think about the past.

I'll take the long way.

I take off on my bike, kicking up sand behind me.

I bank around the corner, tilting into the centripetal force, when the front end of my bike thrusts upward into the air. I fly backward, tumbling into the red dirt. My helmet cushions my head from splatting into the sand. My vision blurs in and out of focus on my airbike, floating six feet over my head.

I groan, rubbing my arm. Before the question can materialize in my brain, the answers emerge from the shadows.

Chantry, Nina, and three other city guards stand over me, blocking my escape.

Nina waves her arm, sending my airbike sailing down the alley, out of my reach. "Going somewhere, Blank?"

I groan, prying myself out of the sand.

"Smile, Zadie!" Nina clicks her communicator at me. "Oh, that's gold. I'm sending this to everyone."

This girl Taylor peeps over Nina's shoulder at the picture and snorts out a laugh.

My face gets hot. I picture waving my hand and dangling them upside down by their ankles. Holding them hostage until they apologize. How sweet it would be to make them regret every bad thing they ever did to me.

It's weird thinking that these people would've been my classmates, if I'd been allowed in school. If I wasn't a Blank, I'd be wearing that same guard uniform, probably patrolling with them. But my genetics betrayed me, and here we are.

"What do you want?" They can't bully me forever, they're guards—they'll have to return to the festival soon.

"That's no way to talk to your superior," Taylor snaps, flicking her black braids over her shoulder. Shimmery gold eye shadow glimmers against her light brown skin. "You better watch your mouth."

Chantry folds her arms. "You've got some explaining to do.

You witnessed a crime. You want to tell us why you ran out before a formal investigation could take place?"

Chantry and I don't look like sisters. We each got our respective mother's coloring; while her skin is fair and burns easily, mine is permanently lightly tanned. Her straight blonde locks are polar opposite to my wavy dark hair. It's only our eyes that reveal our familial connection. We both got our father's deep brown eyes.

"I'm not running from anything. No one asked me about it." And it's not lost on me that of the hundreds of witnesses, I'm the one who gets in trouble for not filing a report.

Taylor anchors a hand on her hip. "Well, you didn't exactly *try* to help, did you?"

Anger boils inside me. The crime was obvious. Dex kidnapped someone, his motives unknown, as usual. Case closed. All these city guards know it just as well as I do.

"Please, it's *Zadie*. She can't do anything right." Nina snorts, flicking my shoulder. A pink sunburn peels across her pale forehead. It looks at least a little painful, and that makes me smug. "I thought you'd have a little shame at this point."

Shame? The Leader is the one who should be ashamed. The Leader, and the Skilled, and everyone who upholds this ridiculous hierarchy.

"Why'd you save me if you hate me so much?" I mumble at Chantry.

Chantry's face stays hard and indifferent. I might as well be any Trinnean citizen, not her blood. I wonder if the other guards know that last week, Chantry punched a Skilled man in the face for calling a Blank worker a slur. She even threatened to throw him in the stocks for a night if she ever heard him say it again. I don't think my sister knows I saw; I'd ducked behind a bunch of barrels the moment I saw her coming. It was the first time I'd ever seen a guard stand up for a Blank. I wish she'd stand up for me.

One of the other guards, a guy named Onyx, crosses his arms. "You know we can punish you for addressing a guard that way, right?"

I swallow. They can throw me off my bike, hurtle it across the alley, and *I'm* the one who gets in trouble?

"I saved you because I'm a guard now, and it's my duty to protect Trinneans," Chantry says in a monotone, not meeting my eyes. "I was doing my job."

Something about her tone makes me doubt her words. Maybe somewhere, deep down, a part of my sister still loves me. I struggle to my feet and half-heartedly touch my fist to my shoulder. "I apologize for my tone, sirs." The words hurt worse than my throbbing head.

"We should punish her," Nina says, her dazzling eyes changing from green, to yellow, to red, to blue.

I cringe, imploring my sister with my eyes. *Please don't let them hurt me.*

Chantry sighs, jotting something on her clipboard. "Find out what she knows about the crime. Then meet me back at the festival for debriefing." My sister climbs onto her own bike. The other guards salute as she speeds away, leaving me in the cobra's den. I'm desperate to beg her not to leave, but I know she'll go anyway. So I keep my mouth shut and pretend my heart isn't on the verge of exploding in my chest.

"We'll need to run an interrogation," Taylor says.

Nina grins, revealing her crooked top tooth. "It's okay. I have an idea."

I absolutely don't like the sound of that.

She snaps her fingers. My airbike floats back down the alley toward me. It hovers several feet over my head.

I flinch, wondering if she plans to drop it on me. Being guards doesn't give them authority to actually *kill* me . . . *right?* I hate being so powerless.

"Let's play a game," Nina says. "I'm going to ask you questions. If you don't answer honestly, I'm gonna throw your bike against that wall." She nods toward the solid clay building to our right. "Would be a pity if you had to walk to the dunes every day, don't you think?"

The others snicker.

I'd have to leave home at one in the morning to walk to work. The watchtowers are past the gate, way out in the desert, even beyond the wasteland village. I can't afford a new airbike. "Please—"

"First question." Nina taps her fingers to her lips, her other hand extended toward my floating bike. "Why does Landon Everhart still hang out with you?"

It's a good question. I don't even know the answer. I guess this interrogation has nothing to do with Dex's crime after all.

"We're friends. We've been friends for years." The jealousy painted across their faces makes me smug.

"Everyone knows that," she snaps. "I want to know why."

"I don't know why."

"Now, now." Taylor wags her finger at me. "No lying."

"I'm not lying. He's been my best friend since we were little kids."

Onyx rolls his eyes. "Okay, Nina. I owe you five silvers."

"Hang on," Nina snaps. "I highly doubt he keeps you around to be his *friend*. What are you *really*? His servant?"

Bile swirls in my stomach. "I don't serve anyone but myself."

"I want to know why he bothers hanging out with you," she continues. "What favors are you giving him on the side?"

"*What*?"

"Uh uh. You know the rules. Answer honestly."

"There are *no* favors on the side. What could I even give him?" Nothing he'd want, at least. "I'm a Blank for hells' sake. I've got nothing to give. Is that what you want to hear?"

Taylor laughs. "Now we're getting somewhere."

"Okay, one more question." Nina lowers her voice to a deadly whisper. Her eyes grow cold. "Why don't you ever visit Nadine?"

The question punches me in the stomach. Of course they blame me for what happened. Maybe they're right to blame me. I close my eyes, letting it wash over me.

Because I'm too scared.

I'm too ashamed.

I've tried to go in there so many times, and each time I can't do it.

I don't know why Nina and the others care whether I visit her; they've never shown concern for Blanks like Nadine before. But I know they care about Chantry. And I know I've hurt Chantry by not visiting Nadine.

Before I can stutter out an answer, my bike spins midair and thuds to the ground. It zips backward until it's facing the others.

Taylor whirls on Nina. "Stop that!"

But Nina's staring at her still hands. "I'm not doing anything."

The engine revs.

"Okay, what in the hells?" Onyx narrows his eyes.

"Whoever you are, you're messing with city guards." Taylor balls her fists, glancing back and forth down the alleyway. "Come out right now, or you'll regret it." My bike rotates to face her. The headlight flashes menacingly, and the authority on her face fades into pure fear.

Nina slowly backs away with her hands up. The others cautiously follow her lead. With a threatening growl, my bike zooms toward them.

"Run!"

They race out of the alley, tripping over themselves to get away. It's almost comical.

Their shouts carry back to me as I scrub my hand down my face. Within a minute, my bike speeds back. It makes a lazy circle around me before sliding to a halt.

I shake my head. "Thank you."

"No problem." Landon materializes on my airbike, with his hand on the clutch and a grin on his face. He hops off and pushes the bike toward me. I don't ask about the invisibility. If a day passed when Limitless Landon didn't gain a new Skill, I'd wonder if he'd taken ill. They lost count when he became a Fourteen and settled on calling him Limitless instead.

"Sorry I'm late." I walk the bike as we head toward the cactus garden. "They ambushed me. I didn't know what to do."

"Yes, Zadie, how dare you be five minutes late when a group of hooligans cornered you in an alley and stole your bike?" he says sarcastically, gently pushing my arm. "How selfish of you."

I laugh, imagining the look on Nina and Taylor's faces if they heard Limitless Landon calling them hooligans.

He grins. "What's so funny?"

"Oh, nothing." I give his arm a push of its own. "You should've seen their faces when the bike started revving at them."

"You know I can't resist teaching them a lesson when they're bothering you. No one is mean to you and gets away with it."

"Well at that rate, you'll need to rev my bike at the entire town."

"I'm on it. Forget Dex, Haunted Bike will be the new Trinnean terror. Oh hey, you've got something in your hair . . ."

Heat rushes through me as he tucks a lock of brown hair behind my ear, dramatically revealing a bright pink blossom that definitely wasn't there a moment ago. The petals open and shut before my eyes, a delicate dance animated only by my best friend's many Skills.

"For you." He presses the flower into my palm, and my breath catches in my throat.

"That totally wasn't in my hair."

"Maybe." Landon gives me a shy smile. "Maybe not. Maybe I found it on the way here and it reminded me of you."

I realize I'm still staring at him, and force my eyes to look away.

Back in the blistering sun, we amble a block down the matted red dirt road. A crisscrossing rusty fence surrounds the small square garden. I lock my bike to the railing. Several days a week, I come here to tend the plants; the landscapers do a terrible job. But my visits with Landon are the ones I savor.

"I feel like we're the only people who ever come in here," I say, scanning the empty park. "I mean, aside from the landscapers."

Landon pushes open the squeaky gate and holds it back for me. "I kind of like it that way. It's like it's . . . our place. No one else can have it."

I hide my cheeks behind my hand so he can't see me blush. "Oh . . . me too." He couldn't be flirting with me. He's Limitless Landon. I need to get it together. He's my best friend, and that's all he's ever going to be.

His eyes meet mine. "No, I mean it." We stop walking and face each other. "Do you ever . . . okay, this is going to sound weird. But do you ever wish you could make the whole world vanish for a moment? Like, that everything would just stop and stand still?"

My mouth runs dry. I'm struck with an urge to reach out and touch him. "All the time."

"That's kind of what this garden is to me. You know?"

I do know. Having this secret nook that's only for Landon and me makes it feel magical. Like when I'm in this garden, I'm safe. "Yeah. I get that."

"Ugh. Sorry I'm being weird. I just . . . I'm glad we could get away." He runs a hand through his messy blond hair, making it look like he got caught in a sandstorm. "The crowds are kind of overwhelming today."

"No kidding. I feel like I'm gonna wake up tomorrow covered in bruises from fifty different elbows."

We keep walking, meandering down the garden trail.

"So uh." Landon scratches the back of his head. A half-smile quirks across his face. "I saw the presentation."

I groan. "Please never mention it again."

"Hey now, I thought you did a good job as the Waterday Rep." He nudges me. "I thought the hat looked cute on you."

Did Landon Everhart just call me cute?

"I looked ridiculous." I nudge him back.

"Not true."

"As long as you didn't take any pictures. Because if you did, I'd have to kill you."

Landon smirks. "If I delete them right now, can I live?"

"I suppose. Just this once."

Smooth white stones cover the ground, with spirals of black stones positioned throughout. It reminds me of a mosaic, like in pictures Ma showed me of civilizations from the past. Before the drought killed everyone outside of Trinnea.

Cacti in all different sizes and shapes line the fence, some sprouting pink and yellow flowers. Others are so prickly, they look almost furry.

"Hey look at these spiky ones." Landon points at a cluster of round, flat cacti. Bulbous red fruit bursts from the ends. "Remind me again what these are?"

"That's a prickly pear. You can eat the fruit."

"Weird." He twists one and it pops off the cactus. "You ever try one?"

"A long time ago. Too seedy for me."

"Well, I default to your judgement on all plant matters." He winks. "I'll give it to Val and see what she thinks."

"Poor Val."

Blanks aren't allowed in public school, so Ma taught me everything she could at home following my release from the bunks. She didn't have many books, so she taught me to read using a tattered old field guide. I've read it so many times, I nearly have every plant memorized.

"Landscapers must've been by. That one looks new." Landon points to a gnarled-looking cactus covered in long skinny prickers.

It's actually not new. Sometimes I think he dredges up my plant facts to make me smile. It works. "Cylindropuntia."

He makes a face. "That's a mouthful."

I slide onto our usual bench beneath the giant saguaro.

"Careful!" He puts his hand against my back.

I've sat here enough times to know not to lean into the saguaro spines, but Landon's concern makes my heart flutter. "You're so overprotective, *Limitless*." I nudge him in the side.

"Ugh. That nickname." He sinks into the seat beside me. I can't help smiling at the pendant hanging from his neck. It's a leaf encased in resin that I bought for him, years ago. He's worn it every day since.

I pick at a loose thread on my jacket. "I'm surprised you were able to detangle yourself from your admirers back there, to come hang out with me." *I'm surprised you wanted to.*

"Admirers, eh?" He arches a brow. "Not what I'd call them."

"What would you call them?"

He gives me another half-smile. "An annoyance. Because all I really wanted to do was come to this garden. And, you know. See my best friend."

My stomach does a full-on somersault.

We sit in silence, soaking up the flowery scent of blossoms. Landon looks straight ahead, fixated on the cluster of prickly pears across the aisle. I know that look; his mind is far away.

"Are you okay?" I ask.

"How could I not be?" He shoots me a toothy smile. "I'm with you." His knee bounces against his hand. I've never seen him so jittery.

Something's changed in our friendship. I can't tell if it's because of me or him. Usually, together, we're a gentle breeze. But recently it's been hot and rough, like the sand storms at the far edge of the wastes.

The silence makes me uncomfortable. With every passing second I'm more likely to blurt out something I can't take back.

I know what I *want* to say. I've rehearsed it a million times in my head. *Hey, Landon, I know you're the hero of Trinnea, and most of the girls and probably some of the guys would do anything to be with you, and I know you could have your pick, and I know I'm a Blank and you're you, but you've always been here for me, and I think I'm in love with you.*

I take a deep breath. "Hey, can we talk about—"

"I need to tell you something—"

We both stop short with an awkward laugh, not meeting each other's eyes.

"You first," he says.

"Okay." But my scripted monologue disintegrates from my brain like paper in water. I open my mouth, then close it again.

He grins. "Well . . ."

"Well." I look into his gold-flecked eyes. The same eyes I remember from so long ago.

When I turned seven, Landon and Valerie showed up at the bunks. It was the first rainstorm in four years, and thunder shook the building. I'd been in bed, trying to convince myself I'd made the right decision the previous year by dooming myself to a lifetime in the mines. Even as a little kid, the whole thing seemed so unfair. My life held such little value to Trinnea, and I couldn't figure out why. They despised me so much, just because I had no Skills. It seemed like a ridiculous reason to hate someone. I bled the same color as them. I didn't feel any different from them. And yet they were in Trinnea, within the borders, blessed by the Leader with plenty to eat; I had to bend over backwards just to get a scrap of food. Like most nights, I lay awake, ruminating over it.

A drenched older woman shuffled through the door around midnight, holding an umbrella over two kids' heads. We all craned our necks around our bedposts to see what was going on. New recruits who'd just signed the Warden's indenture contract weren't treated with such care; the Warden always shoved them into the bunks with nothing but a grimace and a thin blanket. But the glum expressions on these kids' faces screamed defeat anyway.

The woman disappeared into the Warden's office and closed the door. The new boy and girl huddled together a few feet from my bed. The girl's muffled sobs disappeared into her brother's shirt. His puffy eyes were red and blotchy.

I wanted to ask their names, try and offer some comfort. But speaking out of turn led to the Warden's wrath, and I was too afraid.

Even speaking in hushed tones, the woman's conversation with the Warden carried in the dark silence.

"I'm so sorry for the late hour. These poor children have nowhere else to go."

"Are they Blanks?"

"No. Skilled."

"Where's their father?" growled the Warden.

"Dead."

"And the mother?"

"Dead."

"Extended family?"

"None."

The bunks around me were too silent. We were forbidden to speak after lights-out, but there was always noise—rustling sheets, growling snores, the occasional cough. That night, you could hear a pin drop. Everyone was listening, straining to hear Landon and Valerie's pain broadcast to the whole room.

"Their parents' bodies were found together in their shared home," the woman continued. "Leader have mercy on their souls."

A brief pause followed. "Together? What is this, some sort of old-fashioned cult?"

I cocked my head. I'd never known anyone whose parents lived together. Were they monogamous, too? Did that mean these two Skilled siblings shared the same mother *and* father? I'd never heard of such a thing.

"I don't know why you brought them here," the Warden continued. "These are mining bunks. My workers head down to the mines every day. We pay 'em in housing and food, and a small stipend. About ninety percent are Blanks. Wouldn't want those two Skilled kids exposed to *them.*"

The way she said *them* sent a surge of anger rippling through me. I didn't feel any different from the two Skilled kids in the center of the room. They were just . . . kids. Sad kids. Like me.

"I know it's unprecedented. Please. I wouldn't be asking if we had another option. But they're orphans, and they've got nowhere else to go. Just put them up for a few cycles."

"I don't like it."

"You'll hardly know they're here. It's just temporary until the Great Leader finds them a foster home with a Skilled parent."

She sighed. "All right. They'll have to bunk with my workers; I've got no other beds for them. But I'll do my best to keep 'em separated otherwise. Send them to school during the day, when the others go to work."

"That's perfect. Thank you."

They murmured a bit more, their voices too low for me to hear.

The office door swung open, flooding the room with light. Sharp breaths echoed around the room, all of us afraid to be caught eavesdropping. No one made a peep as the woman strode back outside, the pattering rain getting louder and softer again as she opened and shut the door. The Warden dead-bolted it behind her, ensuring her workers stayed put.

The Warden made me vacate my coveted top bunk, stacked five rows high. She gave Valerie my prized bed and Landon the one below it, leaving me the worst slot—row three, right at the Warden's eye level. Tears burned behind my eyes as I ripped the sheets off my old bed and climbed down into my new one.

Throughout the coming weeks, resentment stewed inside me. I hated the new kids. They didn't get hit when they screwed up, didn't have to be quiet. Didn't have to work themselves raw in the mines. And worst of all, they had an out. Within a few months, they'd be out of here forever. Meanwhile, the only foreseeable expiration date on my indenture was death. Technically we weren't prisoners, but we'd all signed the Warden's contract—a lifetime of work in exchange for a lifetime of lodging and food, off the streets of the wastes. We were in it forever, and if we wanted out of the Warden's contract, we had to pay her back for all the cycles of putting us up—a cost almost as high as buying a pass back into Trinnea itself. Anyone who tried backing out of the contract without paying the Warden's debt got hunted down by her lackeys. So as far as the Warden was concerned, we belonged to her. We *owed* her, for saving us from the horrible place outside. And yet to the new kids, the bunks were a minor inconvenience, a blip on an otherwise perfect existence.

I usually forced myself not to think of Ma, because it hurt too badly. I'd probably never see her again. Picturing her face felt like a knife twisting in my chest. But one night, I missed her so bad I cried into my pillow, stifling my sobs so the Warden wouldn't hear.

Landon's hand found its way down from his bunk and latched onto mine. He didn't flinch when his thumb brushed the tough burnt skin on my palm. I peered up to where he leaned over the side of his bunk. A sliver of moonlight seeping through the window illuminated his face. Tear tracks marred his cheeks. He gave my hand a squeeze, and I knew. We were as different as Trinneans could be, yet we were both stuck in this horrible place together, torn apart with grief. And just like that, I wasn't alone anymore.

Ten years later, sitting in the garden, out of the bunks and away from the Warden's clutches, his eyes still fill me with hope.

"Well?" he asks again.

I touch the leaf pendant hanging over his T-shirt. I bought it for him with my very first out-of-bunks paycheck after I got my pass into Trinnea—something to thank him for all his help. I figured it would end up in a drawer somewhere, but he strung it up and wore it as a necklace. I've never seen him take it off. That has to mean something.

I draw my hand back. "Why do you still wear this?"

"I love this thing." Landon touches the leaf. "You bought it for me. And it totally matches my eyes." It definitely does not match his eyes. But that doesn't stop my insides from turning to mush. "Is that what you wanted to ask me?"

"Not . . . exactly." I can do this. I survived the bunks. I survived the Warden. I can tell my best friend how I feel. My feelings might be frowned upon, but they're not illegal. Some

Skilled people probably end up with Blanks . . . maybe. A few. Somewhere. So what if their kids aren't Skilled? Who cares?

"Well. I thought I should tell you–"

His buzzing communicator cuts me off. "Hells, hang on." He reads the message. "I gotta go. Val needs me. They're restarting the festival and she's scared."

I nod, swallowing back the words on my tongue. "Okay." I'm struck with a pang of jealousy. Best friend or not, I'll never be his family–never be Val. My own pettiness feels sour inside me.

"I should probably stay downtown for the rest of the festival, too." He scrunches his mouth to the side. "I don't want to leave. I hate ditching you here."

I force a smile. "You've gotta help your sister." It stings when he stands to leave. I can't tell if my burst of envy is directed at Valerie, for being Landon's priority, or Landon, for having a sister who still loves him.

"Can I make it up to you?" he asks. "Buy you a drink at the Tap Room tonight?"

"I can't tonight; I have work."

"Tomorrow, then?"

I hesitate. I hate the Tap Room. All the city guards get drunk and beat up people like me. Going in there as a Blank I might as well draw a target on my back.

He squeezes my hand. "I'll keep you safe, okay?"

"I don't know."

"Look, Zadie. I just . . . please. Promise you'll meet me tomorrow."

I've never heard him plead like this. Does he want to hear

my awkward confession that badly? "Okay. Meet you there at seven?"

We hug goodbye. He speeds out of the garden at a pace only Limitless Landon and his zillion Skills could muster.

It's only after he's gone that I realize he never got to tell me whatever it was he was trying to say.

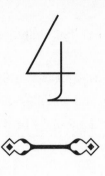

I suppress a yawn as the sun comes up, slowly washing light across the dunes. My muscles ache from sitting on this hard platform for the past ten hours. I stretch, working out the kinks. I'm glad my shift is almost over. My stomach is growling.

After yesterday's festival disaster and the weirdness with Landon, spending the night at work was a relief. Usually monotonous watch-post duty grates on me, but I welcomed something boring. Even the dreaded overnight shift.

When the sun exposes its full, round belly, I do one final sweep of the area before my replacement arrives. My legs dangle over the edge of the wooden platform, five feet off the ground.

Trinnea's in a prime location. Ma says that's why our ancestors survived the drought and famine that killed everyone else.

Located at the bottom of a vast canyon, the steep cliff walls prevent anything from infiltrating us from the sides. They built the labyrinth at the northern tip of the city, with the Leader's palace at the end; nothing is getting through that. That leaves the southern border, opening up to the empty desert. The wall cordons off Trinnea from the wastes and the desert at the southern border, but the Leader still has concerns about safety—hence why I'm here. Watchers sit at the posts and guard them to ensure nothing sneaks into town. Nothing ever does. Well, aside from snakes, scorpions, and the occasional crow.

Legend has it, ghosts of those who perished in the famine linger out here, hoping to cross into Trinnea and bring a second plague with them. The last time a watcher swore they saw a ghost in the desert, it was followed by six cycles of water shortage. Everyone freaked out. I think the whole thing is total nonsense. Ghosts aren't real; the watcher probably just wanted attention. But they pay me to be here and keep a lookout, so here I am.

It's a terrible job no one wants—which is why Blanks usually end up with it. Every day, I pass through the gate that used to keep me out of Trinnea, ride through the wastes, and head out into the desert to take my place at the watch-post. Then when my shift is done, I ride back through the desert and the wastes until I reach the gate, where I show the guards my brands and my ID, proving I'm allowed to enter Trinnea. They think I'm lying at least thirty percent of the time and Ma has to slog out to the border to vouch for me. It sucks.

Red sand stretches as far as I can see. It's strange, being on the edge of endless nothingness. I wonder what it looks like beyond that horizon. Perhaps miles of the same.

I squint, shading my eyes from the harsh desert sun.

Something's moving in the sand. I can't make out what it is.

Whatever it is, it's coming this way.

Rifle slung across my back, I climb up the rungs on the thick wooden post and hoist myself into the crow's nest at the top. The circular space is like a big wooden teacup with barely enough room for one person to stand. From up here, I can see the next watchtower, two hundred feet away. I press my binoculars to my goggle-covered eyes and scan the endless dunes.

A rattlesnake slithers in the distance, slowly working its way toward my watch-post. My shoulders relax. I guess the blistering humidity is enough to make everyone want to seek refuge in town.

I position the rifle on the edge of the flimsy wooden wall and peer through the scope, lining up the snake in my crosshairs. The warm breeze brushes a few strands of dark hair in front of my face.

My finger hesitates over the trigger. I hate this. But a snake within the borders means four years of bad luck. I'm ninety-nine percent sure that superstition's also garbage, but bringing bad luck into Trinnea is the last thing I need.

The snake weaves through the red sand, painting an elegant trail behind it. It pauses, and I swear its beady black eyes lock onto mine.

I tilt the rifle a millimeter to the right and pull the trigger. A crack erupts, the bullet striking an inch to the right of the snake. The rattler takes off in the other direction, winding back into the desert from where it came. I release my breath.

A horn blows somewhere behind me, denoting the end of my shift. About time. Sweat has practically cemented my long-sleeved shirt to my body.

I uncap my canteen and take a swig of lukewarm water that leaves a metallic flavor on my tongue.

Barton's late. Typical.

My brown leather gloves stick to my hands like a second skin as I screw the cap back on. I wonder what Landon's up to today. For the past eleven hours, I've replayed our garden conversation in my mind, wondering what he was trying to tell me. I guess I'll know tonight.

I push a fresh bullet into the magazine to reload the single-shot rifle. Count on Trinnea to arm Blanks with the weakest possible weapons. It isn't lost on me that if something attacked me and I missed the first shot, I'd be dead before I could reload. Not that Trinnea cares.

I'm about to climb down from the crow's nest when a flash of red fabric catches my eye. It flutters, just beyond the dune. My heart jumps into my throat.

It's impossible. I peek through my scope, scanning the desert.

Nothing's there.

I lower my rifle and squint.

What in the hells . . .

A growling airbike races toward my post, kicking up a wave of sand in its wake. It swerves to a stop and the engine cuts off. I take out my earplugs.

The bulky man pulls off his helmet, releasing a swath of graying hair. Barton's another survivor of the bunks. "Hey, Zadie." He shoots me a friendly wave, proudly displaying the circled Xs branded on his palms. "How's it goin'?"

My attention darts back to the desert. Still nothing there. I *swear* I saw it. Something.

"*I'm doing great, Barton, thanks for asking,*" he replies to himself, in a somewhat offensive rendition of my voice.

I snap out of it. "Sorry. I'm kind of overtired." I give him a smile that doesn't reach my eyes.

"Yeah, I got that." He grins. "Sorry I'm late."

I realize I'm subconsciously wringing my gloved hands and thrust them still at my sides. "No problem." I climb down the ladder to the platform, then drop the rest of the way to the ground. My black boots slam into the sand. "I actually enjoyed night shift, for once."

He makes a face. "You getting sick or something?"

Maybe I should tell him what I saw. Technically I'm supposed to report any unusual sightings to the city office. But everyone would freak out about nothing. No use worrying when it was probably just my exhaustion catching up to me. If they think I'm easily fooled by desert mirages, maybe they'll fire me, and I'll really be screwed.

"Nah," I say instead. "Needed the peace and quiet. But now I'm going home to sleep."

"All the guards are on labyrinth duty today, after yesterday's fiasco. You should go downtown and wish them luck."

I snort, passing Barton the rifle. "I'd rather stick my foot into the fangs of that rattler I saw earlier."

"You saw another snake?"

I fidget, feeling slightly guilty for the lie-by-omission. "Yeah. No big deal. Just a rattler."

"Rattlesnakes are a bad sign; we shouldn't take them lightly. You know, the Leader's Manifesto says that's an omen of—"

"Don't start." I roll my eyes. "Seriously, I'm too tired for this. Yammer about the Great Leader to someone else."

Two years ago, Barton started taking lessons to become

one of the Leader's acolytes. I wasn't surprised. Blanks living in Trinnea tend to throw themselves into a hobby—mine was gardening. He dropped out of training after only a month, but he's been insufferable about it ever since.

Personally, I never bought into the Leader's teachings. I refuse to worship someone who banishes you from your home just because you weren't born with Skilled genes. As a little kid, I used to think the Leader would come rescue me from the bunks; when I got older, I realized his decree banned me from Trinnea, which is why I got stuck in the bunks in the first place.

"You're grumpy. Here." Barton tosses an energy bar at me. His boyfriend works at the Leader's outpost, and so they always have a stockpile of food.

My stomach rumbles. "You're a life saver." I rip the wrapper off and shove half of it into my mouth in one bite.

"I mean, I don't like the guy, but I don't know how you can live in Trinnea and not be fascinated with the Leader's messages. Best way to change your enemies is to know them."

Sun spots dapple Barton's skin from so many hours out in the blazing heat. I hate that he worked fifty years in the mines to pay off his own indenture and buy a pass into Trinnea, only to get stuck roasting on the watchtowers every day instead. I don't get how someone who's been oppressed his whole life can pretend to follow the Leader the way Barton does.

"*The Leader's messages* are what locked us out of our homes, banned us from town, and by extension forced us into the bunks for years just to survive. And pressed a hot poker into our hands—twice." I'd never say that aloud within Trinnean boundaries, but there's something freeing about being out in the dunes. "To be honest, I'm pretty pissed off at the guy."

"Keep your voice down." Barton darts his eyes side to side, then lowers his voice to a whisper. "I mean, I get it. You know I do. But you can't just say stuff like that. You'll get thrown right back out in the wastes."

I roll my eyes. "No one's listening anyway."

"Besides," his voice returns to its normal booming volume, "haven't you ever wanted to meet him? Give him a piece of your mind?"

"Don't get your hopes up; no one meets him."

"The Selected Six did."

When I was four, the Leader picked six families—the Selected Six—to come live in the Stone Palace with him as a reward for Trinnea's productivity that year. Ma interviewed for it, but he didn't pick us. Of course. All six chosen families had at least one kid who was a Three or higher. I wasn't even old enough to know I was a Blank yet.

Photos of the Selected families hang in the testing offices downtown, so we'll never forget them, although it's been years; the little kids in the pictures probably look completely different now. Sometimes I wonder about the families he chose, how they're doing. I picture myself living behind those palace walls, away from the harsh desert sun. It must be nice.

"Well, we're not the Selected Six. So you should probably let go of that dream."

"Someone's in a bad mood." He crosses his arms. "I saw your sister's scheduled to be stationed outside the apothecary later. If you wanted to stop and say hi."

I know he's saying it purposely to bug me. I shoot him a deadpan.

He laughs. "Okay, I'm sorry. I had to."

I scan my thumbprint against the keypad embedded in the wooden post, clocking out. Barton may like being relegated to sniper duty, but I don't.

"Sorry, Zadie. Not trying to be a jerk. I'm just trying to make the best of it all."

I power up my airbike and hop on, swinging my leg over the side. It floats a foot off the ground. "Then apparently you're a better person than me."

"Jenny got the Stare, by the way."

I cock my head. "Who?"

"Jenny. The girl who got dragged into the maze yesterday. I've got some connections over at the bunks, so I asked. When she woke up, her mind was gone. Completely entranced, under that spell. I thought you'd want to know."

My stomach sinks. I should have expected it, but the news still stings. If Limitless Landon couldn't save her, then no one could. That poor, poor child. I shoot Barton a sad smile, tapping my right fist to my left shoulder. He returns the gesture.

When Barton's attention is turned, I cast a quick glance back into the empty desert. But whatever I saw—or thought I saw—it's gone.

Stop being so paranoid! Ghosts aren't real!

I tug my helmet over my head and kick off, my airbike growling as I speed through the desert, back toward town. Sand kicks up in my wake.

I stay to the outskirts of the wastes, avoiding the center

where people live; I don't doubt someone would mug me for my coveted Trinnean ID card.

The guard working at the gate is the same guard who's checked my ID three times a week since I started working on the watchtowers. Still, he demands my card and takes five minutes to examine it before begrudgingly waving me through. I speed away from him as fast as possible, not giving him a chance to change his mind.

On a gut impulse, I bank a wide turn and head toward the old asylum. I'm so distracted, I tilt too far to the right. My bike dips into the sand, jolting forward with a bump. I pull over and cut the engine, wiping the sweat off my forehead with the back of my gloved hand.

I am way too tired to be driving right now.

Technically I'm back within city limits, which means covering my brands is breaking the law. With a sigh, I tug off my gloves, shoving them into the zipper pouch glued to my dashboard. The angry zeroes branded on my palms have declared me a Blank since I was age six; when I was fourteen, they burned over them with angrier X's, declaring me a Blank who's allowed to live in Trinnea. The markings feel rough beneath my fingertips. Sometimes I wish I could cut them right off my skin.

A chill skirts across my back.

Someone's watching me.

Slowly, I crane my neck to peer over my shoulder. A young man stares through the dusty asylum window, pressing his palms to the glass. I recognize him; he used to be a Three who worked at an airbike shop downtown.

But now, he's got that terrified frost they always get, like he's looking straight through me at some horror I can't see. Ma calls it the "Labyrinth Stare." No one knows how they end up in this hypnotized state, but they always do. And no one knows how to snap them out of it. Blanks and Skilled alike, practically everyone who enters the maze winds up like this.

I wonder how this man ended up in the labyrinth. Was he kidnapped like Jenny? Did he drink too much grog and wander in? Was he foolishly doing it on a dare?

The man ambles away, back into the depths of the asylum.

A second patient shuffles toward the window. At first, I think it's Nadine, but it's not. Jenny stares back at me, entranced, her lip wobbling as if suppressing a silent scream. Instead of an indenture uniform, she wears a green medical gown. Her hair flows down her back in loose brown waves.

Does she remember anything?

The trance is so thick, it's like she's a ghost.

What did this to you, Jenny? I think of Dex and swallow hard. *Or who?*

I never knew her, but I feel a connection to her. We share a Blank history that others will never understand.

I hop off my bike and approach the building. My feet subconsciously shuffle beneath me. I wonder what Jenny's thinking right now—if she's still able to think, somewhere deep down, past the fog this spell has cast over her. It's sickening to think this horrible trance is what it took for the Skilled to let her back within the town borders.

That could have been Landon. He could've been the one on the other side of the window, staring vacantly at me. Trapped in fear. The thought makes my stomach roll.

I press my fingers to the cool glass. Jenny's face doesn't change. She looks straight through me, her eyes wider than Ma's dishpans. She doesn't even know I'm here. I can't imagine living in a state of permanent fear like that. The thought sends a shiver rippling through me.

The asylum door swings open. "What are you doing here?"

I nearly jump a foot in the air.

My sister exits the asylum and the door locks shut behind her. Chantry's not wearing her guard uniform this morning—just brown pants and a white tunic. "I said, what are you doing here?" I brace myself for another attack, but there's no anger on her face—just a mask of sadness.

"I . . . I just wanted to stop by."

She arches her brows. "And visit Nadine?"

"I—I don't know." Guilt tunnels through me. Chantry visits Nadine every day, and yet I can't even bring myself to set foot inside the building. "Maybe."

Beside me, Chantry crosses her arms and stares through the asylum window. We stand like that for a few minutes.

Sometimes it's like the sweet child my sister used to be and the cold teen she became are two separate people. It's easy to forget we used to play in the sand together as wide-eyed five-year-olds outside one of our moms' houses. But right now, I can see that child in her eyes again. I don't know why, but part of me longs to reach out and touch her. I swallow hard, keeping my hands pressed tight to my sides.

Finally, Chantry breaks the silence. "I can't believe it's been three years."

I wonder how Nadine is doing. She's nineteen years old

now. Does she share Jenny's empty expression? Her permanent fear?

"Me neither."

A nurse in a white uniform gently takes Jenny by the elbow and leads her away from the window.

"Do you think . . . " Chantry fidgets, her eyes still set on the asylum window. "Do you think they'll ever find a way to break this spell on them?"

Honestly, I don't know. It's been so long, and no one even knows how or why this labyrinth trance happens. But I can't bear to say the words. So I lie. "Yes."

Without another word, Chantry hops onto her own bike and starts the engine. She weaves back into town, her back fading into the distance.

I should go inside. I should park my bike in the rack, suck it up, and visit Nadine.

But I'm a coward. I hop on my bike and hit the gas, zipping down the street and leaving the asylum in my dust.

"A date with Landon Everhart?" Ma can't stop grinning at me from across the room as she sets a pot of water on the stove to boil. She gets so giddy when the Leader releases the pipes and we can cook rice and noodles again. "I knew that boy had a thing for you."

"It's not a date." I pull the hot iron through my hair. "And there's no *thing*."

There's no privacy in a one room hut. Even if she didn't have intense hearing, Ma would still know everything I'm up to. My fault, again—if I hadn't been a Blank, she wouldn't have had to sell our old home to pay off my debt to the Warden and buy my Trinnea pass.

"You don't get dressed up like that just to see friends."

"That's because I have no friends, Ma."

She clicks her tongue, stirring brown rice into the boiling water. "You're *my* best friend."

In a way, she has a point. By the time Ma could afford my pass home, I'd been basically on my own for eight years. If you can't take care of yourself in the bunks, you're either beaten to death by the Warden, or someone chokes the life out of you for a piece of bread. I'd become as self-sufficient as I could.

Ma finally saved enough money for me to come home, but by then, I was all grown up. She's been less of a mother and more of a friend to me since.

"Always those long sleeves." She *tsks* at me. "All the other girls your age wear those thin straps that wrap around your neck. What's that called again?"

"A halter top?"

"Yes. You should wear those."

I snort out a laugh. Displaying my back or shoulders to anyone—let alone Landon—is a big fat *hells no*. "There is zero chance of me wearing one."

"You should tell that boy how you feel about him." She points the spoon at me like a dagger. "I'm telling you, from someone who lived through these uncertainties at your age, it's better to get these things out in the open."

"Why, so he can laugh in my face?"

"If he's really the hero everyone thinks he is, then he'd never do that." She grins. "Besides, I'm certain he likes you back."

"Well, I'm certain you're wrong."

"I'm your mother. I'm never wrong."

Usually I brush off Ma's insistence that Landon could some-day fall madly in love with me. She can be delusional if she wants. But tonight, it irks me.

"Stop." I pull on my brown leather coat. "Landon Everhart could get anyone he wants. I'm lucky he hangs out with me at all." I don't know why he's stuck around this long. I was just another desperate Blank at the bunks. He had no reason to talk to me then, and to this day, it's a miracle he still does.

"No. *You* stop, Zadie. The Great Leader didn't bless me with a daughter so you could put yourself down all day."

"If he wanted to give you such a blessing," I mutter, "he would've given me a Skill. See you in a couple hours." I'm out the door before she can argue.

I shouldn't be going to the Tap Room tonight. I'm just gearing up to be miserable later.

I hop on my airbike and weave back into town. Stars cast little pinpricks of light in the black desert sky. Weak dome lights on the ground illuminate the road as I coast between stores and buildings. I take the long way to avoid passing the bunks, but nausea still percolates inside me as I catch its thin metal rooftop in my periphery.

Landon Everhart is the only reason I'd subject myself to this. If the festival wasn't full of enough people who hate me, the Tap Room is a cesspool of them. And they're all emboldened by grog. But Landon was always there for me when I needed him most, so I need to do the same for him. He got me through hell at the bunks.

During the day, I worked in the mines while Landon and Valerie went to school. By the time I dredged my tired feet back up the shaft, soot covered my blue mining uniform and exhaustion pinned my arms to my sides. We exchanged small talk sometimes, when the Warden wasn't watching. But mostly I kept to myself, afraid to do anything that would get me in trouble.

However, one particular day, things between us changed. Nearing the end of my shift, I really had to pee. The Warden gave us sporadic bathroom breaks, but our shift was ending soon, so I knew no more breaks were coming. I crept into a dark corner of the caves, hoping I could do my business and get back to the mine shaft before the Warden noticed I was gone. But as I was feeling around the sharp rocks, my fingers caught something smooth. It was an apple, obviously stowed away by another worker. My heart leapt. I hadn't had fresh fruit since I signed the Warden's contract—and I definitely hadn't had a full stomach since then either. My mouth scrunched to the side; I'd never broken a rule before, but my stomach rumbled with hunger. If I did it quick, no one would know.

I held the apple to my lips, darting my eyes around the dark space. But right before I could bite down, the end-of-shift bell rang. I quickly stuffed the apple into my shirt, praying the baggy uniform would conceal its bulky shape. No one said anything as I joined the line and trekked back up the mine shaft, down the winding path, back to the bunks.

"You hanging in there?" Landon whispered as I passed. He was sitting at the table the Warden had bought especially for him and Valerie, doing his homework.

I slunk toward my bed, terrified everyone could sense my deception. The apple might as well have been a giant flashing light stuck on my body, alerting everyone to my secret. It grew moist, pressed against my sweaty skin, but I didn't dare remove it. "Barely."

I needed a quiet moment to slip the apple out and devour it. A groan escaped my sore body as I heaved my throbbing feet up into my bunk. If I could turn my back quickly, I could hide the apple under my pillow. I glanced up at the Warden's office door, terrified she'd catch me in a double whammy—smuggling food *and* talking to Landon—but it remained closed. The Warden's other workers milled about the room and bathroom, not paying us any attention. I always found it peculiar that Landon always chose to talk to me, rather than the cluster of Skilled workers who usually kept to themselves at the side of the room. The Warden's Skilled employees always kept their distance from her Blank employees, even though we were all stuck in the same place doing the same awful work for the same meager earnings; it was like they still had to show they were somehow better than us lowly Blanks. But not Landon.

"Glad to hear it." Landon winked, and something in my chest fluttered. For a second, I forgot the apple. Looking at Landon made me feel different than looking at anyone else. I couldn't figure out why. But anytime I met his eyes, it was like everything inside me was melting into a puddle. He cared about me. He knew what I was—a Blank, a nobody, someone who was probably going to die in these bunks someday—and he cared about me anyway.

For a moment, we were the only people in the room. "Thanks."

To my horror, hinges squeaked; the Warden's door flung open, shattering our moment. "Inspection!"

My heart stopped. No. Not on the only day I broke a rule. It couldn't be happening.

All the Warden's employees rushed to stand beside their beds, their arms tight at their sides. My heart pounded against my ribs. I crossed my arms over my shirt, attempting to hide the bulge. The punishment for sneaking food into the bunks surely wasn't anything good. The Warden controlled every aspect of our lives in exchange for providing us shelter, and she made sure we knew it at all times. I couldn't hide it; there was no time. Sharp breaths tore through my lungs.

She patrolled the rows of beds, stopping in front of my bunk. Her eyes narrowed. "How do we stand during inspections, Blank?"

I swallowed hard, slowly unfolding my arms. The apple fell out and thunked against the wood floor.

Her lips pulled back into a snarl. She yanked me forward by the collar of my uniform and threw me to the ground. The other workers around us stiffened, watching in silence. "I provide you everything you need, and you think you can hide food from me? Where did you get this? Did you steal it? You ungrateful little−" She flung her foot back to kick me, but Landon jumped between us.

"What are you doing to my food?" He picked the apple up off the ground and dusted it against his shirt. "I brought an apple from school to have as a snack. Zadie offered to watch it while I used the bathroom. You're getting it all dirty."

The Warden blinked. "This is yours?"

"Yes." Landon's gaze was unfaltering. "I already told you."

She looked from me to Landon. Her fingers twitched at her side. I could tell she wasn't sure what to believe.

"The city official promised you'd keep me well fed." Landon crossed his arms, parading wide-eyed innocence. "Apples are healthy. The lady in charge won't like that you took it away from me."

The Warden scowled, but she wasn't about to go against the little Skilled boy entrusted to her care.

"Fine." She grumbled, storming back into her office and slamming the door behind her. She didn't even bother inspecting the remaining beds. The moment she was gone, Landon helped me up.

"You saved me," I whispered.

He winked, discreetly passing the apple back into my hands. "I have no idea what you're talking about."

From that moment on, an understanding passed between Landon and me. We were on the same side. If no one else in this awful place had my back, I could count on him. And I hoped he knew he could always count on me, too.

But something else changed that day. The Warden became unhinged, no longer controlling her temper. She started drinking grog. A lot of grog.

The Warden rarely picked on the Blank adults or her Skilled indentures, but us Blank kids were easy targets. At least three nights a week, she'd drag Blank kids into her office and beat them up, using some obscure rule the kid broke to justify it. But we all knew she did it for fun. As far as she was concerned, we owed her for saving us from the wastes, and that meant we belonged to her. She became a mythical beast to us kids, the monster who came out at night and kidnapped us.

Of course, Landon and Valerie got left alone. I wasn't so lucky.

I'd lie awake, pull my blanket up to my chin, and listen. Most nights, her office door stayed shut. But some nights, the door creaked open, sending goosebumps down my exposed skin. I'd squeeze my eyes shut as her footsteps echoed against the wood floor. Slowly, she'd creep across the room, step by step, deciding on a victim.

The closer her footsteps got to me, the more I'd shake.

"Zadie," Landon whispered from above. "You're going to be okay. I won't let her hurt you."

I could barely hear him. All I could hear were those footsteps, getting closer.

"Zadie, listen to me," he whispered. "You're brave. You're strong. You don't have to be afraid. Think those words as loud as you can."

I gulped. *I'm brave. I'm strong. I'm not afraid.*

I'm brave. I'm strong. I'm not afraid.

I'm brave. I'm strong. I'm—

Fog obscures the small gap in the labyrinth entrance as I pull up outside the bar. Darkness makes the solid clay walls look even more sinister at night. The wooden stage is now deserted and dark, too. There's this superstition that if you stare at the maze entrance for too long after dark, it hypnotizes you and you wander inside. Some even say Dex is the one doing the hypnotizing—that he lurks just beyond the entrance, waiting to cast a spell on unassuming Trinneans who wander too close. I don't buy into superstitions, but I avert my eyes anyway.

The Tap Room is famous for brewing their own grog and being so close to the labyrinth that drunk people have been known to wander in. The maze's lingering magic spikes their barrels and makes the liquor extra potent—at least, that's what their advertisements say.

I cut the ignition. Several bikes lean against the metal rack, glittering and glowing in the moonlight. My silver airbike pales in comparison as I wheel it in beside a neon yellow one with glowing red wheels.

The flickering gold Tap Room sign hangs outside the clay building. Laughter and the sound of bongo drums fill the air. Two guys and a girl lean against the wall, sharing hits on a haze pipe.

I thrust my hands in my pockets and speed walk toward the door.

"Hey, beautiful," one of the guys calls. "You want a hit?" He indicates his pipe.

"N—no, thank you." I keep my head down.

Don't notice my burned palms. Don't notice my burned palms.

I rush past them around the corner.

Two squatty echinocacti flank the doorway. A beefy security guard stands in front of them with his arms crossed. I wring my hands, praying he won't see my brands.

"ID."

As if the circled Xs on my palms aren't bad enough, there's that incriminating black mark on my card.

"I'm over sixteen." I shoot him my widest smile. "Have been for a year."

He narrows his eyes. "ID."

"Okay." I fish through my purse, my stomach squirming. "Hang on."

He's not going to let me in. I can feel it.

I fork over my identification card, keeping my eyes on the red sand beneath my boots.

He scoffs, flicking my ID back toward me. It hovers midair. "We're full to capacity. No room tonight."

"Please." I snatch it out of the air. "I'm meeting someone."

"Not my problem."

I picture snapping my fingers and making those two cacti prick him in the leg.

"Give me five minutes," I beg. "I won't stay."

"Go home, kid. This ain't Blank pity hour."

"But—"

"Zadie!" Landon bursts outside with a wide grin. "You made it."

The security guard startles, then thumps his fist to his shoulder. "Limitless Landon. It's an honor."

"Thanks." Landon's eyes dart from the bouncer to me. "Is . . . there a problem?"

I open my mouth, but the bouncer nervously cuts me off. "No problem at all." He steps back, nodding for me to enter. "Have a good time."

I awkwardly slink past, careful not to brush against him. "Thanks, Lan."

"You know I hate how these jerks treat you."

I follow him through the dank entryway, into the dimly lit bar area. Small circular tabletops float in the air, enchanted by the Tap Room's owner's levitation Skill. People cluster around them with frothy mugs, chatting and laughing. No surprise, several tables are empty. Full to capacity my ass.

My gaze frantically bounces between tables for signs of Chantry's gang, but it's so dark, I can't see anyone's faces. A two-person bongo band plays in the corner, the drums beating in time with my heart.

Landon pulls out a chair for me. "Here, I got us a table."

I drape my jacket over the back and take a seat. His hand brushes my arm and a jolt of heat skates across my skin.

Landon sits across from me and gestures at the waitress. "Can we get two mugs over here?"

"Of course." She sets down two glasses. "On the house, Limitless." She smiles at Landon, but he doesn't seem to notice.

I've never had grog before. I slosh the emerald liquid around the mug, watching the bubbles foam up at the surface. "Please tell me it tastes better than it looks."

"After a couple mugs, you can't taste it anyway."

I take a tiny sip. My stomach roils as the lukewarm liquid hits my tongue. "It's so bitter."

"It's an acquired taste." He winks, sipping from his own mug.

I focus on the metal tabletop, gently bobbing up and down midair.

"I'm sorry I've been acting so weird lately." He fiddles with his leaf pendant. "I've been doing a lot of . . . thinking."

Here it comes. "About what?"

"About my parents."

It catches me off guard. That's the last thing I expected to come out of his mouth. "What about them?"

Landon's never once mentioned his parents. Not in the entire ten years I've known him. All I know is what I overheard that rainy night in the bunks.

"I think they would've liked you," he says.

"Really?" Most people don't like me as soon as they see

the marks on my hands. Blanks are considered abominations–
genetic mistakes. Flaws. Weaknesses. Not the type of people
you want to befriend. Definitely not the type of people you
want your Skilled son to date.

He gives a hollow laugh, slugging back another gulp and
resting his mug on the table. "I just . . . oh man . . . I don't know
why this is so hard for me."

It's like we're both little kids again, only this time, he's the
one with the apple.

"Hey." I reach across the table and squeeze his arm. "It's
okay. You know I'm always here for you."

His eyes meet mine, and something passes between us.
"I know."

I realize I'm still touching him and jerk my hand back. "So,
why were you thinking about them?"

"Well." Landon hesitates, as if fighting some battle I can't
see. His mouth opens, then shuts again. "I need food." He slaps
his hand on the table. "Can't talk about such heavy topics on
an empty stomach. Split an order of fried potato pockets?
My treat?"

Something's definitely wrong. "Sounds great."

"Great. Okay." He's stammering. It's unlike him. "I'll go order." Landon gets up and rushes toward the bar.

I've never known Landon to be anything other than cool
and collected. He always remains in control. Other than that
night in the bunks, I've never seen him cry. Nothing. And yet
tonight, he's so jittery it's like he's ready to shake himself to
death.

Something cold spills onto my lap. I yelp and jump out of

my seat. Green grog drenches my tan pants, while my upside-down, empty mug floats above me.

Laughter slams into my ears.

"I guess drinking isn't your Skill either," Nina says.

"First day with your new mouth?" adds Taylor.

The usual gang sits at the next table, practically choking on their giggles. Chantry remains silent, pulling at a loose thread on her uniform shirt. I press my lips together, fighting back a scream.

"You have an accident, Zadie?" Nina points at my soaked pants. She thinks she's hot shit because her cousin's family were part of the Selected Six.

"Guess we can't come here anymore," Onyx adds. "Seems they'll let anybody in these days."

Chantry mutters something at him under her breath, but I don't catch it.

I can't fight back, they're guards. My eyes dart to Landon, but he's at the counter with his back to me, shooting the breeze with the bartender. *Come on. Turn around. Help me.*

"You're dressed awfully *nice.*" Nina smirks. "Hoping it's a date?"

Onyx laughs. "Aw. That's adorable."

Chantry snorts, but doesn't add anything to the conversation.

I clench my fists, picturing flipping the table and dumping their drinks into their laps.

"Careful," Taylor says. "Don't wanna start anything with us, Blank."

Several people look over, nudging their friends and craning their necks.

I'm so sick of this. I wish I had a Skill that could knock them senseless. Make them pay. Crush them all beneath my heel, see how they like being humiliated.

Even Chantry.

The inequity of it all burns inside me. I wish Chantry got the Blank genes and I got her Skill. Then I'd throw her in the air, dump drinks in her lap, threaten to smash her property against the wall, just like her cronies do to me.

Before I write a check my lack of Skills can't cash, I stomp off to the bathroom. My wet pants slosh with every step.

Focus. I can't let them see me get upset. Not now. Not when Landon's about to open up about something I've wondered about for years.

After dabbing my pants with half a roll of towels, a green patch still stains my right thigh. Great. This will never come out.

I plod back out of the bathroom to look for Landon. Maybe we can finish our conversation somewhere else, away from nosy ears.

The bar is eerily silent. The bongo drummers stare at me from across the room, their hands shaking, fear plastered across their faces. I freeze.

Chantry presses her hand over her mouth.

Onyx is sprawled out on the floor, his arm bent at an awkward angle, blood gushing from a slit in his neck. I barely process what I'm seeing.

A cloud of black smoke materializes around me. I try to

scream, but the smoke engulfs me, choking in my throat. I lurch forward, but something yanks me back.

The smoke clears, solidifying into Dex. He presses a cool blade against my neck. "No sudden movements."

Dex throws his hand out and the Tap Room door flies open. He wraps his arm around my torso, pinning my arms to my sides.

He's going to kill me.

"No . . . let me go . . . please . . . "

As if blown by a violent gust of wind, my feet are ripped from the ground. Everything spins and blurs around me, enveloped by a thick black fog. I thrash my legs, but can't shake his grip.

When the smoke clears, a red clay wall looms only twenty feet away.

The realization sets in and my pulse skyrockets.

"No!" A frantic scream rips from deep inside me. "Please!"

He yanks me toward the labyrinth entrance. I writhe and scream and kick, but he's too strong. My feet drag, leaving jagged trails in the sand.

"Why are you doing this?" I struggle against him. My heart slams in my chest. "Please. Let me go."

The labyrinth opening looms before me, dark and menacing. My mind races. I can't go in there. The maze will fry my brain. I'll be another victim of the Labyrinth Stare. I'll get lost forever.

Sharp breaths rip through my lungs. "Is it because I'm a Blank? Is that why you took Jenny?"

His hood shadows his face, devoid of all emotion. I claw at his black jacket, but he doesn't flinch. His grip tightens around me, a solid, impenetrable muscle. He keeps walking, hauling me closer to the labyrinth.

This can't be happening. I'm going to die.

He could be taking me anywhere. To his home. To the center of the maze to kill me. To just beyond the maze threshold to melt my mind and curse me into that permanent fear.

I wriggle against his grip. "Please," I whisper. "My Ma needs me. I'm a watcher, I have work tomorrow."

He doesn't respond.

Only a couple feet away now, the rough maze walls are close enough to touch. Dark fog swirls inside, sending a chill across my skin. A ghostly wind breezes out of the labyrinth, singing an airy song that haunts me to my bones. I squeeze my eyes shut, preparing for that final step over the threshold.

"Put her down, Dex."

Landon stands in the labyrinth entrance, between us and the maze. His fists are balled so tightly, his knuckles are white.

He steps closer. "I said, put her down."

Dex's upper lip pulls back into a snarl.

"If you don't release her . . . " Landon's fingertips become blades. "I *will* make you."

I don't wait. With Dex's attention turned, I sink my teeth into his arm. The metallic taste of blood stains my tongue.

Dex shouts, throwing me to the ground. My head smashes against the labyrinth wall so hard my vision blurs. He whirls on Landon, his arm curling up; the sand between them dances and ignites, swirling into a tornado of flames.

"Zadie," Landon says calmly. "Run."

He doesn't have to tell me twice. I stumble to my feet and take off. I barely catch them lunging at each other as I bolt away. I run until my chest heaves and my lungs burn and the labyrinth walls are small and distant. Out of breath, I bend over, hands on my knees.

Landon. He's in trouble. I ran away like a coward and left him alone with the Devil of Trinnea.

I hold my fist to my mouth and squint toward the distant labyrinth. Crashes and shouts echo as they attack each other, smoke and flames and light billowing around them. I can't see what's happening. I can't even make out who is who.

"Zadie!"

I spin around. The Tap Room's patrons rush toward me, their voices getting louder.

"What happened?"

"Is Landon okay?"

"Where's Limitless?"

No one asks about me.

"Zadie!" Valerie shoves through the crowd in her night-clothes. "Is Lan okay? Is he still down there?"

I try to answer, but all that stutters out is an incoherent soup.

What have I done?

This can't be happening. This is my fault. I let myself get

captured, I didn't fight back hard enough, and now my best friend is going to die.

Lightning illuminates the desert sky. With a final crack, the earth goes silent.

I press my trembling hand over my mouth. It's over. Either Dex scurried back into the depths of the maze, or Landon fell.

I can't bear the thought of the latter.

I've barely taken a breath before I'm thrown backward, landing on my butt in the dirt.

"This is all your fault." Chantry seethes, stepping toward me.

"I didn't do anything! He kidnapped me."

She kicks the earth, sending red sand sprinkling over me. "Not good enough."

Everyone backs up, forming a circle around us. I bury my head in my arms.

But before she can attack, the crowd breaks into cheers, pointing and gasping.

I whip my head up. Landon hobbles toward us, a limp in his step. The moonlight reflects off his leaf pendant. My heart inflates to the point of bursting. Landon's alive. He's really alive. He's here.

But when he gets closer, my stomach drops. Landon's clothes hang off his body in shreds. A deep gash slices down his arm. He winces as his right foot hits the ground, pain shooting across his face. I can't look away. He's hurting and it's my fault.

"Here, let me help you." Taylor rushes toward him, propping him up.

I take a tentative step forward, but the crowd is already surrounding him.

"Get this boy to the medic!"

"Is he all right?"

"Limitless! What happened?"

I stay near the back, not daring to approach them.

This is all my fault.

Everyone bustles to help him, leaving me behind. I'm powerless. As always.

Chantry stands beside me. "If Landon didn't feel sorry for you, he never would have risked his life to save you."

"I didn't ask him to save me."

She gives a dry laugh. "What, you think he was just going to let you die? He's Trinnea's hero. You're the one always needing someone to rescue you."

What in the hells did Chantry want me to do? I'm no match for Dex and his fire and his smoke and all his Skills. What Blank could compete against that?

If I had Skills, none of this would've happened. I wouldn't need anyone to save me. I hate being so weak and defenseless. I'm sick of it.

I bristle. "What, because I'm a Blank? Is that what this is about?"

"This has nothing to do with being Blank or Skilled, it has to do with *you*, Zadie. You expect everyone to always come pick up the pieces and save you, no matter what that means for them. No matter what everyone else has to sacrifice to do so."

I gape at her, stunned.

"I guess that's you, right?" she continues, unloading like it's been waiting to come out for years. "Always looking out for yourself, and screw everyone else, huh? As long as *you're* safe, it doesn't matter who you hurt, right?"

This has nothing to do with Landon, or Dex, or anything that happened tonight. She's talking about Nadine. I *know* it. But it doesn't make her words sting any less. Especially when deep down, I know she's right.

I could've saved her. It was my fault.

"This isn't about me, Chantry. It never was, and you know it. You hate me because you blame me for what happened with Nadine."

She freezes as if I slapped her in the face. I want to hate her. I want so badly to cut her with my words the way she cuts me. But I can't. She's my sister. I still love her.

Her eyes blaze. "No one's safe when you're around. You just let people get dragged into the maze right before your eyes. Maybe Landon should've let Dex bring you into the maze for good. Maybe we'd all be better off." She struts toward the group, her face flushed, flipping a lock of blonde hair over her shoulder.

Maybe she's right.

I run as fast as I can back to the Tap Room, climb onto my airbike, and hightail it out of there.

By the time I pull up outside Ma's hut, my cheeks are wet with tears. I pull off my helmet and slog inside.

Ma jumps up from her chair by the fireplace. "Zadie? What's wrong?"

"I don't wanna talk about it."

"Are you okay?"

"I hate it, Ma! I hate not having Skills. I hate our laws. I hate the Leader. I hate this town and everyone in it." I stomp into my corner and rip the curtain closed behind me. Collapsing head-first onto my bed, I succumb to sobs.

I wish I hadn't struggled. I wish I'd let Dex carry me into the maze and kill me.

My communicator beeps out my morning alarm and my eyelids pop open. Abrasive sunlight sears into my retinas. I roll over in bed, groaning. I don't remember falling asleep.

I wish I could curl up and sleep off the next two hours before work. But I can't.

I sigh and climb out of bed. My body throbs as an unpleasant reminder that last night wasn't just a terrible nightmare.

"Morning, Ma," I hesitantly call through the curtain. My memory of shouting at her last night makes me cringe. Yet another thing to feel guilty about.

She doesn't respond, but I can hear her humming. Living in a one-room hut has its downfalls. My only personal space is my bed roped off by a curtain, but I love knowing Ma's there. The bunks didn't come with that luxury.

I slip into my boots. "You sleep okay?"

She doesn't reply.

"I'm sorry I yelled at you." I slide open the curtain. "I had a bad night."

Ma stands with her back to me, fixing something on the stove.

I bite my lip. I hope I wasn't *that* mean to her.

"Ma?" I rest my hand on her back. "You okay?"

"I'm fine, dear," she says, her voice melodic. "Just preparing some oatmeal for breakfast."

"Can I help?"

She slowly turns around and I jump back. Her crystal-blue eyes are fully dilated pools of black. As if someone squirted ink into them.

"I'm fine, dear." She smiles a wide, empty grin. Like the lights are on but nobody's home.

"You don't look so good."

"I told you, dear. I'm fine." She doesn't sound fine.

I put my hands up and step back. "I'm gonna go outside."

"Have fun, dear."

I hurry outside, shut the door, and press my back to it. What in the Leader's name is going on? Maybe she's overtired or something. Ma works harder than anyone I know. That must be it.

Warm morning air breezes against my face and I crane my neck back. The first thing I notice is the sky. The usual rich blue is a pale pink. It seems to glisten in the sunlight, as if made of glass.

Strange. I've never seen it that color before. Maybe there's a storm coming.

I shoot Landon a quick message on my comm: *What are you up to today? You feeling okay after last night?*

When two minutes pass without a reply, I tuck the device back into my pocket. I hop on my airbike and make a beeline into town. I can get some errands done to kill time before work. By the time I get home tonight, Ma will be back to normal.

As I get closer to Center Square, I have to slow down.

People are everywhere, bustling up and down the streets. Each one is smiling that same stupefied grin.

It's my imagination. I'm being paranoid after last night.

I park my bike in the rack by the apothecary.

"Hello, Zadie."

Chantry smiles at me in her guard uniform. She's the last person I want to deal with right now.

I tense. "Hey, Chantry."

"Beautiful day." Her smile doesn't falter. "I love this weather, don't you?" Black orbs shine where her brown irises should be.

I don't dare take my eyes off her. "Okay . . . Sure." Am I dreaming?

An older woman ambles up the street hauling three overflowing grocery bags. She's a One who worked at the testing offices when I was a kid.

"Here, let me help you." Chantry grabs the bags and carries them to the woman's airbike. By hand. I haven't seen her lift so much as a pencil since her telekinesis Skill developed.

"Leader bless you," the woman says, giving Chantry a hollow grin. Her eyes are black.

I quicken my pace, speed walking through town. Landon will know. If anyone will know what's going on, it's him.

I check my comm, but he still hasn't answered my message.

I zigzag between buildings, shouting my best friend's name. People of all ages shuffle by me, all sharing that dazed look. They're walking, working, using their hands—no Skills in sight.

This is wrong. This is all wrong.

"Good morning, Zadie. You look lovely today." Nina walks past, her blackened eyes focused ahead, a smile stretched across her face. This is getting creepy.

Jagged breaths rip through my lungs, but I can't stop until I find an answer. I run up to Landon and Valerie's massive house and rap against the door. They'll know what to do. If nothing else, I can hang out inside for a bit. Maybe everything will be back to normal by then.

My hands subconsciously clench and unclench while I wait. They've got to be here. It's still early.

No one answers. Catching my breath, I press my ear to the side.

Nothing.

Fire hells. This is so bizarre.

I race around a corner and back downtown, my boots sliding in the sand. The rusty garden gate comes into view. Maybe Landon's in there.

A blonde-haired girl crouches behind the gate, yanking weeds and humming to herself.

Valerie.

I don't even question why she's suddenly showing interest in gardening. Praise the Leader. She'll know where Landon is.

"Val!" I rattle the gate. "Valerie. Where's Landon? Do you know where your brother is?"

Her hands stop rifling through the weeds. When she faces me, her eyes are deep pools of ink.

"Who?"

"Landon," I burst out. "Your brother."

She shakes her head slowly, her smile never slipping, like it's been stitched across her face. "I'm sorry, I don't have a brother."

7

Valerie goes back to weeding and humming, the notes floating through my ears.

This is impossible. Val's messing with me.

I run back downtown to where Chantry and Taylor stand side by side, chatting.

"Hello again, Zadie." Chantry smiles. "How are you?"

The warmth in her voice unnerves me.

"I need to find Landon," I stammer. "Limitless. Where is he?"

Taylor's forehead crinkles. "What's a Limitless?"

"Come on!" I slap the side of the building in frustration. "You have to remember."

No Landon. It's impossible. It's like he disappeared overnight, leaving no trace he ever existed. I'm the only one who hasn't completely lost my mind.

"The weather is lovely today," Chantry says.

I grit my teeth. "Yes, you've told me."

"Not a cloud in the sky." She cranes her neck. "It's so beautiful."

"Dammit Chantry, snap out of it!" I snap my fingers in her face, but she keeps staring upward.

The cloudless sky glows a faded shade of pink. A white

shiny glare reflects back to me where the sun hits. It warps at the side, like I'm holding a pink glass bowl up to the sun and looking into it. I'm imagining things. This isn't good.

It makes no sense. None of this does.

The Great Leader will know what to do. He's the only one who can fix this mess. I'll activate his screen and beg him to help me—help us. Blanks aren't supposed to contact him, but this is an emergency. He has to find Landon and bring him back.

Something rumbles in the distance. The earth comes alive, shaking beneath my feet. I jump back as six tripod-shaped airbikes devour the street in front of me.

They reach the stage and weave in a circle around it, whooping and shouting. A cloud of red dust kicks up in their wake.

I crouch behind the apothecary and peer out. Whoever these people are, I've never seen them before. And I recognize nearly every Trinnean face.

It's not possible. There's nothing outside of Trinnea. There's the labyrinth and the Palace on one side, the wall on the other, and the desert beyond that. That's it. If these people aren't Trinnean, where did they come from?

The bikes jerk to a stop, one at a time like dominoes, and cut their engines. Spellbound Trinneans come out of the shadows and drift toward the stage, sleepwalking in the daylight. Taylor and Chantry follow, their footsteps slow and rhythmic.

"Chantry," I hiss. "Stop." I grab the back of her silver guard's jacket, but she slips out of it in one fluid motion, leaving me clutching her coat. She joins the others, another sheep in the flock.

I slink down and stay hidden, ready to bolt.

Ma enters the river of people, flowing like a current into the square. *No.* She disappears into the masses.

Taylor, Chantry, Nina, the Warden, Valerie, everyone I know trickles in as if pulled by invisible ropes. I search their faces for signs of life, for eyes that aren't black or mouths that aren't upturned into hypnotic grins, but they're all gone. Every single one of them.

One of the bikers, a skinny man with a golden beard, struts onto the stage.

The screen. The communication screen should be floating above the stage as always. It's gone. My stomach turns to lead. *Where's the Leader?*

"Good morning, Trinneans." He has no microphone, but his voice carries. His five comrades, three men and two women, stand in front of the stage with their arms crossed, daring anyone to step closer. "I am here to inform you that your *Great* Leader has forsaken you."

I slap my hand over my mouth. But the rest of Trinnea watches like dolls, their smiles perfectly set across their faces.

"We are your new leadership," he booms. "This is the new age. Big changes will come to Trinnea, and you shall be the first to bear witness."

Big changes. I swallow hard. For some reason, the two words sound like an engraving on my tombstone. Every time a new law is put in place, it's nothing good for people like me.

"You may call me Sir," the man says. He gestures at each of the five other bikers below the stage, the three men and two women. "You may call each of them Sir."

I tense as the entire crowd nods in unison. Accepting this. Smiling about it.

It doesn't make sense. Our Great Leader wouldn't have abandoned us. He'd have no reason to. Just like Landon wouldn't have abandoned us—wouldn't have abandoned *me*. I know him better than that. He'd never leave his town—his sister, his only family—behind. Whoever these *Sirs* are, they kidnapped Landon and somehow put every Trinnean under a spell.

Every Trinnean except me.

"You may have noticed the bubble around Trinnea." Sir gestures at the shiny, pastel sky. The shimmering surface stretches from the sky into the sand. It cuts off right before the maze. A sharp breath catches in my throat. It's a dome, sealing the city inside.

"That is your boundary. From now on, you do not venture beyond the boundary." Sir lowers his hand until his finger points into the crowd.

As if tugged forward by an invisible hook, a One named James trudges forward. I recognize him immediately. He owns the botanical shop at the edge of town, near the bunks. Ma bought cactilixer from him at the Waterday Festival.

Face vacant of any emotion, he trots toward the translucent wall.

James reaches the bubble and steps right through. As if walking through an incinerator, his body turns to ash. I bite back a scream. Black dust wisps through the air, all that's left of the botanist. The crowd remains unfazed, their faces blank.

Fear cements my feet to the ground. I can't let the Sirs see me. Something tells me they wouldn't like that my eyes aren't blackened with submission.

"Let this be a lesson, Trinneans." Sir scans the crowd. "Do not disobey."

In unison, all two thousand Trinneans pound their fists to their shoulder. In *respect* for their new self-appointed leaders. We're all prisoners. And none of them care. It's like they all caught the Labyrinth Stare without ever setting foot inside. Only instead of looking horrified, this hypnosis leaves them permanently content. It's somehow scarier.

"Now, the day is young, and there is much work to be done. You will continue with your daily labors and report back at sundown for an update. We will be circling Trinnea throughout the day to keep watch. That is all."

The crowd breaks, their smiles unyielding as they meander to their homes or shops. I have to go with them. If I don't, the Sirs will notice. I slip into Chantry's guard jacket, praying it will help hide my identity. When things go south for the Skilled, it's always a thousand times worse for Blanks.

Keeping my head down, I join the throng of people as they filter away from the square. Shoulders jostle and bump me, but I don't dare make a sound.

I am brave. I am strong. And I am not afraid.

The crowd winds toward one of the Sir women. My pulse ticks under my skin, ready to burst.

I am brave. I am strong. And I am not afraid.

I force my legs forward, keeping pace with the mindless crowd.

I am brave. I am strong. And I am not afraid.

We pass her, and I release a wavering breath. I've spent years hiding my hands, praying no one notices the brands marking me a Blank. Now, it's my eyes. Maybe the brown is close enough to black if no one gets too close.

I hope.

I force myself to breathe. I need to get to the watchtowers. If I pretend I'm under their spell, act natural, maybe I can figure out a plan during my shift.

More than anything, I wish Landon were here. Thinking about him makes a pit form in my chest. I'd give anything to know he's okay.

The Sirs jump on their bikes and drive away, breaking off in different directions. Their hollers and whoops fade as they weave down side streets and out into town. I guess their threat of keeping tabs on us wasn't an empty one.

Elbows and hips bump me as we wind through the square. I keep my arms pressed to my sides, not letting my skin brush theirs. They drift past, smiling and silent and empty. Blanks are always isolated, but right now, I've never felt so alone.

Anxiety coils around my windpipe.

My hands fumble with the padlock as I unlock my airbike. Slowly, I chance a glance back toward the stage. The crowds are gone, and the Sirs have moved on.

Beyond the shiny bubble, the maze looms. I wonder why they cut the town boundary here, excluding the labyrinth. Maybe since the Great Leader has deserted us, he doesn't need the maze to protect him anymore.

Something glimmers in the sand. It catches my eye, all the way back by the far side of the stage. I hold my breath, not daring to breathe. Doing my best to remain inconspicuous, I tilt my bike against the rack and cautiously sneak back into the square.

Inches from the bubble, I crouch and brush aside the red sand. Landon's leaf pendant glimmers in the sun.

He was still wearing this last night after his fight with Dex. Sometime before he disappeared, it ended up half buried in the sand, right by the labyrinth entrance. Could someone have dragged him inside? Maybe the Sirs wanted to eliminate him as a threat to their power.

A flash of movement catches my eye. My breath catches in my throat. On the other side of the bubble, Dex stares back at me, leaning against the red labyrinth wall. With a swish of his arm, he disappears in a cloud of black smoke. The smoke drifts into the maze until I can't see it anymore.

The boundary isn't just holding us in. It's keeping him out.

8

For the first time ever, there's no one guarding the gate, so I drive straight through it on my way to work. I zip around the outskirts of the wastes, avoiding any possible interactions. My airbike skids to a stop at the watchtower. I cut the engine and park it beside Barton's. The older man's silhouette crouches on the platform.

Landon's leaf pendant is securely fastened around my neck. "Sorry I'm late." The pale pink bubble edge glistens only a few feet away. I shudder at the proximity.

"No worries." Barton leaps down from the platform and wipes the sweat off his forehead. "Pulled an all-nighter anyway, what's a few more minutes, eh?" He grins, wiggling his bushy gray eyebrows. His smile quickly fades into a frown. "Hey, where'd you get the guard jacket?"

It takes me a moment to process his brown irises gleaming back at me. Full of life. I don't even remove my helmet before nearly tackling him to the ground, throwing my arms around his neck.

"It's you." Tears threaten to spill from my eyes. "Praise the Leader. It's really you."

Barton stiffens, then awkwardly pats my back. "Um, yeah.

Who else would it be?" He chuckles. "You think everyone's lining up for the night shift?"

I sniffle, refusing to let him go.

"Hey." His forehead creases. "You okay? Did something happen?"

"You didn't see? The . . . the announcement? The changes? The . . . everything?"

"I have absolutely no idea what you're talking about. What announcement?"

I gape at him. He doesn't know. It didn't affect him. I don't know whether to laugh or cry or just bathe in relief over the fact that I'm not the only one.

It hits me.

The Sirs enchanted the whole town, but somehow Barton and I are immune. "The curse doesn't affect Blanks."

"The what?"

My jaw slowly drops. It makes so much sense.

I could go to the bunks and the wastes and recruit ten dozen people to help me. There've got to be at least fifty Blanks indentured to the Warden in there. In the wastes, there are even more, although most are sick and starved.

"The hypnosis." I shake his shoulders. "The Sirs put a curse on everyone in Trinnea and they're all mindless, under some sort of trance. It's like the Labyrinth Stare, but worse. They do everything the Sirs say with a smile; it's so creepy." I point at the pink wall. "Didn't you notice the bubble?"

His face scrunches. "You can see it too? I thought I was dehydrated. Seeing mirages and all that garbage."

"Landon. Landon Everhart. Do you know who that is?"

He rolls his eyes. "You say that like anyone could live here and not know Limitless."

"Praise the Leader. We have to save him."

"Save him from what? What are you—"

"Come on." I sling the rifle over my shoulder and drag him onto the platform. "We can see from up here." I'm climbing so fast, I almost slip on the ladder rungs. Hoisting myself into the crow's nest, I point the rifle toward town and peer through the scope. I can't see very far over the wall, but I can see enough. There must be some proof I can show him. Something that's changed.

From back here, everything looks fine. White wisps puff from the bakery's smokestack and ant-sized airbikes whiz up and down streets.

Barton stands on the platform below me, hands on his hips. "Listen. I've had a rough night. I'd like to get some sleep before dinner at least."

"You don't understand." I throw my head back and groan. The motion thrusts my helmet off and it tumbles down, smacking into the platform edge and careening into the sand. It slides straight through the pink translucent wall.

Barton sighs. "Clumsy Zadie." He jumps off the platform to retrieve it.

My heart lurches. "No!"

He's already stepping through the bubble. Barton grabs the helmet, shakes the sand off it, and chucks it at me. "Think fast." He steps back through as if nothing happened.

The bulky plastic slams into my chest. I wrap my arms around it, still gawking at him.

It can't be.

I lower myself into the sand as Barton puts on his own helmet. The shiny wall glimmers innocuously back at me. I take a deep breath, close my eyes, and shove my hand through it.

Nothing.

I tentatively peek my eyes open, waving my fingers on the other side.

I don't feel anything. It just feels like air.

I step through.

Nothing happens.

"No way!" I step back and forth, bouncing between one foot in Trinnea and the other beyond the dome.

Barton quirks an eyebrow at me. "You sure you're all right?"

"Blanks can go through. It can't hurt us. We're not prisoners. The tri-bike Sirs can't—"

"Whoa, whoa, whoa. You said tri-bikes?"

"Yeah, I'd never seen one before, with two engines in the back and the seat in the—"

"I saw six of 'em late last night when I rode in for my shift. They were down by Center Square." He shakes his head. "Real shifty-looking folks."

"What were they doing?"

"Smashing the Great Leader's communication screen."

I gasp. "That's impossible. How'd they break it?"

"I mean, smash isn't the right word. They obliterated it. I didn't know it was physically possible either."

"Did you try talking to them?"

Horror crosses his face. "Say something to the hoodlums?"

I sigh. He's right; confronting a Skilled gang is a death

wish. Ma always said if I pass someone at night, keep my head down and don't make eye contact. Even Barton's overacted devotion to the Leader isn't enough to make him risk his life. "What else did they do?"

"Didn't stick around, had to clock in. I figured the Leader was punishing us or something, taking himself away for a while. Failed acolytes aren't supposed to address the Leader directly, so I thought—"

I tune him out. The Sirs said the Leader had forsaken us, left Trinnea forever. But if they were the ones who broke the connection, that doesn't make sense. Why do it in the dead of night unless they wanted to keep it a secret? The Leader didn't take himself away; he was taken from us. Maybe he doesn't know we're in trouble.

". . . and I've tried before, but—"

"You don't think . . . " I interrupt him. "The Sirs disabled our connection to the Leader so we'd think he abandoned us? So we'd feel alone and lost and obey the first people to assert power? Maybe the Leader never left at all. Maybe he's in the Stone Palace right now, wondering why no one's reaching out." Usually, my resentment toward the Leader gnaws through me like an infection, but we're all beholden to his protection. It keeps us alive. He's the only person powerful enough to save us from these Sirs and their curse.

"What type of person would do such a thing?"

"Same type of people who'd put a whole city under a spell and kidnap their hero in the middle of the night."

He blinks. "You really aren't kidding."

"Fire hells!" I want to scream. "No, I'm not kidding. If you want to see for yourself, go downtown right now. See what they do when they realize you aren't hypnotized."

"Okay, okay. I believe you. So what do we do?"

I hate the Leader and his laws, and I hate the idea of turning to him for help, but he's our only hope right now. If he doesn't save us soon, the Sirs could kill us all. It's only a matter of time before they murder more Trinneans. If they discover Blanks aren't entranced, we'll be the first to go.

"We need to reach the Leader, and fast," I say. "He'll help us. He'll know how to bring Landon back, too."

Barton grabs an energy bar from his pocket and rips off the wrapper. "No one's getting through that communicator screen. They destroyed it."

"You're being awfully blasé about this."

"What do you want me to do?" He throws his hands up.

"There has to be some way to reach him."

"There isn't."

"There's no secret screen somewhere?"

He shakes his head. "Nope."

"Another communicator?" I'm losing hope fast. "A magical . . . something?"

"Only way you'd get to him is to march right up to the Stone Palace yourself."

The realization turns my mouth to ash.

"Don't try it," he warns. "No one could last a day in that thing without losing their minds. Even Limitless only goes in for a couple minutes."

My blood runs cold. "There's one person. Who lives in there, full time."

"You can't mean Dex."

I rack my brain for other options, but there's nothing. We're screwed. Dex is the only way to find the Leader. He's the only one who knows how to survive the maze.

"We don't have another choice."

"He's a criminal, Zadie. A killer. We don't even know if he's human. You know most people say *he's* the monster entrancing people in there? The one responsible for cursing Jenny and everyone else with the Labyrinth Stare? And you wanna run up and befriend the guy?" Barton takes a massive bite, his mouth bulging with food. "You don't need to go in there, your mind's already mush."

"He lives inside the labyrinth. He'll know how to survive it."

"He'll never help you, if that's what you're suggesting."

"I don't have to convince him to help me." I swallow hard. "I have to let him take me."

"He's not the only obstacle, Zadie." Barton pinches the bridge of his nose. "That maze is a death trap designed to stop anyone from getting through. Even if you maintain your sanity, you'll die in there."

"Maybe between the two of us, we can change Dex's—"

"Whoa, whoa, whoa." Barton steps back. "What's this *us*? I'm not going in there."

"You're not gonna help me?"

"Go into the maze? Come out with my mind all messed up?" He shivers. "Probably safer wandering into the desert to starve. Sorry, Zadie. Frankly, I think you're making a big mistake."

"But Landon! And the town. And the Leader . . . " My voice cracks. "You're gonna make me do it alone?"

"You don't have to do it at all. It's a suicide mission. And since when do you care about Trinnea?"

I close my eyes. "Landon's gone. My sister's a zombie. Ma's under their spell." I wonder if he caught the unspoken words at the end of my sentence. *I don't have anything else to lose.*

He bows his head. "I understand."

We hug each other tightly. Despite our fifty-year age difference, Barton's one of the few people who's always understood me. Our time in the bunks, our years living as Blanks in a city that doesn't want us, was a shared history most people could never understand.

"So is this . . . goodbye?"

"Nah." Barton smiles, but I can tell it's forced. "It's more of a see-you-later." The look in his eyes says otherwise.

"See you later, then."

"Are you ever going to tell me the story behind the guard jacket?"

"It's Chantry's. I . . . it's a long story."

"Ah. Your sister." He climbs onto his bike and starts the engine. "Take care of yourself, Zadie."

"You too. Don't let the Sirs see you. Stay inside."

"Will do. If you see the Leader, tell him I say hi. And send him this message on behalf of every Blank out there." He raises his middle finger.

I laugh. "You got it."

Barton thumps his fist to his shoulder. I return the gesture. And then he speeds away on his airbike, weaving into the distance until he disappears.

I don't dare go back into town before sundown. The Sirs

will be watching the stage, and I can't let them see me before I reach the maze entrance. If they catch me before I pass through the boundary, it's all over.

I stay at the watchtower, my legs dangling over the platform, but I can't focus on work. Every distant noise makes my muscles tense. This is so screwed up.

I spend my entire shift second guessing my plan. Why did I insist on doing this? There has to be another way. Something Barton would agree to help me with.

There is no other way, I remind myself. The labyrinth is the only way.

Nausea swirls inside me. Dex will probably kill me the moment I enter the maze. If he doesn't, I'll end up one of those vacant-eyed patients in the asylum. And even if by some miracle I reach the end unscathed, the Leader might not help me. He could turn me away at the door—didn't his policies already do that once?

I fist my hands in my hair. Ma lost everything to save me from the bunks. Landon risked his life to save me from Dex. Chantry faced Dex's wrath at the Waterday Festival when he tried to attack me. I can't abandon them now.

I decide against recruiting the other Blanks. There's too much at stake to risk involving strangers I don't know or trust. I can't waste any more time. Whatever happens, I need to reach the Stone Palace.

An hour before my replacement is scheduled to arrive, I climb onto my airbike. I don't clock out—too suspicious if the Sirs are watching our timestamps.

But I don't leave the rifle on the platform like I'm supposed to; I keep it slung over my back. I'll need every defense I can get.

The sun glows orange in the distance, sinking into the horizon. Zipping through the sand on my bike, I make a quick stop at home. I tiptoe inside, cringing as the door hinges squeak. If Ma's home, I'm screwed. I don't trust anyone under the Sirs' control. But, praise the Leader, the house is empty.

I yank open the stove-side drawer and grab our two sharpest knives. Ma won't be able to chop onions for a while, but she'll live. I slide them into my leather boot buckles and take a flashlight too. My communicator is only at half power, but I don't have time to charge it. This will have to do.

It crosses my mind to bring spare clothes, but I'm already bogged down. I need my hands free in there. I don't want to carry a bag.

I almost laugh at myself for being naïve enough to assume I'll even survive longer than a day in there. Hells, I'll probably be lucky if I last ten minutes.

After scarfing down two energy bars, I stuff another handful in my pocket. I don't know what else to pack. Maybe I'm stalling.

A lump balls in my throat as I survey the empty house. I'll probably never see it again. Never see my Ma again.

I scrawl out a quick note telling her I love her and leave it under her pillow. I don't mention where I'm going. I don't even sign it. My heart is heavy as I walk outside, closing the door behind me.

Every hypnotized Trinnean will be flocking downtown for

the Sirs' evening assembly. I can use the crowd for cover. All their attention will be on the speaker.

I zip downtown, forcing my brain to stay numb. The Sirs' tri-bikes lazily prowl the area, weaving between buildings. Every time I see one, my fingers tighten around my handlebars. One look into my eyes will tell them I'm not under their control.

I stay on the side streets, letting the dusky evening conceal me. Sliding onto the main road, I quickly cut my engine and park outside the Tap Room. I pray the growing darkness will hide my brown eyes as I reluctantly leave my helmet behind.

People shuffle past, staring vacantly ahead. No one's loitering outside the bar tonight. They're all strictly business, silent and smiling. I keep my head down, making my way toward Center Square.

The pink bubble wall glimmers under the final drop of sunlight. I crouch behind the stage, cringing as my rifle clanks against the wood. A Sir stands with his back to me, surveying the Trinneans flocking into the square.

I peek behind me, over my shoulder. Darkness obscures my view into the maze. I gulp. The monster responsible for the asylum's patients lurks inside. So does Dex, the Devil of Trinnea.

Maybe they're one in the same.

The energy bars sit in my stomach like bricks.

I can't stop hearing Barton's voice, saying it's a suicide mission.

I'm going to lose my mind and end up in the asylum with Jenny and Nadine. The maze will hypnotize me. I'll be terrified forever, permanently shocked.

Maybe I won't even make it back out. Maybe I'll be the next Farrar Jensen, lost to the labyrinth.

It's impossible.

I'm going to die.

This is the end.

My anxiety won't shut up and let me think.

I tell myself it's okay—that at least I'm doing *something*—but it doesn't calm my speeding heartrate.

More and more people fill Center Square, flooding in from every corner of the city. All six Sirs stand by the stage, stiff as statues.

I have no other option. If I don't enter the labyrinth, I either wait here for the Sirs to find me, or run away into the desert to starve. Neither of those options results in safety for me or the people I love. I have to do this.

The longer I wait, the greater the chance someone sees me. But every second I hesitate, my fear grows deeper, pinning my feet to the ground.

Ma wanders into the square, her eyes black and empty. Only two days ago, she squeezed my hand in this square as the Leader unleashed his springs. Landon made a daring rescue of a Blank girl, only to save me from the labyrinth the next day.

He won't be around to rescue me this time.

"People of Trinnea," the gold-bearded Sir begins, his back to me, "I am glad to see all of you."

I chance a peek around the back corner of the stage, sizing up the crowd. Ma stands in the front row, transfixed on the speaker.

Recognize me. Show me you're not lost. Please.

Her eyes flick toward me.

"Ma," I mouth.

Her arm stretches outward, her finger extending into a point. For a moment, I forget my plan. A flicker of hope ignites inside me. Maybe she's here. Maybe she's not gone.

But to my horror, she screams.

I push to my feet as the entire population of Trinnea flashes their black eyes toward me. Their fingers point at me in unison.

The Sirs whip around. The man with the golden beard lowers his brows.

Before I can second-guess myself, I'm running. My rifle clanks against my back. I can't breathe, can't think. All I know is I can't be here. I plow through the pink bubble. The crowd noise dulls to a muffle behind me, their voices warped.

I stop, the thin barrier separating me from the menacing crowd. Ma watches me without the slightest hint of sympathy.

I am brave. I am strong. And I am not afraid.

I slide my leather gloves on. There are no Blank laws in the labyrinth.

I look into Ma's empty eyes and pound my fist to my shoulder. Then I charge into the labyrinth, disappearing into a cloud of mist.

PART TWO
THE
LABYRINTH

I run down a corridor and around a corner until I can't see the square anymore.

I strain my ears, but no footsteps follow. Just thick, heavy silence. The silence is deafening.

My communicator buzzes. The screen flickers on and off, buzzing and beeping. I press some buttons, swipe my finger across the screen, but nothing happens. The maze's magic has jammed my signal. This isn't good. I shut it off and tuck it back in my bra.

Massive red walls tower over my head, as high as I can see. Mist clogs the narrow path, barely wide enough for me to stretch my arms. The dank stench of mold permeates the air, and the darkening night envelops me. I click on my flashlight and squint, but can barely see two feet ahead. The light reflects against the fog.

It all looks the same.

What have I done?

Eerie silence smothers me, closing in around me.

I whirl around, my pulse racing. Walls. Solid red walls. Everywhere. Walls and fog and darkness. I'm lost already. I'm going to die.

No. I squeeze my eyes shut. *Don't panic.* I'm still alive. Landon came in here yesterday for me, and I can do the same for him. I can't go back. The only way out is to go through. I rub Landon's pendant, wishing he was here.

Soft footsteps thump behind me. I whirl around, brandishing my flashlight like a sword. My pulse pounds in my ears. "Hello?"

No one's there.

"Dex?" I take a cautious step forward. Gravel crunches beneath my boots. "Are you there?"

I need to find him before anything else finds me. I have no idea where I'm going.

Something taps in the distance and I jump. But when my flashlight scans the gravel, the corridor is dark and empty.

I don't know if the sounds are real or in my head. Maybe this is how people lose their minds. Maybe this is where the trance sets in. Is it already happening? Have I already started getting the Stare?

Focus. I can't freak out.

"Dex!" I raise my voice. "It's me, Zadie! The Blank you tried to kidnap yesterday."

Sharp breaths tear through my lungs. I creep straight ahead until I reach an intersection. One path leads in a gentle right curve, while the other juts off sharply to the left. I wring my gloved hands around my flashlight, wondering which one leads to imminent death.

My heart hammers. This is so bad.

"Dex, come out!" I cup my hand around my mouth. "I need

to talk to you!" This is going to backfire. For all I know, he'll have no interest in taking me to the Palace—he probably takes Blanks into the maze to murder them.

Something whooshes past me and the hair on my neck prickles. "Who's there?" I squint, but can't see anything. "Dex?"

A wisp of black smoke curls through the air.

Ice snakes through my veins. It's him.

The smoke thickens, billowing at my feet and stretching upward, blotting out the light. I sling the rifle off my back and aim at the smoke, forcing my body to stop shaking. He can't think I'm defenseless. I can't let him kill me without hearing me out first.

Dex materializes from the darkening fog, tall and menacing. My voice dies in my throat. Recognition dawns on him and his lip curls into a sneer.

I try to speak, but the words freeze in my mouth.

Dex flicks his hand. My rifle melts, the metal dripping into a molten puddle at my feet. The strap hangs limp over my shoulder. I gape at the metallic mess, my lungs constricting inside me. That's it. I'm screwed.

I make a desperate grab for the knives in my boot, but he waves his hand; I stop mid-reach, frozen in place. My muscles won't move.

My heart slams. I have no defense against him. I am at the mercy of the Devil of Trinnea.

He rips my gloves off my still hands and examines my brands. My skin goes clammy under his touch. I flinch and shut my eyes.

"Shouldn't have come here," he snarls, pulling twine out of his pocket.

With another wave of his hand, the paralysis subsides but the cold metal twine starts to wrap itself around my wrists. If he's tying me up, he wants me captive—not dead.

"Wait!" I blurt. "Stop. I won't fight you."

He snorts. "You *can't* fight me. Might as well accept that right now."

"You don't need to tie me up. I'll come with you."

Dex glowers down at me, the bottom half of his body enveloped in smoke. Shadows mask his face. The twine stays locked over my wrists.

"What is it you want from Blanks like me?" I squeak out.

His dark eyes focus, unyielding, on mine. Whatever is left of his humanity has burned from his gaze. But he doesn't reply.

"You want to kidnap a Blank? Here." I hold up my bound hands, offering them to him. "Take me. I'm willing."

At first I don't think he's going to respond. He'll probably kill me on the spot.

His eyes narrow. "You're not in a position to make bargains."

"I know." I swallow hard. "But if you need a Blank, I'm your last hope. You're never getting back through that bubble wall to get another one."

"We're done talking." He tugs me forward by the twine binding my hands. I stumble, but stay on my feet, making myself deadweight.

"No. Hear me out. You want to drag Blanks into the labyrinth, right?"

He yanks me forward again, but I grind my feet into the

gravel. Anger flashes across his face, and he grabs for my hands, but I struggle against him and pull away.

"Stop it." Dex snarls. "The journey to the Palace will be much longer if we have to do this the whole way."

My heart leaps. "You're going to the Palace. That's where I want to go too."

He considers me a moment, suspicion painted across his face. "I do not believe you."

"I'm serious. My name's Zadie, and I really need to get there. You're the only one who knows the way."

Two thin white scars stand out against his olive skin, disappearing into the dark stubble shading his chin. It strikes me how young he is; he can't be much older than me.

"I need to get to the Stone Palace," I continue. "I'd never have come in here otherwise. Please. I'm desperate. And I'm guessing you need me as much as I need you, or else you wouldn't be trying so hard to get Blanks into the maze. And now that there's a bubble wall, you'll never get back in to get another one. I'll do anything to get there. Please."

"Don't lie to me." His low voice drips with venom. "If you can't come quietly, I will drag you there."

"That's really not necessary. I'll come quietly! I'm willing. I swear. You don't know what they've done to my town. To my best friend. My mother. My sister."

He pauses a moment. "I do know what they've done."

"That's right!" I remember him standing beyond the bubble, watching. "You saw it. You saw the Sirs, everyone walking in a trance. I need to see the Leader, I need him to fix this."

He doesn't reply.

"Please."

I want to ask why he needs a Blank so bad, but I don't want to push it.

"It's a perfect plan I'm your gal I won't struggle or fight you or anything." My words all mush together into one long sentence. "Seriously, you can't tell me you'd prefer dragging me the whole way—" I hold up my bound hands "—to just walking with me willingly, right?"

"You want to come with me, through the labyrinth, all the way to the end. Voluntarily."

Want is a strong word. "Yep."

"And you're telling me you won't run away."

"I won't. Where would I even go?"

"You'll do everything I tell you."

"I will."

"This isn't a game. The maze is designed to kill anyone who sets foot inside."

Assuming Dex doesn't kill me first. "I know."

We watch each other, suspicion burning in his gray eyes. It's like he's staring right through me, seeing every secret written on my soul. I force myself not to look away, defying every instinct in my body screaming at me to run.

"Okay," he says finally. "You come willingly. I'll take you to the Stone Palace." The twine slithers off my wrists and falls to the ground.

"Deal." I hold out my hand. He looks at it for a moment, but turns his attention to my weapon instead.

He flicks his hand. The melted remains of my rifle solidify before my eyes. The metal molds itself back together, hardening into its familiar form. It's as good as new—maybe cleaner. I hold the barrel, examining it. "Thank you." Relief washes over me as I loop it back over my shoulder.

"Don't thank me," he says. "I've been looking for a good weapon. And I don't trust you not to shoot me in my sleep, so I'll be taking that rifle."

I back up, shielding it with my body. No. He can't take my gun. That will leave me with only the knives in my boots against every evil lurking here. "It's my only protection."

"Do you want me to bind your arms and legs and carry you there?"

My face gets hot. "No."

Dex holds out his hands, looking expectantly at me. I imagine snapping my fingers and watching chains wrap around *his* arms and legs. He'd beg me to release him, offering to escort me to the Palace with no complaints.

But that's not reality.

Reluctantly, I slide the strap off my shoulder. I feel uncomfortably light without it. "How do I know *you're* not going to shoot *me* in my sleep?"

"If I was going to kill you, you'd be dead already." He slings my rifle over his shoulder, gesturing toward the path. "Let's go."

This is a horrible idea. For a half second, I consider bolting back out of the maze, finding Barton, and leaving Trinnea to the vultures.

But Ma and Landon need me. I'm their only hope.

I grab my gloves off the gravel and slide them on. Forcing my legs to move, I follow Dex. We set off into the bowels of the labyrinth, my footsteps echoing behind his. I have to trust that he's telling the truth about leading me to the Palace—and trusting the Devil of Trinnea sounds like a very bad idea.

I need to calm down.

"How long until we reach the Palace?"

Dex keeps plowing ahead, his pace steady. I shift, wondering if he heard me.

"A week."

Dread balls inside me. I have to survive in here, with him, for a whole week.

I'll never last that long.

10

An eerie chill smothers the air, leaving permanent goosebumps on my skin. Darkness descends over us like a shroud. I shine my tiny flashlight ahead, casting a small beam of light onto the gravel path.

Twenty minutes ago, Dex forced me to take the lead, muttering something about not wanting his back to a stranger. The feeling is mutual.

He hasn't spoken a word to me since, other than barking out directions when we reach an intersection. But even without his soft footsteps crunching behind mine, I could sense his presence.

"Left," he orders. I turn without question.

Every path looks the same—same width, same fog, same massive red clay walls towering fifteen feet over my head. If I stretch my arms, I can brush both walls with my fingertips. The clay has hardened over centuries, and it's tough as rock. Maybe this is how people lose their minds. Winding through the endless passages, seeking an exit that never comes.

I swallow hard. I wish Landon were here.

We continue straight, the slim crescent moon shining a dim light along our path. I haven't seen anything or anyone this whole time. Whatever monster or magic is responsible for the asylum's patients, we haven't encountered it yet.

Unless the person scrambling people's brains is the one plodding behind me.

"Are there really monsters in this maze?" I ask.

"Yes."

I bite my lip, wondering if he caught the hidden meaning in my words—*are* you *the monster in this maze?* If Dex is the only evil in the labyrinth, maybe I have a chance.

"You live here, right?" I ask.

Our footsteps are the only noise cutting through the silence.

I try again. "How long have you lived here?"

"Small talk wasn't part of the deal."

My mouth snaps shut.

I spend the next forty minutes trying to memorize the turns. Right. Left. Left. Straight. Right. After a while, he gets sick of directing me and takes the lead. I don't let myself fall more than two steps behind. I can't risk getting lost in here. My rifle taunts me, slung over Dex's back a mere foot away but still out of my grasp. My exhausted limbs feel like iron.

Dex jerks to a stop in the middle of the path and I nearly smash into him.

"We'll sleep here. Five hours." He slumps to the gravel and leans against the red labyrinth wall. "Don't be foolish enough to run away."

I wasn't anticipating a break. "Okay."

I sink down against the opposite wall, my butt hitting the

gravel. Dex tilts his head forward. His black hood shades his eyes, but I can feel him watching me.

I fidget, not daring to let myself drift off.

As if reading my mind, Dex snorts. "Go to sleep. I'm not going to hurt you."

Right, like I'd believe that. He could kill me anytime. But then again, he could have easily knifed me in the back as we walked. He's bringing me to the Stone Palace for a reason.

But what is *the reason?*

No. It doesn't matter. He's taking me to the Palace, and that's the only way I can save Ma, Landon, and Chantry. That's the only detail that matters.

I try my communicator again. The jumbled screen mashes all my photos and messages together.

"Won't work in here," Dex mutters.

Reluctantly, I put it away.

My eyelids droop and I jerk my head up. It won't do me any good to be tired tomorrow. I need to stay alert.

Dex doesn't move a muscle. He's a coiled spring, ready to burst to life at any moment and slaughter anyone in his path.

I force my eyes to close.

I am brave. I am strong. And I am not afraid.

Exhaustion drapes over me like a blanket.

I am brave. I am strong. And I am not afraid.

I am brave. I am strong . . .

I am . . .

Ssszadie . . .

My eyes pop open, my heart pounding against my ribs. I click my flashlight, scanning the dark pathway. No one is there.

My pulse slows back down. I must've dreamt the whisper. I don't know how long I was asleep, but it feels late. A thin layer of clouds blocks the moonlight, drowning me in pitch blackness.

He's gone.

"Dex?" I whisper. "Where are you?"

I'm alone.

I click my flashlight off. The last thing I need is to draw attention to myself. I get to my feet, squinting into the darkness. He couldn't have abandoned me—he needs me.

"Zadie!"

My heart leaps at the familiar voice. Ma emerges from the darkness, shining a thin flashlight beam onto the ground. A balloon inflates in my chest.

It's not possible. I'm imagining her. She's a mirage.

I stiffen, unsure what to do. But when her quivering hand brushes my cheek, she's as solid and warm as always.

"Ma!" I throw myself at her, burying my face in her shoulder. "Praise the Leader. How'd you find me?"

"I came looking for you."

"The curse. Did you break the curse?" I hold her at arm's length. Black ink no longer floods her irises, but they're not their normal brown—they're as yellow as the sun. "You're not my mother!" I rip out of her grasp, panic jolting through me.

She sighs, a guilty expression washing over her face. "You're right. I'm sorry."

"Who are you?" I flex my fists, too aware of how powerless I am. "What do you want?"

"I'm a sand guardian."

"A what?"

"I'm sorry I tricked you. I needed to get your attention without you immediately running away from me. I'm here to help you."

"H—help me? Did . . . did Landon send you?"

She smiles. "Yes."

"Prove it."

"He said something about a conversation you started in the garden and couldn't finish in the Tap Room."

I hold my fist to my mouth. He must know I'm here. I'm not alone. "Where is he now?"

"Poor boy seemed so desperate to find you," she continues, "but he's been captured in the maze." I wince at the confirmation of my worst suspicion. "I have something you can use to save him. We don't have much time. Come on."

"What about Dex?"

"I distracted him long enough to get you away. We need to hurry before he comes back."

The sand guardian takes my hand. Her skin is leathery beneath my fingertips, like Ma's. This creature's resemblance to her unnerves me. She even smells like Ma's garlic and spices.

"How do you make yourself look like her?" I ask.

"I can alter my appearance. I pulled her image from your mind."

That should disturb me, but I'm too relieved at the offer of help. "Well, thank you for coming."

"I hurried to find you tonight, before he could take you farther." She leads me around the corner. "Almost there."

My tired feet stumble over the gravel, but I don't stop. Finally, the woman tugs me to the left. "Here."

We enter a round clearing about the size of my house. In the center of the open space, the most beautiful plant I've ever seen sprouts from the ground. Its bushy branches stretch as high as the maze walls and dangle all the way down to the gravel. Soft light glows inside it, illuminating the whole clearing. Bright red, green, blue, yellow, orange, and purple streaks twinkle in its otherwise smooth, thick woody stem, like they were drawn there. Leaves drip from its long sweeping vines. Sparkling pink and white flowers gently fall from the white wooded branches like raindrops painted in glitter. Different colored berries dangle from the wood. I recognize every type of bush that grows in Trinnea; this isn't one of them.

"What is this place?" I whisper, stepping closer to the massive plant.

"It's a rainbow shrub."

I run my fingers down the smooth wood. "It's beautiful." Up close, the bulbous berries aren't berries at all. "Are those . . . necklaces?"

She nods.

Strings of gems and jewels hang from each branch. I tentatively stroke a chain of luminous pink pearls, cradling them in my palm. "But . . . why?"

"Each visitor who finds the sacred shrub earns the right to wear one. While a necklace sits around your neck, the mysteries of the labyrinth cannot harm you."

"I can take one?"

"Only one, but yes. Choose carefully. It will protect you." At her words, the shrub's branches gently lower to my level, each offering a necklace more beautiful than the last.

I press my fist to my shoulder at the woman. I hope she understands my gratitude.

A string of jade beads dangles from the edge of the nearest branch. The next is a string of black diamonds, followed by a gold chain adorned with tiny silver roses. I make my way around the tree, examining each one. They all twinkle and glimmer under the trunk's glow.

Finally, my eyes snag on a string of tiny sapphires. They remind me of the rich blue Trinnean sky, pre-bubble. "This one."

"Beautiful. Do you want me to help you put it on?"

"I think I can get it." I detach the chain from the branch, careful not to hurt any of its leaves.

The necklace grows, stretching just wide enough to fit, like it was made for me. I slide it over my head, the stones cool against my skin. I've never had my own jewelry before.

The sand guardian watches me.

Something in her eyes changes. I step closer, trying to make out what it is, when the necklace tightens, yanking me back. The sudden jerk pushes the wind from my lungs.

"What's going on?"

The woman's mouth curls into a grin.

Sssszadie . . .

The familiar whisper makes the hair on my neck stand up. My necklace constricts around my throat like a serpent. I yelp, tugging at it, but the chain won't budge.

"Help me!"

The woman's pupils narrow into slits. Laughter fills the air.

No. She tricked me.

I pull at the stones with all my strength. Terror shoots through me. I gulp for air that won't come.

The necklace is too strong. It lifts me off my feet. I thrash and kick but it doesn't relent. I reach for one of my knives. My gloved fingers brush the hilt, knocking it out of my boot. It falls to the ground, out of reach. My vision blurs, fading in and out of focus.

A scream chokes in my throat. The woman's laughter swims through my ears as I struggle against the chain. I make a desperate grab for my second knife, but can't reach. White light floods my eyes. My lungs burn, screaming for air.

I'm going to die. I'll never see Landon or Ma again. It's all over.

A shriek pierces the air.

The chain around my neck loosens. Something jerks me back and I'm falling. My body smashes into the earth. I can barely make out blurry movement around me.

I clutch my neck, gasping for air. All I can think about is breathing. Sweet, wonderful oxygen floods my lungs. I savor it, my throat still on fire. My vision refocuses.

Two figures stand over me.

More refocusing.

No. It's one figure. It's Dex. "What in the hells were you thinking?"

I struggle, trying to stand, but settling for crawling on all fours. As if putting on glasses and seeing for the first time, the magical shrub blurs into reality.

A spindly, dead gray stick pokes up in the clearing, its branches creaking like pointy, lifeless fingers. As if a current of cold air bursts into the clearing, a chill shoots through me. Those aren't necklaces, but dozens of knotted vines. They slither themselves loose until they're dangling innocuously from the bush's branches. A thick vine lies motionless on the ground, two feet away, its tip frayed from Dex's knife. All of the shrub's light and warmth and color is gone.

I clumsily crawl away from it in case it tries to kill me again.

"Where . . ." I rasp, my throat like sandpaper. "Where's . . ."

"She's gone," Dex says coolly. "I told you not to wander off. I didn't think you'd be naïve enough to ignore me."

"You . . . left." The words burn in my sore throat, interrupted by sharp breaths. "You were . . . gone."

Dex plucks my fallen knife from the ground. "I see the rifle wasn't the only trick up your sleeve." The blade melts in his hand, dripping silvery pools onto the gravel. "And I was taking a piss. I came back and you were nowhere to be found. Next time you don't listen, I won't save you. I'll leave you there to die."

My muscles are gelatin. My throat feels like I swallowed a gallon of acid. Every inch of me aches. "You . . . won't . . . leave me behind. Our . . . agreement–"

"Our agreement entailed you following basic instructions. You said you understood how dangerous this place is. Yet you went gallivanting off with the first stranger who said hello–a very bad idea in here."

Exhaustion mingled with the knowledge that I almost died clogs my mind, not leaving room for fear. All I know is I can't move, and for whatever reason, Dex needs me too much to abandon me.

"You . . . need . . . me."

"I need a Blank. I lose you, I'll get another."

"You . . . can't . . . get back . . . into Trinnea . . . to find one. The . . . bubble wall. You . . . need me." I crawl to the edge of the clearing and prop myself against the wall. The clay is cold against my back.

Dex doesn't respond. I can tell he knows I'm right. But that doesn't make him less pissed.

Wisps of black smoke curl up from his feet. He looms over me, his arms crossed.

The numbness in my mind wears off like a short-lasting drug. I'm eight again, facing down the Warden. The image of her standing over me, sneering, reaching for me, flashes in front of my eyes. Everything closes in around me. The breath is snatched from my lungs. I'm small, so small.

Dex's brow creases. "What? Why are you looking at me that way?"

My lip trembles, but the words die in my mouth.

Dex reaches into his coat pocket and chucks a canteen at me. I barely catch the round plastic container before it smashes into my skull.

"Drink. You look like you're going to be sick."

I hesitantly uncap it and sniff, not daring to take my eyes off him.

"It's water," he growls.

I tilt it back, pouring the lukewarm liquid into my mouth. My throat cools. "Thank you."

He's close enough that I can make out the white scar stretching from his left eyebrow down to his mouth, entrenching a path through his otherwise dark stubble.

I almost died. My rifle and my biggest knife are gone. I only have one hidden blade left. Worse, the sand guardian lied about Landon; I'm no closer to finding him. I don't even know if he's alive. Hopelessness sets in, filling me with a growing sense of despair. "This place is terrible."

Dex laughs dryly. "Let me make one thing clear. This labyrinth is designed to keep people away from the Palace. It will kill you, incapacitate you, any chance it gets. If you want to survive, you need to smarten up. If you can't keep your part of the deal, I won't keep mine."

I have to push through. For Landon. For my Ma.

"Okay." I struggle to my feet. "I'm ready. Let's go."

11

We walk for hours without interruption. Voices breeze past us. Each time I flinch, but don't stop. I won't fall for the labyrinth's tricks again.

The silence between us only amplifies the tiniest echoes of the maze—from our pattering footsteps to the wind's soft whisper. At every creak or crack, my muscles tighten.

"Who was that sand guardian woman?" I ask.

I've grown used to Dex ignoring me, but I haven't stopped trying. I have six days left to make an escape plan. I need to learn his secrets of the maze.

I try again. "Is brain-picking her Skill? Is she even human?"

Nothing.

I plaster my sweetest, most innocent smile on my face. "Please? The time would pass quicker if you'd talk to me."

"I highly doubt that," he mutters.

Dex paces briskly beside me. There's something about him that looks un-whole.

When I was really young, long before the bunks, I had a porcelain doll named Jade. One day, I accidentally dropped her on the ceramic tiles and her face cracked, shattering into pearly bits. Ma glued the pieces back together. From far away, Jade looked as good as new. But when I held her up close, I could see the microscopic cracks in her veneer. It was barely there, but still visible—the evidence that she'd been broken and put back together. For some reason, I see the same thing when I look at Dex. I can't fight off the curiosity prickling in my brain.

"Why are you trying to bring Blanks to the Stone Palace?" I ask.

He snorts. "Why are *you* trying to reach the Palace?"

"I already told you. I'm trying to get the Leader to fix Trinnea, get rid of the Sirs, and break the curse. He's the only one who can."

"I don't believe you."

"Well, believe it or not, that's why I'm going."

"You're a Blank. You really want me to believe you entered this labyrinth, willingly, to save a city that hates you?"

"That's awfully . . . blunt." He's right. I'd let Trinnea burn if Ma, Landon, and Chantry weren't there. I wish I was better than that, but I'm not.

"I think you have another reason," Dex says. "Maybe a person?"

"My Ma. And my sister."

"I don't think that's it—at least, not all of it."

I squirm. Landon is Dex's nemesis. Dex could use Landon's and my friendship against me, use me as bait. I can't risk him finding out. "Nope."

"Fine." He shrugs. "Don't tell me."

We turn down a new path and Dex abruptly stops.

"Wait here," he orders.

"Where are you going?"

Dex ignores my question. "I wouldn't wander off again if I were you, not unless you want to die slowly and painfully. I know what lurks in this quarter of the maze, and it'll make you wish that bush strangled you to death."

"But what if something comes after me?"

"You can't be alone for five minutes?"

"I'm a defenseless Blank." I rip my gloves off, showing off my burnt palms. "And unless you've forgotten, *you* took my rifle and destroyed my knife." As soon as I've made my point, I shove my hands back into my gloves.

We stare each other down. I'm hoping he'll cave and return my weapon. But of course, he doesn't.

"Here." Dex swoops his hand upward. Fire erupts in the hallway, burning eight feet tall and blocking me in. Two more blazes appear, obstructing the road straight ahead and the sharp left turn a few feet away. The flames warm my skin, but don't spread.

"How long will you—"

Dex vanishes in a cloud of black smoke, drifting straight through the flames. I watch the flickering orange for a moment, hoping he'll float back through, but he doesn't. I am alone.

Wrapping my arms around my body, I wait. I don't dare let my guard down. I feel so vulnerable. Too exposed.

Alone at night in the bunks, I used to pretend I was invisible. If no one could see me, they couldn't hurt me. The Warden couldn't find me.

During the day, I had to wear my hair in a long braid down my back to signify my indenture with the Warden. She liked making it clear to everyone that we belonged to her, and we were forever in her debt. But at night, I'd let it free, covering my face in a brown blanket of hair. It was one thing I could control.

"What are you doing?" Landon asked from his bunk above mine, his face wrinkled with confusion.

"Hiding."

"From what?"

"The dark."

I could tell from the silence that followed that he read between the lines. Darkness meant the Warden would come prowling around, looking for Blank kids to torture.

"Don't be scared."

"Easy for you to say. You don't have zeroes on your palms."

"Zeroes or not, darkness is the same for everyone. It's temporary. The sun goes away at night, but it always comes back in the morning—no matter what." His whisper drifted through the darkness down to me. "The light always comes back for you."

Maybe it was the way he said it, but I heard another meaning in his words—*I'll* always come back for you. Landon was my sun, the brightness in my darkness. The glowing center around which I revolved.

"You promise?" I whispered.

"Yeah. I promise."

But this time, Landon didn't come back for me. I wish I knew where he is. I'd even settle for knowing he's safe.

If he's alive.

I have to hold onto hope that my mission will work. Still, doubt claws at me. I could get to the Stone Palace and the

Great Leader won't help. He could've already washed his hands of Trinnea and everyone in it.

The Selected Six are there. Maybe if the Leader won't help me, they will. They're Trinneans by blood after all. I wish we could contact them somehow.

But most of all, I wish Landon were here. He'd know what to do.

At night in the bunks, we all had to be in bed by nine. Landon would tell Valerie bedtime stories, and I'd sit in my bunk below and listen. No one else would get away with talking after hours, but the Warden's rules weren't for these two prized Skilled children.

"Tell me the one about the princess," Val pleaded.

Landon grinned, reeling off a tale about a princess stuck in a high tower and the hero who rescued her. Sometimes, the hero was a lovesick man. He'd use his Skill to float the princess effortlessly down to earth, into his arms. Sometimes the hero was a woman, a fierce warrior who melted the tower with her hands. Whoever it was, they'd save the princess and live happily ever after.

The heroes all had one thing in common; they were Skilled. I knew where I fit into this imaginary world: I was the weak, helpless princess waiting for my savior. I used to pretend Landon was the hero, trekking through the forest and fighting monsters to rescue me. He'd pull me down from the tower—in this case, the middle bunk bed—and hold me in his arms. Even as a kid, I knew my crush was forbidden. The Warden didn't allow any of her indentures to have intimate relationships with anyone, but a Blank loving a Skilled was practically blasphemous in her eyes. I kept my forbidden feelings to myself, taking solace in Landon's stories instead—even if they were laughably unrealistic.

In the real world, no one rescued Blanks from anything. Landon's stories were a fantasy. A bittersweet reminder of my role in the world.

I tap my fingers against my thighs. My stomach rumbles. I haven't eaten all day.

Sssszadie . . .

My heart rate kicks up several notches.

"I'm not afraid of you." I unclasp my last knife from my boot and brandish it like a sword, keeping my back against the wall. "Whoever you are, you don't scare me."

"Oh, put that away, silly girl. A simple blade can't harm me."

The sand guardian slumps against the opposite wall, pursing her lips. Her yellow cat eyes twinkle with boredom. So much for Dex's fire wall.

It's surreal seeing the monstrous incarnation of my mother in the daylight. I don't lower my blade. "Get away from me."

"You're a jumpy one, aren't you?"

"You tried to kill me. Leave me alone."

The sand guardian shrugs. "You shouldn't trust him, you know."

"I don't trust him any more than I trust you." Dex better hurry back. "I'm not falling for your tricks again."

"I'm not here to trick you. But no matter. I'll leave you to see for yourself." She winks at me. With a whoosh of sand, she disappears.

That was too easy. And telling me not to trust Dex—does she really think I'm that oblivious?

A cold rush of air sweeps through. The flames guarding the path to the left flicker for a moment, then burn out.

I tense. Walls of fire still rage in the roads leading ahead and back from where we came. But for some reason, the sand guardian wants me to go to the left. Dex's warning flits through my head.

"I'm not falling for that," I call, hoping the sand guardian hears me.

I creep closer to the newly cleared path and peek around the corner. Déjà vu pulses through me. There's a small square space, similar to the one with the murderous shrub.

But instead of a killer plant, a rectangular mirror stands in the center of the clearing. It looks like the one Ma has at home, only with fewer smudges. If the sand guardian wants me to go in there, it's definitely a trap.

I rip open an energy bar and take a bite. I'm not setting one foot inside that room.

With a whoosh, black smoke billows into the hallway. I quickly stow my knife back in its hiding place. I never thought I'd be happy to see the Devil of Trinnea, but the moment he appears I'm flooded with relief.

Dex's eyes widen in panic. He flings his hand toward me and the wind thrusts me against the wall. "How did you clear the fire?"

I try to move, but an invisible force pins my limbs in place. "I didn't!"

Dex tears my right glove off and rubs his thumb over my brand. "Are you Skilled? Is this fake?"

"No!"

"Don't lie to me."

"I'm a Blank, I swear! I didn't put out the fire, the sand guardian did."

"She was here?"

"Yes!"

He shoves my arm back to me. The invisible force relents, and I stumble away from the wall.

"Why do you care if I'm Skilled or not?" I snap. "Obviously you're more powerful than me, shouldn't that be enough?"

I want to ask where he went, but I'm just grateful I'm not alone anymore. I rip the wrapper off a second bar and shove the whole thing into my mouth in two bites.

Dex watches me with perplexity.

"What?" I ask, my cheeks bulging with food.

"I thought you'd run." He leans against the wall. "I was expecting I'd have to track you down and drag you back here with chains around your wrists."

"You must really think I'm eager to run off and get myself killed in here."

"You're afraid of me. Don't think I don't see the urge to run plastered across your face every time you glance my way."

"You held a knife to my throat at the Tap Room. You're known for kidnapping people and dragging them into this horrible place where they lose their minds. Why ever would I be afraid of you?"

"You want a reason to be afraid? How about I leave you here?"

How *dare* he? "Nope. You won't do it. You need me." I pop the last bite into my mouth and turn my glare away from him. Two can play at this game. His threat is empty, and if I have to call his bluff every time he opens his mouth, so be it.

Finally, curiosity overcomes my annoyance. I point at the doorway. "So, what's in that room?"

He heads inside. "We can rest here. Five hours."

"With the scary mirror?"

"With the mirror," he says. "I wouldn't say scary. Not comparatively."

I follow Dex into the small space. It isn't lost on me that if the sand guardian returned, we'd be cornered inside. I subtly position myself so that Dex is between the doorway and me.

"It can't be an ordinary mirror," I muse, stepping around it.

Dex sinks to the ground by the doorway. He opens an energy bar and bites into it as if I'm not there.

"Or, you know, ignore me," I mutter, too low for him to hear. "That works too."

An ornate silver frame grayed with tarnish supports the rectangular glass. My reflection looks at me with weary eyes. "Is this thing going to sprout arms and try to strangle me, too?"

I've barely spoken the question when my reflection smiles. Words scrawl themselves across the mirror in choppy script, as if someone breathed on it and wrote with their finger in the fogged glass:

Landon Everhart is alive at the Stone Palace.

My heart stutters. "Is this some sort of sick joke?" The

mirror couldn't know about my friendship with Landon. It's trying to manipulate me, lie to me.

The sand guardian knows about Landon. This could be another one of her tricks.

I peek over my shoulder. Dex's mop of dark hair obscures his eyes, but I can tell he's staring intently at the ground.

The words on the mirror start to fade.

"Who are you?" I press my palms to the glass. "Are you the sand guardian?"

But the self-aware person on the other side fades back into mirroring my movements—a simple, harmless reflection in the glass. Maybe it *was* telling the truth. Maybe Landon *is* alive at the Stone Palace.

It seems too far-fetched to be true. Landon's never completed the whole maze. Plus, it takes a week to reach the end. He couldn't have gotten there overnight.

Unless someone dragged him there against his will. The Sirs enchanted everyone in Trinnea overnight; their powers could've also transported Landon far away by then.

Faded letters covered in moss and mold spell something out across the thick frame. Using my sleeve, I scrub away the grime and tarnish.

I recognize the words as Sandrinese, although my proficiency in the ancient dead language is rusty. Ma taught me what she could, but it's not the same as formal classes. It takes me a few minutes of squinting and thinking through the prefixes before I translate it:

The answer to the deepest question written on your soul.

If this is real, and not another maze trick, then the mirror answered the question that's been tearing at my heart for the last two days—*where's Landon?* He's alive. I have to believe it's real.

"So, that's why you're going to the Stone Palace," Dex says smugly. "I knew I'd find out if I brought you here."

"No. You don't . . . no. That's not it. I—"

"I should've known after the way he came running to save you the other night."

"He's just . . . he's my best friend. We're not . . . no. We're friends. Platonic."

Dex swoops in front of me, blocking the mirror. "Landon Everhart is your best friend."

"Yes." I slink down. "Please don't hurt me."

His dark eyes lock onto mine.

"Everhart is scum." Dex shoves past me. "Let's go."

"But you said we could rest here!"

"I changed my mind." He barrels toward the exit.

"Wait." I squint at the mirror. Dex's retreating reflection writes its own message in the glass:

Shae is still alive, but barely.

"What does that mean?" I call as Dex disappears out of the room, into the labyrinth. "Who's Shae?"

He doesn't look back.

12

Dex knows my secret. This solidifies it; the moment we reach the Palace gates, I need to ditch him. I won't give him the chance to use me to get to Landon. But getting past him won't be easy. I don't know what I'm up against.

I mentally list his Skills as we walk. He's got some doozies. I know about the fire, the metal manipulation, the black smoke, the ability to freeze my muscles so I can't move, and the whole shoving-me-against-the-wall-without-touching-me thing. If I want any shot of escaping, I need to figure him out.

"Are you a Five?" I ask, trying my best to sound innocent.

To my shock, he actually answers. "I'm a Six."

"Fire hells." No wonder he's the only one strong enough to threaten Limitless. I've never heard of anyone having more than four Skills, other than Landon—and he's an anomaly.

But that means he's got a Skill that I don't know about. That's a dangerous secret to have.

"So, what's the sixth one?"

He doesn't reply.

I force the fear not to show on my face. If Dex was going to curse me with the Labyrinth Stare, he would have done it already. *Right?*

"Oh come on," I jog to catch up to him. "I know about the smoke, the fire, the metal, the locking up my muscles so I can't move, and the shoving without touching thing. What else you got?"

Dex speeds up, my rifle clacking against his back. He strides down a corridor to the right, then immediately changes course into another left turn. I struggle to keep up.

A soft buzzing fills the air, getting louder with each step. It's like a swarm of crickets is chirping somewhere in the maze walls.

We take another turn.

I nearly trip when I see it. The towering red walls on our left and right split off to the sides. A rock wall cuts across the middle, overflowing with green moss and brown vines. Boulders and pebbles of all sizes fit together like a crooked puzzle, creating an eight-foot-tall barrier between us and whatever lies ahead. A green wooden door cuts through the center.

Whatever it's blocking, it isn't good. I'm struck with an inexplicable urge to turn around.

"Maybe we should find another way."

But Dex doesn't stop. "Keep up."

Swallowing back my fear, I follow him toward the door.

The buzzing intensifies with each step, as if a million tiny insects wait on the other side.

Chipping green paint coats the door's surface. A rusty handle shaped like a curved lily pokes out. It looks like no one's been through here in years.

I jiggle the handle. "Oops, it's locked. Guess we can't go in."

Dex smirks at me. He backs up and flicks his hand, that

damn Skill again. As if pushed by a wave of air, the door swings open, its rickety hinges squeaking.

I brace myself, but nothing happens.

"C'mon." He heads through the doorway.

I follow him into a wide, overgrown field awash with sunlight.

No, not a field. A garden.

Overgrown bushes bursting with leaves fill the large space. Wildflowers cascade down the rock walls and up tree trunks. Sprawling vines wrap around everything. Everywhere I look it's like a volcano of green erupted, spilling plants across the earth. Like someone dumped a truckload of assorted seeds in here a decade ago and forgot about it.

"Careful what you touch," Dex says, breaking off ahead.

The ancient stone path beneath our feet winds into the depths of the garden. Weeds and grass sprout up between the cracks.

Trees dripping with vines and fat pitcher flowers surround us, their green stalks stretching toward the clouds. Crickets and bugs hum and buzz. It feels so magical. Everything is alive, vibrant. A sickly sweet aroma perfumes the air. It's like I stepped into a rainforest from Ma's lessons about faraway lands from the past.

I've never seen any of these outside of Ma's plant guide. Nothing but cacti grow in Trinnea, and they're mostly in the public gardens. Only two days ago, I sat beside Landon on that garden bench. I touch his leaf pendant hanging from my neck.

Black Moon Flowers grow to my right, their crescent-shaped

bodies flushed with a pink glow. They're a hallucinogen known to make people orchestrate their own deaths.

I can't help wondering what Landon was trying to tell me that day. Something about his parents—about me.

Clusters of acidic Amphorae Root jut out from the earth, like claws dripping in purple goo. Its secretion can burn through the thickest steel in seconds.

I wish we'd finished our conversation. I'd give anything to go back to that day.

Appleweed grows along the rocks. Its thin vines stretch and bend to infiltrate any crack it can find. It looks innocuous enough, aside from the fact that its roots can strangle the thickest tree.

I should have spoken up. I should have told him how I felt when I had the chance. Now, I don't know if I'll ever see him again.

Ice Lilies sprout from the ground, their white frames hunched over like a frail person shivering in the cold. Ingesting a bite slowly freezes a person from the inside.

When I see him again—if I do—I'm going to tell him. I won't give him a chance to speak first. I'm just going to lay it all out on the table.

Woodvine weaves in splintery thickets around us. Its thorns are longer than a dagger and sharp enough to pierce iron. It's deadly. Like the others.

This isn't an ordinary garden. This is a death trap.

I keep my arms tight at my sides, carefully surveying the ground before each step.

We continue down the path, under canopies of vines. I can't

see the rock wall anymore. Everywhere I look, there's nothing but plants. We must be near the center of the garden.

Life thrums around us, hissing and buzzing and rustling. A strange feeling washes over me. Like the plants are watching us. Waiting for something. I stay alert, my body tense.

Clumps of white cylindrical flowers grow to the right, several feet off the trail. Berries black as the night sky pinched with a blood-red speck hang beneath them. I know them immediately: Devil's Bell. They say if a single drop of juice touches your skin, it will stop your heart within seconds.

Dex continues along down the path. I need a failsafe in case he turns on me. If I ever want a shot of fighting back, now's possibly my only chance.

"Hey, Dex?" I smile sweetly. "I need to relieve myself."

He groans. "Can't you wait?"

"It's really urgent. I don't think I can."

"Fine. Make it quick."

"Thank you."

But he's already black smoke, wafting to the other end of the garden to give me privacy. I need to be fast. Careful not to brush any leaves, I slink off the trail.

With every footstep, I shuffle and maneuver to avoid touching anything. Death by toxicity is not a pleasant way to go. My heart jumps into my throat when something flutters against my arm, but it's only orange Dustfern. My skin might itch later, but better than gruesome death by poison.

When I'm so concealed by flora that I can't see the path anymore, I unclasp my knife from my boot. Double checking my leather gloves for holes, I rub my blade across the lethal

Devil's Bell leaves. I slice into the black berries, letting their juice douse the metal. When it's coated in poison, I wipe the excess on the grass. Perfect. I carefully wrap it in its leather sheath before hiding it back in my boot.

If he tries anything, one swipe is all I'll need to kill him.

Elated with myself, I tiptoe back toward the path.

At least, I think it's the right direction. Those purple flowers don't look familiar. Then again, everything looks the same. It's all leaves, flowers, trees, shrubs, and vines everywhere I look.

I double back to the Devil's Bell to reevaluate.

Something rustles in the bushes behind me.

"Dex?"

The rustling stops. No one's there.

I go to step in what is hopefully the right direction, but nearly topple over. A thick green root coils around my left ankle like a snake, as if it had grown there. I try again, pulling with all my might. I dig my fingernails underneath it and wrench at the root, but it won't budge. Panic shoots through me.

"Dex! Can you come here?"

I reach for my poison knife, but the root yanks me forward. I stumble, landing on my butt in the dirt.

The buzzing and hissing intensifies. I can't fight the feeling that the plants are talking about me.

Its grip tightens like a shackle. I wince, straining against it. The root lurches, dragging me by the ankle.

I scream at the top of my lungs. Branches claw and scratch my clothes as the vine drags me farther into the garden. I flinch to the side, narrowly missing impaling myself on the Amphorae Root.

I kick off my left shoe, freeing my foot. But two more vines latch onto my bare ankle. I lunge for my knife in the discarded boot, but the plants drag me away before I can grab it.

I desperately grapple for a branch. Prickers dig through my gloves, ripping into my skin as the vine pulls me straight through a patch of Dustfern. Gravel scrapes into my back. I can't let it drag me to my death.

Insects and plants buzz around me, the noise deafening in my ears. The dirt and grass become wet patches of mud, sloshing over me. Dank swamp odor swirls through the air.

I grab a stem and wrench it from the ground. Sharp spikes protrude from the gnarled branch—Woodvine.

I barely process the dark pond ahead until a cold flood washes over my feet. My ankles disappear into the water, then my knees. I scream until my lungs burn, but Dex is nowhere to be found.

He said he wouldn't save me again. Did he mean it?

My arms flounder for anything and latch onto a root. I can't let it take me under the water. I'll never make it out alive.

The vine is viselike around my ankle. It pulls harder, cutting off the circulation to my bare foot. My whole body strains, clinging to the root with every fiber I've got. The buzzing turns to whispers around me.

Ssssszadie.

Let go, Zadie.

Stop fighting. Just let go.

I catch a flash of the sand guardian's dress out of the corner of my eye.

My sweaty fingers slip. With one solid tug, the vine yanks

me into the water. I thrash my arms but can't grab the shore. A gulp of water burns my throat as the vine drags my head below the surface.

13

Cold water engulfs me. My arms flail, struggling to find land. The sunlight fades into the distance until nothing but darkness surrounds me. Muffled sounds from above dull to silence as the water swallows me whole.

The vine stops pulling. It's not dragging me; it's holding me here. Drowning me.

I blindly feel for anything to grab, but my fingers meet nothing but water. I yelp, releasing a breath of precious air. Bubbles float to the surface, taunting me.

I'm going to die. I'm going to drown and no one will know. I'm too weak, too powerless. This is the end.

I'll never see Ma again.

Landon. I'll never see Landon again. Never find out what he was trying to tell me. Never know how he truly feels.

I jerk my arms and something sharp digs into my skin. My hand wraps around the Woodvine thorn, stuck in my shirt fabric.

My lungs scream for air.

I take the thorn and hack into the vine. The plant tugs and writhes, jerking my leg back and forth. I don't relent. White spots dapple my vision.

A crack reverberates in the water as the vine snaps. With my final drop of energy, I propel myself to the surface. I'm fading. The light grows closer. Everything spins around me.

I burst through the surface, gasping for air.

I can't swim. I kick as hard as I can, paddling my arms and struggling to keep my head above water. Finally, I throw myself onto the shore. Cool pond sludge splashes my cheek. I practically cry with joy. I don't care that my hair is slick with mud and I'm drenched to the bone. I'm alive. Praise the Leader.

I claw my way toward my discarded boot. My poison-coated knife is still firmly in place. I breathe out a heavy sigh and slip my wet foot inside.

Branches crack and rustle ahead as Dex dodges around the Dustfern bushes. The moment he sees me, his body visibly relaxes. "You're wet."

"Thanks for noticing." I push to my feet, dripping with pond scum. "I wasn't aware."

I expect him to yell at me for slowing us down.

But he raises an eyebrow, fighting back a laugh. "Let's go. Before you fall into another pond."

"I didn't *fall* into a . . . never mind."

"Let me guess. You went off the trail and touched the plants. So, basically, exactly what I told you not to do. Violating our deal again."

I roll my eyes and stomp past him.

"That's what I thought," he calls after me.

"What?" I whirl around. "You gonna say *I told you so*?"

"Don't need to. You already know."

"Funny. Hilarious. I almost drowned and you did nothing. Some hero you are."

"I never said I was a hero."

"Oh don't worry, I'd never mistake you for one," I snap, shoving a lock of mud-soaked hair behind my ear. I expected no less from him, but it still stings that he was going to let me die.

Dex leads me back to the trail. My feet slosh in my boots with every step. Mud and grime coat every inch of my soaked body.

I grab my waterlogged communicator from my bra and press the buttons. The screen stays black. It's dead. So much for that plan. I leave the broken device in the dirt. One less useless item to carry.

Dex's nose wrinkles. "You reek."

"Well, maybe you should have come when you heard me screaming. Then I wouldn't have gotten dragged in."

"Maybe you shouldn't have wandered off the path, like I told you."

That's right, Dex. Keep talking. I have a poison blade in my boot with your name on it.

"Besides," he continues, "you got out fine on your own. Looks like you *are* capable of surviving without Everhart panting after you."

I stop dead. His words take me aback.

The plants buzz around us, but more subdued now, like a whisper. By the time we reach the rock wall at the other end of the garden, the sun is an orange sliver shrinking over the horizon.

Dex pushes the door open with a flick of his hand. I never

thought I'd be so grateful to see those towering red maze walls again. Good riddance, death garden.

Gray clouds blot out the moon overhead. The night breeze blows against my wet clothes, prickling goosebumps across my skin. My mud-caked hair has dried into stiff clumps. I wish I had a change of clothes. I'd give anything for a hot bath.

We take a wide left turn and Dex abruptly stops. "We'll rest here—"

"For five hours. I know." I sink to the ground with a groan. Every muscle aches with exhaustion. My stomach rumbles.

Dex sits against the opposite wall, watching me. A hint of curiosity gleams in his eyes.

Something mushy sloshes in my pockets. I dig out the soggy remains of my energy bars. Hells, I can't eat them now, not when they're soaked with dirty pond water from the death garden. Who knows what that would do to my body. I sigh, leaving them on the ground. Guess I won't be eating for a while.

Scaly red patches dapple my skin from the Dustfern. I'm grateful the vine didn't drag me through worse, but my skin feels like it's cracking off my body. Everywhere. It even got through my clothes. I dig my fingernails into my skin, furiously scratching.

Dex raises an eyebrow at me.

"Don't say it," I mumble, practically ripping my itchy skin off.

The night air feels ten degrees colder in these drenched clothes. I huddle into myself, fighting back the chills.

Dex rakes his hand upward. Fire jumps to life between

us, crackling with flames. Warmth floods through me and my teeth stop chattering together.

"Thank you." I scooch closer, letting the fire warm my freezing, itchy limbs.

"Don't thank me." He tosses me an energy bar. "Here."

Food. Praise the Leader. I want to ask where he got this, but I'm too hungry to care. "Thank you."

"For the record, I did come when I heard you screaming. By the time I found you, you were fine."

"Oh." I guess it makes sense. He *did* look relieved when he saw me alive. But I guess it's like I told him originally; he needs me as much as I need him. Obviously he doesn't want me to die. "Well, thanks, then."

Something in his face changes, like he's looking straight through me. "Stop thanking me."

Crackling embers jump, dancing in the flames. The flickering orange casts an eerie glow across Dex's face. In this light, he looks almost regal. Like a dark, fallen king. Someone who would be strikingly handsome if his features weren't marred by evil and scars. I wonder how someone like him, a Six with all the advantages in the world, wound up a cold-hearted killer.

Did he only try to save me because he needs me? Or is there a spark of humanity somewhere deep inside him after all?

"Are you the one destroying people's minds in here?" I don't know why I asked. I know he'll never answer.

The flames reflect in his gray eyes. A muscle in his mouth twitches.

"There are lots of stories about you in Trinnea," I continue. "They say you're an embodiment of fear. That your heart is made of shadow and darkness, and your soul is tainted by pure evil." I shift, averting my gaze to the ground. "They say if the devil ever laid eyes on you, he would run."

I feel his eyes on me. "And you believe those stories?"

"I . . . I don't know."

He considers me, his hands clasped pensively beneath his chin. "So, what are you asking?"

"You saved my life once, tried to help me a second time. Gave me food. I don't think that's what a monster would do."

"I need to bring you to the Stone Palace, alive. Wouldn't do me much good if you're dead."

"So that's it, then? That's the only reason?"

Dex doesn't reply. He keeps his eyes fixed ahead on the crackling flames. Ma once said you can tell a lot about a person from looking into their eyes. For some reason, when I look into Dex's, I don't see evil staring back at me.

"I want to know the truth. Are you the monster they say you are?"

"I am a monster, Zadie. You'd do well to remember that." He swishes his hand through the air and the flames burn out. "Enough talking. Five hours. Then we go."

It's only after he drifts off to sleep and I'm stuck wide awake, staring at the sky, that I realize he didn't answer my question.

My eyes crack open. Dex stands over me with his arms crossed. "Time to go."

I groan. "Already?"

"I said five hours, and you slept twenty minutes past that. I was more than generous."

"Wow, twenty whole extra minutes. How kind."

"I figured you were in a huge rush to get back to lover boy."

"He's not my lover boy," I grumble, sleepily getting to my feet.

I trudge after him around the corner. My Dustfern patches faded during the night, praise the Leader. A dull itch still prickles beneath them, but it's tolerable.

Morning sun burns bright, warming my still damp clothes. A yawn rips through me as I clumsily follow after him. My footsteps hit the gravel softly and unsteadily, my mind still foggy with exhaustion. Dex, however, paces briskly ahead.

"Can I ask you something?"

He sighs. "What?"

"Do you like living in the labyrinth?"

"Is that a serious question?"

"I mean, yes?" I shrug, several paces behind him. "You don't seem to mind it."

"Are you suggesting I live here because I've chosen to? Prime real estate?"

"Haven't you?"

We've barely rounded the second corner when Dex stops short. It's a good thing I've kept my distance, or I would've crashed right into him.

My senses spring to life. "What's wrong?"

Dex ignores me. He grunts and mutters to himself, flailing

his arms and batting away the sticky purple web that has woven itself across the pathway.

I watch with curiosity. I guess I should be used to the strange mysteries of the labyrinth by now, but this one seems especially random. "Do you need help?"

"No," he mumbles, swatting at the purple rope. It hisses, swatting back at him and sticking to his clothes.

I stand several steps back, one foot in front of the other. "Is it poisonous or something?"

"No." Dex kicks at it, and it gloms onto his boot. "Just a hells-forsaken piece of . . . "

"Why is it there?"

"To bake pies—what do you mean why is it there?" He scowls, brushing the encroaching web off his pant leg. Every time he wipes one away, another slides off the wall and sticks to him. "It's trying to block our path."

I raise my brows. I mean, it's effective enough, I guess. Kind of silly, though.

With a final roar, he breaks the web down the middle, clearing the pathway. The web hisses before slithering away like a million skinny snakes and disappearing beneath the red wall.

Dex's shoulders rise and fall as he catches his breath. He whirls toward me, completely exasperated. Pieces of web cling to his hair and cover his jacket like a bunch of cooked purple noodles.

"To answer your question, no. I don't like living in the bloody labyrinth." Dex flicks a purple chunk off his shoulder, glowering at it. "Let's go."

I stare at him for a moment. Then I burst out laughing.

He deadpans at me, pieces of web curling through his hair. "Yes, it's very funny."

I can't help it; I double over, rolling with laughter.

Dex crosses his arms. "Are you done?"

Hands on my knees, I close my eyes and take a deep, shaky breath. "Yes. Sorry." I open my eyes, and there Dex stands, another purple noodle slithering up his arm. And I lose it again.

I don't even know why it's so funny. I don't think it would be funny if it was literally anyone else but him. Or maybe if I wasn't completely overtired. But here's this sulking, angry, monster of a man, fighting tooth and nail against a bunch of sticky purple noodles. It's ridiculous.

Dex tilts his head back. A pink flush crosses his cheeks. "Zadie. Come on. We've got to keep moving."

"Okay. Sorry." I swallow back my final giggle. "I'm sorry." My face is flushed and my eyes wet with tears from laughing so hard. "I'm good."

"You done?" He plucks the last pieces of web off his jacket, throws them to the ground, and crushes them beneath his boot.

"Yes."

"Good." Dex turns, and I swear the slightest hint of a smile twitches at the corner of his mouth. He keeps plugging down the path. I chug along after him, several paces behind, when he flicks another strand off his sleeve; it pelts me in the arm, sticking to my jacket.

I peel it off, leaving it in the pathway behind us. If I didn't know better, I'd say he did that on purpose.

I give a half-smile to his back. Maybe the Devil of Trinnea has a sense of humor buried deep down after all.

We spend a good hour walking with no more traps. I'm not sure when Dex started walking beside me, but we're keeping pace together now, in silence.

I wonder what's going on in Trinnea today. I hope my Ma is okay. Thinking of her stuck behind with the Sirs energizes me. I have to keep going. For her.

Four days until we reach the Stone Palace. Four days until I meet the Leader and figure out what happened to my town.

Four days until I'm rid of Dex forever.

Four days until—Leader willing—I see Landon again.

"What are you smiling about?" Dex murmurs.

My ears burn. "Nothing."

"Don't tell me it's Everhart again."

I roll my eyes. "Can I ask you a question?"

Dex's silence implies a no. But I ask anyway.

"Why do you hate Landon so much?"

"I already told you. Everhart's scum."

"Is it because you put everyone under the Labyrinth Stare in here, and he's been thwarting you?" I speed my pace to catch up to him. "It totally is, isn't it?"

Silence.

"So, why do you scramble everyone's brains, but only kidnap Blanks?"

"Blanks are easier to kidnap."

"C'mon, there has to be a reason you treat us differently."

"You aren't used to being treated differently? I thought you were a Blank."

My face gets hot. "I mean, yes, but—"

"Didn't see a braid on you. Don't most Blanks end up working for the Warden?"

I hate talking about my past. Just thinking about the bunks makes my skin clammy. But I haven't given up on learning Dex's sixth Skill. Something tells me that if I want Dex to let me in, I have to return the favor.

"My Ma bought out my indenture and got me a pass back into Trinnea three years ago, when I was fourteen."

I wait for him to acknowledge what I've said. But, typical, Dex doesn't reply. He keeps walking. So I continue.

"She saved up for eight years, from the moment I was banished from the city. Worked three jobs, barely slept. Sold her house and most of her possessions. I guess at one point she'd saved enough to buy my pass home, but it wasn't enough to pay back the Warden, so it took a few extra years. My sister Chantry helped, too, and so did Landon. He gave my Ma all his earnings. Together, they raised enough money to buy off my debt."

Dex's head inclines slightly. The barest hint of a nod.

"I remember the day she came to the bunks to get me. I'd been working in the mines. The caves are really poorly lit, and I slipped and twisted my ankle. I could barely walk, let alone do my duties. So I tried to hide my limp. I know what the Warden does to her workers when they're injured and can't work anymore—she gets pissed at the lost income and breaks both their legs before abandoning them back in the wastes. It's basically a death sentence."

For a moment, I forget where I am. All I can smell is the

rotting mold of the mines. My lungs constrict, that suffocating feeling like everything is caving in on me. It might as well be happening right now.

"So, what happened?"

"I faked it all the way back to the bunks. Every time I stepped on my left foot, pain shot through my leg. My eyes watered, my whole body was on fire, but I couldn't let it show."

"That's . . . impressive."

"The Warden called me into her office. I was really scared. *Putting them out of their misery*, she'd call it, whenever she threw an injured worker out of the bunks."

Dex's hands clench. It's subtle, but I notice it anyway.

"I remember hoping it would be fast." I clasp my hands together to keep them from shaking. "But when I stepped inside, a woman with short brown hair was waiting. Her eyes were red rimmed from crying. It was like the ghost from my dreams. I just looked at her. I couldn't comprehend what they were saying. The Warden told me that Ma had paid off my debt, and I didn't believe it. Ma gave me the pass into Trinnea and led me to the city office, where the lady in charge burned the Xs into my palms, over the circles I'd had for years. I barely felt it. I kept waiting for her to tell me it was all a joke. I managed to walk, but I felt so numb. I leaned on Ma's shoulder the whole time. And when I got out into the sunlight, I fell to my knees and sobbed." I smile. "It's the happiest memory I have. There are no words to describe the feeling of seeing the sun as a free woman, thinking you'd die in the Warden's debt."

"I see." We walk in silence for a few moments. "So you've been free for the past three years."

"Technically, if you count living as a second class citizen *free*. Also, the town hates Blanks, but there's a group of people who *really* hate *me*. It's like, I was out of the bunks and back into my own personal hell. They love tormenting me." I don't know why I'm telling him all this. He's probably not even listening.

We turn a corner into a clearing.

"Why?"

I sigh. "It's a long story. I—"

Dex flings his arm out, thumping me in the chest. I stop walking.

A long, thin table draped in an elegant white lace cloth spreads out before us. Eight delicate white chairs surround it. At each place sits a set of formal china plates, bowls, and a teacup. Tall white candles burn in the center of the table, with hot wax dripping down their sides. It's like someone set it for a fancy banquet but the guests haven't arrived yet.

I gulp. *Maybe we're supposed to be the guests.* "I don't like this."

"We need to get out of here." Dex nods at the path on the opposite end of the square room. "Let's go."

He plows ahead, but I don't move. "I really don't think we should."

"That's the only way through. But we need to hurry, and I mean now. Do you want to reach the Palace or not?"

"Well yes, but—"

"Come on!" He grabs my arm and tugs me through the clearing. His pace quickens until we're running toward the door.

"Hurry!" he orders.

I pick up my pace, the opening getting closer.

Out of nowhere, Dex freezes. I screech to a stop, slamming into him.

"No," he whispers.

A sickly cracking splinters through the air, like stepping on thin ice.

I jump back. "What? What's wrong?"

Gray stone hardens over his feet. Then his legs. It snakes its way up his body, through his torso, his neck, his face. The light vanishes from his eyes. A statue stands before me.

I slap my hands over my mouth to block the scream. No. He can't die. I'll never survive the maze alone.

"Dex." I tap his arm, solid and rough beneath my fingertip. "Please. Wake up."

My heart races. He triggered this somehow.

"Dex!" I rap his shoulder. "Come on!"

Ssszadie . . .

I whirl around.

The sand guardian saunters toward me. Only, instead of taking the form of my Ma, she's a teenage girl dressed in black. Two thick gray horns protrude from the sides of her head where hair should be. Her yellow cat eyes sparkle.

"You did this to him." I thrust my quivering fists up, a feeble attempt to protect myself. "Turn him back."

"Won't you join us for tea?" She pulls out a white chair, beckoning me to sit.

Us?

"You must think I'm really gullible."

"I'm having friends over for tea," she says. "You should join us."

Thick fog rolls in around the table. Six figures materialize, each bearing the same yellow irises with slitted black pupils.

Some of the figures watch me, while others keep their faces blank and empty. I could make a run for it. Maybe I could reach the doorway and hide in the maze's many corridors.

"Come, Zadie." The sand guardian smiles. "We don't want the tea to get cold."

The other six creatures approach the table. Each one looks slightly human, but warped.

The smallest figure hovers a foot in the air. She wears black tights and a tattered, dirty pink dress. Sleek, black hair cascades down her shoulders. But instead of a little girl's face, she wears a golden mask with the face of a horse.

Beside her stands a glassy-eyed woman in a long black suit. A bird's nest rests on her head like a crown. Flowers grow and curl from the center.

The creatures take their seats, leaving the chair at the head of the table for me.

"Zadie." The sand guardian nods at the empty seat.

"Turn him back." My voice cracks. "Please. I need him."

"If you want to save him, you'll join us for tea."

Against my better judgement, I let her take my elbow, leading me into my seat.

"There." She pushes my chair closer to the table. "I'm so glad you could join us."

My pulse races. Everyone watches me with dead eyes. "Okay," I whisper, "I'm here. Will you fix him?"

"I will," the sand guardian says. "For a price."

I really don't like that she's standing behind me. "What's the price?"

The words barely leave my lips when black liquid floods into my teacup. A wisp of steam curls from the surface.

"I told you." The sand guardian reaches around me, unfolding the cloth napkin and resting it over my lap. "One cup of tea."

I peer into the teacup. Whatever that black liquid is, it's not tea.

All my internal alarm bells blare.

"If I drink this . . . you'll turn him back?"

She takes her own seat at the other end of the table. It isn't lost on me that all of the other cups are empty. "Yes. If you drink every last drop."

I sniff the tea. My nose crinkles at the sickly sweet stench. I can't. There has to be another way.

"What *is* it?"

The sand guardian smiles. "Your only chance of reviving your friend."

"Is it . . . poison?"

No one answers me.

My stomach curdles. They watch me, waiting. If I don't do it, I'll have to try and solve the maze by myself. I'll have to survive the next few days in here, alone.

If the monster doesn't find me first.

The rock looks just like Dex, all the way down to that sullen expression and the indents where his scars should be. For some reason, I'm overcome with a wave of sadness seeing him that way.

Holding the teacup handle in one hand and the saucer in

the other, I bring it to my lips. The porcelain cup rattles against the plate in my shaking hands.

I'm certain this potion will kill me.

Before I can talk myself out of it, I close my eyes and drink it anyway.

14

Something soft cradles my head.

Where am I?

My muscles are anchors, pinning me to the cushy bed. I blink my groggy eyes. A fan spins over me, wafting a cool breeze into the room. Wooden beams crisscross under the high ceiling.

I jolt upward.

There was a table. Someone poured me tea. It's all blurry, like fingers grasping at wisps of smoke. A dream.

"Good morning, sleepyhead," Ma sings, sauntering into the room. "You ready for your big day?"

I prop myself up on my elbows. "B-big day?

"Don't want to be tardy." She clicks her tongue. "I told you not to stay out late last night."

"I was at the Tap Room with my friends. They wanted to celebrate." The words sound foreign. Like my brain spit them out on cue.

Ma sits on my bed, the mattress squeaking. I feel like she should have more wrinkles. Doesn't her face have more wrinkles?

"Everyone's waiting for you, dear. Don't want to miss your inking."

My inking. Because today is the day I get inked as a city guard.

I swing my feet over the side of the bed, and the shaggy brown carpet brushes my bare toes. A large mahogany dresser is propped by the door. Comfy-looking white puffy chairs flank a round glass table.

My bedroom.

I recognize the huge room, but somehow, it feels like I'm seeing it for the first time.

Ma bustles back into the kitchen. I get up and walk around my room, trying to shake off this weird feeling. My legs ache, like I haven't moved them in a month.

My room looks normal enough. I pick up the coins on my dresser and examine them, the silver cold against my skin. A framed photo shows me in a fancy black jacket, my arms around three other girls—Chantry, Nina, and Taylor.

They're my best friends, my brain reminds me.

I smile, setting the picture back on the bureau. Of course. Last night, we were at the Tap Room together. I had a whole pitcher of grog to myself. Maybe that explains the bitter dryness cementing my tongue to the roof of my mouth.

A silver guard's uniform is pressed and laid out on my bed. The gold *Guard Captain* pin gleams back at me, pinned to the collar. I'm supposed to be wearing that right now for my induction. My eyes flit to the clock by the window. Hells! I'm already late.

I reach for the uniform, but stop. Something tugs in my gut. An instinct.

I hold up my hand. As if someone threw it at me, my clothes sail across the room, into my grasp.

Because I'm a Four. Obviously.

I shake my head, hurrying into my uniform. The exiting guard captain is going to punish me if I act like this on duty.

I head into the main room and inhale deeply. Ma's spacious kitchen is bursting with a buttery aroma. "That smells glorious."

"I made you biscuits and honey for your big day." She sets a plate on the table.

My stomach rumbles, cavernous and empty. I'm so hungry. It feels like I haven't had a full meal in days.

I break the honey-soaked biscuit and stuff a handful into my mouth, but stop mid-chew. My hand looks different, somehow. I set the food back down and examine it, rubbing my thumb across my palm. Strange. My skin is so *smooth.*

I shake my head. I *really* shouldn't have drunk that much grog last night. Horrible decision, seeing as I have to stand in front of the entire population of Trinnea in a couple hours.

I'm about to stuff the second biscuit into my mouth, whole, when a light knock echoes in the room.

Ma rushes to the door, wiping her hands on her apron.

"Oh, Landon!" Her voice echoes from the hallway. "I didn't know you were coming."

My heart jumps.

"Morning, Ms. Kalvers. You look lovely."

I wipe my sticky hands on my napkin and smooth my hair, wishing I'd taken a moment earlier to look in a mirror.

"Zadie!"

Landon stands in the doorway, beaming. His messy blond hair stands up at every angle.

I grin the moment I see him. "Hey you. Long time no–"

His lips are on mine before I can finish. My insides turn to liquid. I wrap my arms around his neck, running my fingers through his soft hair.

He pulls back. "I missed you so much."

"It's only been a few hours," I tease, giving his chest a light shove.

Landon puts his fingers under my chin, tilting my head up. "You feel okay this morning? You had a lot of grog last night."

"I'm still a little . . . dizzy." I guess that's the right word for it. "Disoriented."

"Let me take you to the inking. You shouldn't drive your airbike if you're feeling sick."

The thought of squeezing into his bike seat with him makes my chest all fluttery. "Free ride? I'll take it."

He winks at me.

I pop the rest of the biscuit into my mouth. "Ma, we'll see you downtown?"

"I wouldn't miss it," she calls from the other room.

Landon follows me outside, his hand on my lower back. "You excited for today?"

"A little nervous, to be honest. I feel like we spend our whole lives waiting for the inking and now that it's here, it's surreal." I bite my lip. "What if I'm the worst guard ever?"

Landon plops a bulky helmet on my head. He presses a quick kiss to my cheek. "Yeah, you with that super speed?

You'll put the other guards to shame." He climbs onto his bike and slides toward the front, patting the rest of the seat behind him. "Hells, you'll probably put *my* record to shame, and that's been solid since I finished duty last year."

I get on the bike and wrap my arms around him, letting his warmth bleed into me. That fuzzy, confused haze melts away. This is so right.

He powers up his bike. "Hold on!"

I squeal with delight as we zip toward Center Square.

I bury my face into his back, inhaling his scent. He always smells like sage and cinnamon.

His bike whirs as we zip through town, kicking up a trail of sand in our wake.

We turn a sharp corner, past an old square building with broken windows. My stomach flips. "Stop!"

Landon hits the brakes and the bike lurches forward. He spins toward me, alarm written all over his face. "You okay?"

I squint at the building. Those windows. There's something about those windows. Like there's a ghost peeking back through, pressing its invisible hands to the glass. "What is that place?"

"The old hospital?" His face scrunches. "Zadie, are you okay? It's just some abandoned building. No one's used it in years, maybe decades."

"I guess I . . . forgot. Sorry."

I crane my neck to watch the decrepit building fade from view as we speed away.

Within minutes, we pull up by the stage. The Great Leader watches from the screen, a wide smile splitting his wrinkled face. Hundreds of people crowd the square, eagerly awaiting the inking ceremony.

I hop off Landon's bike. He winks at me before heading toward the rack to lock it up. Within seconds, I'm surrounded by people.

"Zadie!" Chantry wraps her arms around me.

A tall, older girl comes up behind Chantry, resting her elbows on my sister's shoulders. "Hey, Zadie."

"Nadine!" I tackle her in a hug.

It strikes me as odd that I'm so surprised to see her. We hung out last week. Still, it feels like I haven't seen her in years. She *was* my friend. Chantry's girlfriend.

I'm taken aback by my own thought.

Was? She's right here. She *is* my friend. She *is* Chantry's girlfriend.

Stop being so weird! You're not that *hungover.*

Chantry slaps me on the back. "You gotta talk some sense into Taylor."

"We have to hit the Tap Room again tonight," Taylor says. "I swear, I was two seconds from getting that hot bouncer's comm number."

Chantry releases an exaggerated sigh. "He was just doing his job."

"Was not! Zadie, he was flirting with me. Right?"

"He totally was," I say. Although, the moment I say it, I can't remember Taylor talking to a bouncer at all. I can't remember anything about last night.

What's wrong with me?

"I can't believe you guys still hang out at the Tap Room." Nadine laughs. "It's a cesspool."

"Obviously," Chantry says. "That's why it's so great." She kisses Nadine's cheek.

"Yeah Nadine, you should come with us next time," I add.

"People of Trinnea!" the Great Leader's voice booms. "Let's start the ceremony, shall we?"

Chantry links her arm with mine and we head toward the stage to join the rest of our class.

It's alphabetical, so Taylor stands near the front. Chantry and I stand next to each other in the middle.

A city official takes the stage. He offers the Leader a quick shoulder thump and bow before rattling off a speech about fulfilling our Trinnean responsibility. I've got a whole year of guard duty ahead of me, but at least I'll have my best friends by my side.

Chantry nudges me with her elbow, nodding into the crowd.

Landon stands in the front row with Ma, filming the ceremony on his communicator.

"He's totally in love with you," she whispers.

"I wish." My brow furrows. Why'd I say that? "I mean, yeah, he is."

"Maybe you should marry him. Then I could say Limitless Landon is my brother-in-law."

I make a face. "Marry him?"

"Oh come on. *Some* people still get married. It's not *that* weird." She shrugs, her eyes trailing through the crowd until they land on Nadine. "I've thought about getting married."

"Newly appointed guards!" the city official addresses us. "We will now make our way down the line for the inking. At attention."

We snap our feet together in unison.

His narrowed eyes scan the crowd. "Where is that hells-forsaken Blank with the ink?"

"Excuse me. Sorry." An older man in the Warden's navy blue indenture uniform weaves through the crowd. "Sorry. Pardon me."

"Out of the way, Blank." A guy shoves him hard. "You're blocking the view."

The Blank man stumbles, almost dropping his jar of dark blue ink.

A woman's face contorts into disgust as he plods by.

Barton.

"Barton!" barks the city official.

I stiffen. How'd I know that?

"You're late! The whole ceremony had to wait for you." He slaps Barton in the face. My hands subconsciously ball into fists.

Barton lowers his head. "I apologize for my tardiness, Sir."

Sir. Sir. Sir. The word sends a wave of nausea rolling through my stomach.

The Sirs.

"Don't let it happen again."

Barton and the official make their way down the line as the new guards recite the oath and receive their ink. When they reach me, I straighten my spine and look straight ahead.

"Do you hereby swear your allegiance to the Leader's Guard for the next year? That you vow to serve the Leader and Trinnea to the best of your ability, protecting his land and its people from threats and harm at all costs to you?"

"I do."

The official dips his thumb into the blue ink and smears a stripe across my forehead. It's warm against my skin.

They move on to Chantry. "Do you hereby swear . . . "

"Thank you," I whisper to the old man.

Barton gives me a nervous smile. "You're welcome." Something inside me unwinds.

"Barton!" The official yanks Barton's arm so hard he stumbles. "You're getting paid to work, not chat, Blank."

"Stop," I murmur.

"Punish him!" shouts someone in the crowd.

The official throws Barton to the ground and kicks him in the side. Barton grimaces but doesn't fight back.

Several people in the crowd cheer, egging him on. Barton grunts, curling into himself.

"Stop," I say a little louder. The man doesn't stop. He just keeps kicking and kicking. Venom floods through my veins, enflaming me with rage. "I said, stop!" I fling my hand upward. The official sails across the stage, slamming into the solid labyrinth wall behind us. He falls to the ground with a thud.

Shocked murmurs and gasps fill the air.

"Zadie," Chantry whisper-yells, lowering her brows at me. "What is wrong with you?"

I step back. "I don't . . . " I trail off, zeroing in on the labyrinth entrance.

I went in there.

Images flash before my eyes. A glowing shrub. A garden.

A long table set with eight porcelain cups.

Dex.

One cup of tea.

Your only chance of reviving your friend.

Every last drop.

"No." I step back, struggling to absorb it all. "No no no. This . . . no. I'm a Blank."

Chantry cocks her head. "What?"

"This isn't real."

The faces in the audience blur together into one solid mass. Everything spins, the edges bleeding together until I can't tell anything or anyone apart.

"I have . . . have to go back."

"Zadie, listen to me." Landon's gripping my upper arms.

"Where am I?" I'm sitting on that bed again. In that huge bedroom that isn't mine. Terror surges through me.

Ma, Chantry, Nadine, and Taylor stand beside the bed.

"You're not real," I squeak out. "None of this is real."

"Zadie." Landon takes my hand, stroking his thumb across my palm. My smooth, unmarked palm that's supposed to be burned with the truth. "We're as real as you are."

"No you're not." I jerk my hand away. "I have to go back. Please, let me go back. I'm trying to save you. All of you."

"Zadie." Ma smiles, sitting beside me. "Don't you like this life? Here, with us?"

"We're together now." Landon brushes a lock of brown hair behind my ear. "Isn't that what you always wanted?"

"You have Skills, too," Chantry says.

Ma nods. "Yes. And friends. Money. All this." She gestures at the huge bedroom around me. The bedroom would fit two of Ma's huts back home. "Why would you want to go back to all that pain?"

"I'm here now, too," Nadine says. "You don't need to feel guilty anymore. I'm right here."

I was a Blank. Everyone hated me. I had to last four more days in the labyrinth with a killer who loathed me. The whole town was in trouble. They were under a spell. My life was terrible.

My life *is* terrible.

"You can stay with us," Landon says.

"I . . . I can?"

"Of course, sweetie." Ma squeezes my hand. "You'll be so happy here with us."

"You never have to go back there," Landon says.

My hand finds his. For a moment, I can see it. I can picture myself here, wherever I am, in this alternate reality forever.

I can be a guard and have real, actual friends. I can have Landon. Ma isn't worked to the bone. I have Skills—*four* Skills.

"We love you, Zadie," Chantry says. "Don't go."

"You and I can be together forever if you stay," Landon says. "Isn't that what you want?"

My insides twist. "You . . . want that?"

"I want that more than anything." He presses his hand to my face. "Zadie, I'm in love with you."

I love you too. I've always loved you. I'll stay here with you forever. The words hover on the tip of my tongue.

I squeeze my eyes shut and hold my hand over his, savoring his warmth against my cheek. "I want that more than anything." I inhale deeply; the air doesn't fill my lungs. "But you're not real."

He looks at me like I slapped him in the face.

Shattering my heart into a million pieces, I push him away. "I can't. We can't. I have a job to finish." The words rip through me like knives. "I want to leave."

Landon's face contorts into fury. His eyes burn with hatred, his irises morphing into a sickly yellow. Before I can process the fear churning inside me, he shoves me back onto the bed.

My head hits the pillow. Only, instead of a soft cushion, it slams into something hard. Pain splinters through my skull.

My eyes wrench open.

Gray bricks surround me, towering high over my head.

Where am I?

I jerk upward, examining the small circular room. A round window displays black night sky and red labyrinth walls outside. Dust settles in the cracks between the stones checkering the floor. A wooden door with a brass handle is embedded in the wall. The thin foam mat beneath me slowly puffs back up, erasing the indent left by my body.

I suck in a hollow breath. I don't know how I got here. I don't know where I am.

My rifle lies on the floor beside me. I brush the barrel and the metal is cold against my fingertips. Dex would never have surrendered it. I must still be dreaming. What if I never wake up? I'll be trapped in this place forever.

The door creaks open. "You're awake?" says a deep voice.

I startle.

Dex cautiously puts his hands up, no longer encased in stone. He stands in the doorway, his silhouette shadowed by light in the hallway behind him.

I try to speak, but my voice comes out raspy. Panic jolts through me. It happened. The labyrinth stole my voice. The sand guardian's tea must be the culprit scrambling people's minds and cursing them with the Labyrinth Stare.

"The potion takes a while to wear off," he says. "Don't try to talk. Get some sleep."

My pulse thrums beneath my skin. The potion screwed with me, messed with my judgment.

I don't want to be alone. I don't want to sleep, don't want to enter that world again.

"It's okay." Dex reaches toward me. For a moment, I think he's going to touch my face. But his hand drops back to his side. "You're going to be fine. You can go back to sleep."

I don't want him to go.

Please. I need someone here. With me.

Don't go.

Don't leave me here alone.

I scream the words, but they don't make a sound.

Dex strides out of the room, closing the door behind him. His footsteps get softer and softer until I can't hear them anymore. The light on the other side of the door burns out.

I sink back into the thin foam pad. Five minutes ago, I was surrounded by people. People who loved me. People who begged me to stay with them. Now, I'm alone again.

It felt so real. Only instead of waking up from a nightmare, I woke up to one.

I've barely wrapped my arms around my face before the tears pour out.

15

I don't remember falling asleep, but when I wake up, blue sky shines outside the tiny window. I sit up, every muscle in my body throbbing. My eyes burn.

I'm alone.

I miss my Ma. I wish I knew she was okay—or alive.

My heart feels like it's been shredded, lying in bloody chunks inside my chest. I keep picturing Landon telling me he loved me. And me pushing him away.

I remind myself that it wasn't really him. But that doesn't make it hurt any less.

The maze is screwing with my mind. Unhinging me, one painful piece at a time. Maybe this is how it starts. This is what everyone feels before the Labyrinth Stare sets in. Maybe there's no monster after all. The maze itself is the cruel monster, destroying the sanity of all who wander inside.

Everyone warned me about the labyrinth. My entire life, all I ever heard was to stay away from it. And here I was, thinking I could somehow survive it. How naïve and arrogant I was to think I could manage after all the strong, Skilled people who tried and failed.

I snort, marveling at my own foolishness.

I don't know where Dex is. Hells, I don't even know where *I* am. For all I know, the sand guardian lied to me. Maybe the Dex I saw last night was another trick. Maybe she locked me in here and I'm doomed to hallucinate these nightmares until I starve to death.

I sniffle, pushing to my feet. My rifle lies on the floor beside the mat.

I hesitantly poke it, expecting another trick. But nothing happens.

Dex wouldn't have returned it to me. He must have dropped it here by mistake. Or maybe he abandoned me and left the rifle as one final courtesy. I sling it over my back, relishing the familiar weight.

I can do this.

I am brave. I am strong. And I am not afraid.

My own voice creeps into my head, low and deadly.

But you're not brave, Zadie. You're not strong. And you're definitely afraid.

You're a coward, Zadie. A big, scared, coward.

I close my eyes and take a few deep breaths. Focus. I can't give up. Not yet.

I try the door. Surprisingly, it's not locked. It creaks open, revealing a down-winding staircase made of stone. At least I'm not trapped in here.

I walk to the other end of the room and peek out the window to get a sense of my location. The small space is just big enough to fit my head through. Vertigo swirls inside me at the sight of the gravel, several stories down. Steadying myself, I back away.

Okay. I need a plan.

The room is small, but packed. A few trinkets are scattered across the floor, including a collection of dusty marbles and a stack of moldy books. A burlap sack of potatoes leans against the wall, surrounded by sealed glass jars of what look like pickled fruits. Cardboard boxes are stacked beside them, each one labeled with words like *Crackers* and *Sugar*.

This isn't just a tower. This is a home.

I crouch and gently peel open the nearest cardboard crate. Two hundred energy bars fill the box. At least I won't starve. I stuff a handful into my pockets.

Several crinkled sheets of paper are tacked to the nearest wall. I stand and examine them. My brow furrows. Lines zigzag across the pages, creating corners and turns. Rooms. Angles.

Fire hells. I slap my hand over my mouth. It's a map of the labyrinth. I study it, tracing the paths with my finger. This is it. This is how I'll get out. I just need to find the right direction.

Hinges squeal and I whirl around. Dex stands in the doorway with his arms crossed.

"This is where you live," I say. "Isn't it?"

Dex's jaw tightens and he nods.

"Why did you bring me here?"

"Would you have preferred I left you to the sand guardian?"

"No." I shudder, never thinking I'd be so grateful for Dex's company. "Definitely not." I touch the map. "How long did it take you to make this?"

"Five years."

"You've lived in the maze for five years?"

"I've lived here a lot longer than that."

I trace the trail labeled *Waterfall: Exit.* "Have you ever brought a Blank all the way to the Palace?"

"No. Thanks to your friend Everhart."

"Why *are* you trying to bring Blanks to the Palace?"

He doesn't reply.

I want to ask more. Dex has been terrorizing Trinnea for several years now. The legend of Dex is a mystery, a tale of evil passed among Trinneans like grog. But the more time I spend with him, the more the legends feel like lies, or at least exaggerations. Still, I tread carefully.

"Did you build this place?" I ask, running my fingers over the cracks in the bricks.

"No. I found it this way, years ago." He strides past me and looks out the window. "What did they make you see?"

"What?"

"The potion. What did you see?"

I don't want to relive it. The images of Landon holding me, Nadine smiling beside me, Ma living in a comfortable home, slice through my heart. "It's . . . complicated."

"You were out cold for three days."

"Three whole days?" It didn't feel like more than a few hours.

Dex stares out the window. "When it happened to me, I was out for a week."

I slide to the stone floor on my butt. "It happened to you?"

He doesn't respond. I want to ask what he saw when he drank the potion. What do things look like in Dex's perfect world?

"They made me wake up in my Ma's home," I say. "Only . . . it wasn't. It was huge, the size of Landon and Val's place." I laugh dryly. "That alone should've cued me in that it was a fantasy."

Dex sits across the room from me, his back against the wall. "What was the fantasy?"

"It was foolish."

He gives a hollow smile to the floor. "Fantasies generally are."

I don't want to talk about it. But I can't hold it in.

"Well, you know what my life is like now."

Dex nods.

"In the fantasy world, I was a Four. I had friends. My sister was actually speaking to me, and my friend Nadine wasn't stuck in the asylum. My Ma wasn't overworked. We had a real home, with actual rooms. My current bedroom is roped off with a sheet, if you'd believe it."

Dex gestures his hands around the bare, stone-walled room and quirks a brow.

"Yes, okay. Point taken. My room isn't so bad."

"So, that's it? That's what you saw?"

"Not . . . quite." I bite my lip, debating how much I'm willing to share.

Dex looks at me expectantly.

"Landon was there, too. He asked me not to leave. We were together. He . . . " My voice breaks. "He said he loved me."

"I see."

I blink back a fresh set of tears threatening to break free. "Sorry. I don't really want to talk about it."

"Understood. I apologize if I overstepped."

I fidget my fingers in my lap. "What did you see when you drank?"

Dex picks up a blue marble from his collection and examines it. "I saw my family."

He has a family. Obviously he does—everyone does. But still, that knowledge surprises me. It's a different side of him. Do they live in Trinnea? Do they know their son is a killer?

"What are they like in real life?"

Dex tosses the marble back into the others with a clack. "They aren't around anymore." He gets to his feet. "If you're feeling better, we should get moving. Grab some energy bars for the road. I'll fill the canteens." He sweeps from the room.

I hurry after him, bursting into the hallway. "Wait! Dex!"

He halts halfway down the winding staircase. "What?"

"Why did you give my rifle back?" I immediately regret the question the moment the words leave my mouth. Maybe he'd forgotten about the rifle, and now he's going to demand I hand it over.

"It was getting heavy and I was sick of carrying it."

"Is that really why?"

"You've nearly gotten yourself killed three times now, and I can't bring you to the Stone Palace if you're dead."

"Dex . . . "

He rakes his hand through his hair. "You drank that awful potion to save me. I don't think you're going to shoot me, okay? Take some energy bars; we're already running behind. There's a water trough out back if you want to wash up before we leave." He hurries down the remaining steps, his footsteps echoing in the narrow corridor.

I keep watching the empty stairwell long after he steps out of view.

Something sinks inside me. In a weird way, I'm touched. Even before the sand guardian turned Dex to stone, I think I always saw him that way. Like a hardened, impenetrable rock. A stone cold statue. For the first time since we've met, I think I see a crack in his veneer.

But I can't take any chances. I untack the maps from his wall, fold them up, and stuff them into my pocket.

I run my hand over my boot. A knot tightens in my stomach. My poison knife is securely in place. I pray to the Leader I won't have to use it.

16

We set off back into the maze, my rifle comfortably strung over my shoulder. Our pockets bulge with food from Dex's stash.

For the first time in forever, my skin isn't caked with sweat and grime. I'd never been so grateful to bathe—even in a rusty bucket full of freezing water. My soaking wet shirt sticks to my skin. At least it'll dry quickly under the scorching sun beating down on us today.

Dex gives me a weird look. "Who bathes with their clothes on?"

I adjust my rifle, not meeting his eyes. "Me."

"Yeah, I can see that. Want to explain why?"

"Not really."

"It's weird."

"Are you saying you'd prefer me naked?"

"No." A red tinge spreads across his cheeks. "I was just saying it's odd."

I scrunch my mouth to the side. "Can I ask you a question?"

"If I say no, you're going to ask anyway, so let's skip that step. Go ahead."

"If you'd gone through it before and knew it was there, how come you didn't avoid the room with the table in it?"

"Oh. *That* type of question."

"Were you expecting a different one?"

"The maze passages stay the same, but the tricks and traps tend to move, and new ones crop up all the time."

"That's creepy."

"Yes. Now can I ask you one?"

"Shoot."

"Why'd you bathe with your clothes on?"

"Fire hells! Drop it!"

We turn a corner and stop dead. Dirt and leaves cover the ground, with a gravel path winding through the middle. Thick tree trunks stretch upward, their leafy branches pointing toward the sky. Threadbare chairs and faded velour couches are propped along the walkway, leading through the woods. It's like we stepped into a bizarre forest that grows furniture.

"What's this one?" I flex my hands. "More necklaces?"

"No. A toll road."

"A what?"

He sighs. "Come on. Let's get it over with."

I follow him, trudging down the path to the first set of chairs. A piney aroma wafts through the air. "What's it going to do?"

"I don't know. Something to try and keep us from getting through." He takes a seat in a faded green armchair, leaving the high-backed pink one beside it for me. I perch at the edge, my butt sinking into the lumpy cushion. My rifle sticks straight up behind me like a metal spine.

Purple smoke weaves through the air, spelling out a word. *Secrets.*

"It wants our secrets?"

"I guess," he says. "Do you want to go first?"

"Oh, uh, sure." I clear my throat. "Let me think." This isn't so bad. "Um, when I was a little kid, I broke Ma's favorite ceramic dish. I was spinning around the room, being silly, and I knocked it down. The thing shattered everywhere. I told her the neighbor's cat snuck in and did it—he used to slink into our open window sometimes. I still don't think she knows it was me." My knee bounces against my hand. "There. That good?"

Dex watches me, hesitation written on his face. "I don't know."

The chairs jerk downward. My stomach drops. Hardened dirt and forest debris envelop the chair legs, burying my ankles, then my calves. Slowly, I sink further into the ground.

Sharp breaths rip through my lungs. "It's burying me alive!"

"Mine too." Dex throws his hands up. "Don't move."

"Did I do it wrong?" I jerk upward, straining, but the quicksand is too strong.

"Stop struggling. It'll make it sink faster."

I don't know how he stays so calm. Frantic, I force my hands to lie still on my knees. "Okay. I'm not struggling. Now what?"

"I think you need a deeper secret."

I rack my brain. "I don't know! I'm thinking!"

"Okay. I'll go." Dex's knees disappear beneath the earth. "I sacrificed a little girl to save my sister's life."

I stop writhing. "What?"

The chairs slow down, mollified by his secret.

"Your turn!" he snaps. "Hurry!"

"Um." My mind races, still absorbing what I just learned.

They speed back up. The ground engulfs my legs, all the way up to my waist.

"Zadie! Come on!"

"I'm in love with my best friend."

"That's not a secret!"

The chairs sink quicker. I try to wriggle my legs, but the heavy earth encapsulates them. The ground swallows my stomach, working its way up my torso. My pulse races. The maze wants more.

"Keep going! Deeper secrets! Now!"

"Um!" I cringe as the cold dirt hits my chest. "It's my fault Nadine entered the labyrinth."

The soil covers my breasts, my shoulders.

I clench my fists beneath the soil. "She's in the asylum because of me."

The chairs stop moving.

Dex hoists himself out of the ground, his black pants coated in a thin layer of brown dirt. He holds out a hand and pulls me out.

"You okay?"

I brush the dust off my pants. "Yeah." I don't feel okay.

Dex doesn't ask about my secret. I'm guessing it's because he doesn't want to explain his.

We wind up the trail to the next set of chairs—a squatty brown one and a slender paisley one. They face each other at an angle, a few inches apart.

"Do we have to sit?" I ask.

"It won't let us pass if we don't."

I can't bear the thought of being buried alive, and I'm all out of secrets.

"I'm going to try." I keep walking, straight past the ominous chairs, and smash into something. I wince, rubbing my knee.

It's just air. But when I hold out my arm, my fingers brush a hard surface. An invisible wall. Of course.

Frustration wells inside me. This labyrinth does not want me to reach the Palace. I can't let it win. "Fine. Okay. I'll sit." I collapse into the brown chair. "Happy?"

Dex takes the other one.

Purple smoke curls through the air.

Blood.

The moment the last letter weaves itself, a slick blade materializes on the ground between us. The knot inside me loosens. I'm not afraid of cutting myself, not afraid of the pain—not when I'm in control.

"Do you want me to go first?" he asks.

"No." I pick up the knife. "I can do this."

Preemptively cringing, I drag the blade across my forearm. Pain sears through the cut. Blood blossoms from the slit, dripping red teardrops down my skin. "Is that good enough?"

"I don't know."

I wipe the knife on my pants, leaving a streak of red across the already dirty fabric. The rest of the blood fades from the metal, leaving the blade shiny and new. I pass it to Dex.

He slices into his own skin without hesitation. Blood trickles out, oozing down his arm.

"Okay, good. That's done." I go to stand, but something

holds me down. My heart races, waiting for the chair to start sinking. It doesn't.

Dex presses his lips together, straining against the chair. "I don't understand."

I struggle against it, wriggling my torso, but it's like my butt is glued to the seat. "I think we need to cut each other."

"No. Absolutely not."

I hold out my other arm to him. I'm offering it freely—still in control. "It's okay. Go ahead."

He slices a tiny line in my forearm, and a sting jolts through me. My blood instantly vanishes from the knife.

I examine the cut. "Not bad. Your turn."

He stiffens, holding the knife back out to me. All the color drains from his face.

"Dex?" I touch his arm. It's tense as a rock. "Are you okay?"

He gives a terse nod. My forehead wrinkles. He's not upset—he's *afraid*. The Devil of Trinnea is afraid.

"It's okay," I say. "I'll be gentle."

He squeezes his eyes shut. Something in my chest twists. "Hey." I rub his arm. "It'll be okay. I promise."

"Just do it," he snaps.

I open my mouth, then close it. He reminds me of . . . me. It's the fear I get when the Warden walks by, when someone moves too quickly to touch me. It's the feeling of being small, too small, trapped in a past I can't escape. A world that gets smaller and smaller, threatening to cave in around me. And it's practically radiating off him. For the first time, it's like I understand Dex—at least, a little bit.

As gently as I can, I take his hand in mine. His pulse hums

beneath my fingertips. "It'll be okay." I slice the blade through his skin with one smooth stroke. Blood drips from the cut, leaking onto my fingers.

"Okay, all—"

Dex jumps to his feet, and the chair lets him up. "Let's go," he growls, plowing onward.

For all the horrors in the maze, it seems silly that Dex the Six fears a simple blade. Blanks fear knives. Not Dex. Not the Devil of Trinnea. It's a strange fear for someone who can melt metal with his mind.

I shouldn't know this. It's like I peeked into someone's window, into their home. I feel dirty.

The realization squirms inside me like I swallowed a handful of worms. I have the power to bring him to his knees, right here in my boot. I subconsciously scratch the back of my leg, brushing the hidden hilt of my knife. It suddenly feels heavy. Like there's a barbell in my shoe.

I'm struck with a strange feeling: *I don't want to hurt him.* It's weird; I shouldn't care about him, because he doesn't give a damn about me.

I follow him to the final set of furniture—a gray loveseat with scratched wooden legs and a faded white armchair with roses stitched into the fabric. Praise the Leader, it's the last toll.

Dex's fear shook me up. The labyrinth could demand anything next. A hand? An eye? What if it asks for something I can't give?

For the first time since entering the maze, I wonder how far I'd actually go to save them. I'd like to say I'd give anything for Ma, Chantry, and Landon, but I'm weak. There are some things I wouldn't do. After all the things they've done for me, I'm too cowardly to return the favor.

Guilt tunnels through me as I picture turning around and walking out with my tail between my legs. I survived the garden, the necklaces, the potion, all by sheer luck—and Dex. But the toll road has made itself perfectly clear: we both pay, or we don't pass.

"You ready?" he asks.

"Yeah." It's a lie. I've never felt so un-ready in my life.

But before we can sit, the purple smoke scrawls through the air.

Best memory.

"It's . . . going to take our best memory?"

Dex stands stoic beside me. "The price to pass."

"So . . . the moment we sit down . . . "

"Yes."

Neither of us moves.

I should be thrilled. It's not going to cut me open—at least, not physically. A memory seems a small price to pay, compared to the alternatives. But I can't bring myself to sit.

I don't have a lot of happy memories. If the chair demanded misery, I'd plop down and let it suck the bunks, the Warden, and the bullies out of my head forever. Good riddance.

But I have one memory. One bittersweet, beautiful memory.

"Can we go a different way?" I already know the answer.

"No. There is no other way."

I remember the air. It smelled so much cleaner and sweeter the afternoon Ma came to save me from the Warden. I remember how my heart swelled and tears poured from my eyes as she held me outside the bunks, a free woman. She presented me with my pass back into Trinnea, and I knew, for the first time in years, that I was going home. I remember it so clearly. It's the memory I've replayed in my head every time my life seemed hopeless. I've clung so hard to that thread of happiness.

The labyrinth is going to steal that from me.

And I have to let it. I can give Ma and Landon this. I owe them much more.

I force a smile, despite the hollow pit in my chest. "Okay, let's do this. Last one."

"Zadie. Wait. I need . . . I need you to hear it." He fists his hands in his dark hair. "Before the maze takes it from me."

I'm taken aback. I've been in this hells-forsaken place a few days; he's been here a good chunk of his life. I wonder what the maze has already taken from him. What prices he's had to pay.

"Okay. Tell me."

He hesitates.

"It's okay." I touch his arm. "Just tell me."

"I was six. My little sister Shae woke me up in the middle of the night. She used to get these awful nightmares, and my Ma would get frustrated since she kept everyone awake. Ma worked ridiculous hours at the Coin Tavern, so I'd try to keep Shae from bothering her."

I know the Coin Tavern. It's a block away from Center Square. So he did grow up in Trinnea. He wasn't born in the maze. Curiosity prickles inside me.

"But this one night, Ma heard us talking—we had really thin walls. She made a pitcher of hot sweet-milk and brought us outside. It was seventh-month, warm and dry but not humid.

The perfect temperature. I remember being shocked at the quiet. There were no airbikes, no shouting crowds. Just the night wind. We spread our blankets out on the sand and lay down."

It strikes me that other people had childhoods outside the bunks. Childhoods that didn't involve the Warden's beatings and hard labor in the mines and being banished from the only home they knew.

"We watched the stars for an hour, lying on our backs. Ma made the sand spin around us in weak, soft tornadoes. Shae fell asleep on my shoulder. I don't remember Ma carrying us back inside, but we woke up in our own beds." He looks away. "That's it."

"That's a nice memory. What makes it your favorite?"

"I don't know. I guess because two days later . . . " He trails off.

I swallow hard. Two days later, something terrible happened. I can see it in his eyes.

"Tell it to me over and over again if you have to. Don't let me forget that memory."

I go to squeeze his shoulder, but my hand falls to my side instead. "I promise. Don't let me forget mine either, okay? It was the day my Ma came to the bunks and—"

"Bought out your debt. You hurt your ankle in the mines and hid your limp. They branded you, but you didn't feel it—you were too shocked. The moment you got outside, you couldn't stop crying. I remember."

I blink. "I . . . didn't think you were paying attention."

He nods.

"Well, let's get to it."

My butt barely hits the seat before the memory of Ma saving me from the bunks fades before my eyes. I grab at the wisps as they evaporate like smoke through my fingers. The details quickly slip away: the look on Ma's face, the cool air against my skin, bustling Trinnea unfolding before me without the Warden looming over my shoulder.

It slowly disappears until I can't remember what I was thinking about in the first place, leaving only a dull sense of sadness behind.

"Is it over?" I ask.

I glance at Dex in the seat beside me. His eyes are wet and glassy. "Yes."

17

Out of the forest, the path narrows into the familiar red-walled corridors. A blanket of gray clouds covers the sky. It matches my mood.

I feel numb. Like the labyrinth has stolen my ability to feel anything anymore.

Dex and I have barely spoken since the toll road, other than recounting each other's stolen memories. He told me about the day Ma came to buy my freedom from the Warden. It feels more like a story, something that happened to somebody else. I can remember every painful, sordid detail about being abandoned beyond the Trinnean gate as a little kid, about working in the mines, about cowering in fear in the bunks—but not the day I left. I am stranded in a sea of sad memories. What a cruel trick for the maze to play.

I touch the leaf pendant around my neck. I can't forget why I'm here.

After a few hours, we stop to eat. The long hallway stretches straight for as far as I can see, with a few breaks in the wall where passages break off to the sides.

I rip the wrapper off an energy bar. "So . . . are we almost there?"

"Almost. A couple days left."

I'm feeling antsy. I stretch my arms, holding one out across my chest and then the next. My skin stings from the cuts, but the blood has dried. Stiff maroon patches stain my sleeves.

A soft whisper hisses somewhere behind me.

I freeze. "Did you hear that?"

"No."

I must've imagined it. I get back to stretching, careful not to reopen the wounds.

A whisper whooshes past me again.

"Okay, that time you must've heard it."

"I didn't hear anything."

I pick up my rifle and squint through the scope. A thick layer of fog floats through the air.

No one's there.

"I think we should go."

Dex grunts. "Fine." He takes a swig from his canteen and wipes his mouth on his sleeve.

We continue down the long path. I keep my shoulders hunched and my arms tight at my sides.

Ssszadie . . .

I whirl around, unstrapping my rifle in one fluid motion.

Dex stops. "What was that?"

"You heard it too?"

"I heard a–"

Gravel crunches in the distance.

"Who's there?" Dex flexes his hands, ready to conjure metal or fire or whatever number six is. I keep my rifle aimed and ready.

Footsteps patter softly. I can't see anything past the fog, hanging low and misty in the air.

"Show yourself!" Dex orders.

The footsteps pat lightly in time with my heart. Uneven. Like a person walking with a limp.

"Let's keep going," Dex says. "Whoever it is, they're not moving too quick."

But I don't dare lower my rifle or take my eyes off the road. "I don't like this."

A shadowy silhouette appears, getting darker and more solid as it approaches.

"I *really* don't like this."

The slender figure emerges from the fog. I bite back my scream—a skeleton stands before us. It's either a corpse, or another incarnation of the sand guardian, or something else entirely.

The creature staggers as its bony feet hit the earth. It stops, setting its dark, hollow eyes on us.

"What is it?" I whisper, lining the creature up in my cross-hairs. "What's it going to do?"

"I . . . don't know."

More silhouettes appear behind the fog, their outlines solidifying until an army of at least fifty skeletons stands thirty feet up the path.

I lower my weapon an inch. There's no way I can take out all of them. "What do we do?"

"Nothing." Dex keeps one foot squared in front of the other. "Yet."

They're not moving. Empty holes replace the spaces where eyes should be, but I can feel them searing into my skin.

The first skeleton makes a low gurgle. The sound echoes between the labyrinth walls and sends a chill rippling through me. Setting one bony foot in front of the other, it takes a step toward us. I bristle, bracing for something to happen.

The first figure cocks its head. With a sickening scrape of bone against bone, the skeletons charge.

"Run," Dex whispers, grabbing my arm. "Run!"

He throws a burst of fire over his shoulder as we sprint down the path. The skeletons' footsteps patter behind us.

"Where do we go?"

"This way!" He pushes me down a path to the right.

The skeletons follow.

"Fire hells!" Dex stops short. Dead end. "This way!"

We take off down the opposite corridor.

Dex waves his hand, throwing the five closest pursuers flying through the air. I aim my rifle and pull the trigger, nailing one in the skull. The recoil pushes me backward as the monster crumbles to the ground.

"We're getting off track," Dex shouts. He hurls another wave of skeletons away from us. "They're leading us off the trail."

We blaze around the corner, kicking up gravel. I'm so defenseless. "I need to reload my rifle."

"No time." He sends a fiery ball at the encroaching skeletons. The flames pass straight through the creatures. "Hells!"

I glimpse over my shoulder. My pulse hammers beneath my skin. They're getting closer.

"What do we do?" My sweaty fingers fumble with the extra

bullets in my pocket. One falls to the ground with a plunk, left behind as we plow forward.

Dex flings his arm out, sending four more skeletons flying. They smash against the labyrinth wall, showering bones across the gravel. "This way!"

I follow him down a path to the right. I'm so useless. He's doing everything. I hate this.

I turn the corner and tear through my pocket for spare bullets. I look up just in time to see the skeleton lunging at me.

"Zadie!" Dex yanks me back, his other hand sending the creature soaring. "What in the hells are you doing?"

"Trying to reload my rifle!"

"You're being a liability!" He sends two more sailing down the corridor.

My face heats. "Sorry."

"I'll get them. Get out of here."

"What about you?"

"There aren't many left. I've got this."

"But—"

"You're defenseless. I can't focus on taking them down if I'm protecting you."

His words sting. *Always needing someone to rescue you,* Chantry's voice echoes in my head. It's like I'm back in Trinnea, a useless Blank in a sea of Skilled.

"Where do I go?"

"Take that first corner, then two rights and a left. There should be a clearing with a tower." Dex throws another skeleton with a flick of his fingers. "Wait for me there. Don't touch anything, don't go anywhere else."

"I'm not a baby," I mumble. But his attention's back on the monsters.

I race down the hall and around the first corner. The bone screeching fades into the background. I slow to catch my breath, rage flooding through me. I throw my head back and scream, slapping the red labyrinth wall.

I'm useless. Reliant on metal, flawed weapons because I'm too weak to defend myself. I slam a new bullet into the magazine with more force than necessary.

I hate this. If I had Skills, I wouldn't be a liability. In my head, I send all those skeletons flying through the air with one swipe of my hand. I'm fighting alongside Dex, not cowering and running away.

I hope he's okay.

I swat the thought out of my mind. He'll be fine; he's Dex.

My feet trudge along as though my shame materialized into sticky patches on the ground, slowing me down. Two rights and a left, look for a tower.

There's no fog swirling in these corridors, and the sudden change unnerves me.

My useless rifle hangs over my shoulder. Dex wouldn't have sent me here alone and defenseless if it's dangerous. At least, that's what I tell myself.

A rancid stench fills the dry air. I crinkle my nose.

My foot crunches down on something hard.

A bone lies in the gravel beneath me. Not just a bone—a foot bone, lying inches away from the rest of its skeletal body.

I jump backward, raising my rifle.

But this skeleton stays firmly planted on the ground. Some

of the bones are embedded in the earth, as if they've been there for years. Time has tinted them yellow.

I carefully step around the bones, keeping my back to the wall. The bones don't move. This isn't an enchanted labyrinth skeleton; it's a dead body. My stomach curdles.

The person's legs are stretched behind it, its arms reaching out in front. Whoever this is, they died running away.

I force myself not to ruminate over that.

I keep walking, taking the next right. Two more yellow-tinted skeletons are strewn across the path. One skull lies a foot away from its spine. Again, they're pointed toward me, fleeing whatever chased them this way. I gulp.

Whatever it was, I'm walking toward it. But if these people died years ago, their cause of death has been here a while. Dex knows this maze. He wouldn't have sent me toward the danger.

Would he?

I keep my rifle out, holding it in my shaking hands. If nothing else, I can whack it over someone's head.

I creep down the path, my muscles stiffening at every sound. The smell gets stronger with each step.

Another right turn.

Six skeletons line the path, their bodies collapsed over each other. It's as if the newer ones died climbing over the older ones, desperately trying to escape. My knuckles turn white around the barrel of my rifle. No movement. I step around them, careful not to brush any bones.

There are so many of them, all ancient and decayed. I'm tiptoeing over centuries of the labyrinth's victims.

I peek around the final corner.

Bones and corpses litter the hallway, their bodies in various states of decay. The overbearing stench of death assaults my nose. I gag, burying my face in my elbow.

I can't make out how many dead bodies there are. I step between and around them, searching for any bit of gravel not laden with the dead. A few still have patches of hair and rotten skin. Their lifeless eyes stare vacantly up at me, sending another wave of nausea rolling through me. I search their faces for signs of life. Who *are* they?

Finally, the path opens into the clearing. I speed up, practically throwing myself into the open space to escape the rotting corpses.

A thin black tower stands in the center with four tall spires protruding from the roof. The sun reflects off it, casting a bright glare. A cluster of brown, flaky bushes grows at its base. I release a heavy breath. This is exactly where I'm supposed to be. All I have to do is wait for Dex.

A final, single corpse lies a mere ten feet from the tower. Its lifeless, rotting hand stretches toward the path. Reaching for something it never grabbed.

I scan the body for signs of stab wounds, bullets, cuts, anything.

But there's not a mark on it.

18

I shuffle my feet. Dex is taking too long. Maybe something happened to him.

Four openings lead back into the labyrinth, and who knows what's down each one. I feel so vulnerable out in the open, waiting to be attacked. Whatever killed those people could be watching me right now.

Dex better hurry.

I debate retracing my steps, rifle locked and loaded, and taking out all those skeletons. See how much of a *liability* I am then. But I don't want to see the corpses again, and I told Dex I'd wait here. I'll give him a few more minutes. At least I have Dex's map. I bite my lip, scanning the area.

I am brave. I am strong. And I am not afraid.

A chill emanates through the square. It's colder in here than out in the maze. I'm not sure what to think about that.

Sssszadie . . .

The whisper is so soft, I barely hear it. Goosebumps prickle down my arms.

No one's there.

A flash of movement catches my eye. I tense, brandishing my weapon. Near the top of the tower, a tiny circular window breaks through the black bricks. A boy's face peers back at me from inside. I'm struck with déjà vu; there's something familiar about him. I squint, but he darts away from the glass.

He's likely another sand guardian trick. But what if he's a regular kid who lives here like Dex? Dex has lived in a similar tower for years. It's a big labyrinth—there could easily be another. And if it is a regular kid, shouldn't we check on him? Or recruit him to help us?

Cautiously, I approach the tower. It's at least a story taller than Dex's, and half as wide.

The shiny black stones clearly reflect my face, as if they've been vigorously scrubbed. I hesitate. Trusting anything in the labyrinth seems like a terrible idea. But all those corpses died in the corridors, not inside this building. Maybe it's safe.

A half-oval wooden door is embedded in the wall. I grab the sleek black handle, waiting for something to happen, but nothing does. With a deep breath, I rip it open.

"Zadie!"

I'm swept off my feet and thrown backwards. I sail through the air and slam into the ground, wincing as my rifle crushes my arm against the earth. The tower door slams shut again.

"What are you doing?" Dex shouts. "Do you have a death wish?"

I groan, maneuvering away from the thing poking into my back; when I see that it's a bone, I full-on dry-heave and chuck it across the clearing. "You told me to come here!"

"I said wait for me here, not go inside!"

"You didn't specify that!"

"Is *don't touch anything* not specific enough for you?"

I glower at the ground. "Not really."

"Sorry I threw you." He offers me his hand. "But if I hadn't, you'd be dead. Are you okay?"

I nod and let him help me up. "What is this place?"

"It's a trick."

"I should've expected as much," I grumble, rubbing my sore arm. The boy in the window must have been an illusion. I'm so gullible. Here I am, yet again, needing someone to save me from my own mistakes.

"People come here and see a sanctuary, a place to rest," Dex says.

"I thought it was another tower like the one you live in."

"So their trick worked on you. But anyone who enters *this* tower gets cursed in the most horrible way imaginable."

"The curse kills you?"

"Worse." Dex skulks away from the tower. I follow him around the clearing. "It traps you here. Once you go inside, every step you take beyond the tower cuts a year off your life."

A whole year, for one step? I think of the skeletons in the hallway. "So depending on how old you are . . . "

"Yes. If you're young, you can get farther away. But you will die, regardless. You either stay at the tower forever or walk twenty, forty, eighty steps and die. Painfully, I might add. The most excruciating death imaginable."

Those poor people in the corridors. I swallow, imagining fleeing the tower only to perish within steps. I escaped that same fate by half a second. Anger wells inside me. "You couldn't have warned me?"

"I was a little busy with the skeleton army. Protecting *you*, by the way."

I laugh dryly, wondering if he was protecting me or protecting his commodity. "You need me to reach the Palace just as much as I do. Stop pretending to be such a hero."

"I already told you." His voice is low and dangerous, his forehead inches from mine. "I never, ever said I was a hero."

The tower door creaks open, exposing a sliver of darkness from inside.

Dex shoves me behind him and draws his knife. "Who's there?"

I line up the door in my crosshairs, my finger twitching against the trigger.

"Show yourself!" Dex booms.

I peek over his shoulder. The door is cracked open, but nothing's happening.

Dex's brow creases. "We should go."

I nod, following him toward the path.

The tower door whips open. Dex draws his knife as I raise my rifle. A boy jumps out, his eyes wide and his hands raised. It's the kid from the window.

The moment his feet hit the earth, the boy's face contorts into sheer agony. His mouth trembles, but no sound comes out. He falls to his knees in the gravel.

I keep my rifle hesitantly aimed at his head.

"Who are you?" Dex demands, not lowering his knife.

I shouldn't falter. This has to be another trick. But I'm struck with pity for this boy. Tattered clothes hang in shreds off his body. He's got to be around eleven, but he's so dirty, it's hard to tell. When he stops wincing in pain, he pushes back to his feet. He raises his hands in defeat, looking sheepishly between Dex and me.

"Who are you?" Dex snaps his fingers. "Answer me."

The boy gapes at us, but doesn't reply.

He's got a crescent-shaped birthmark under his left eye. I swear I've seen him before.

No. Way.

"Farrar?" I squint, lowering my weapon. "Farrar Jensen?"

The boy's eyes light up and he nods.

Dex looks from the boy to me and back. "You know each other?"

"Fire hells!" I shove past him, throwing my arms around Farrar. "Everyone in Trinnea thinks you're dead. Praise the Leader."

A smile splits the boy's face. I'm so happy to see him, I don't care that his sweaty arms are wrapped around me and he smells like years of festering B.O. I found Trinnea's Lost Boy. He's alive. Dex isn't the only person who can survive in here. It's possible.

Finally, I pull back. There are so many questions I need to ask.

I remember the pictures they strung up all over town. He was so young then. "You've gotten so big." I can't stop grinning.

Farrar taps his fist to his shoulder and I return the gesture. I've never actually spoken to him before, but he's a Trinnean. I have a feeling he has no idea who I am, but he'll take any familiar face.

Dex sighs. "We've gotta get moving."

I swat my hand behind me, then turn back to the boy. "How old are you? You've gotta be at least, what, eleven by now?" I mentally calculate how many years it's been since he disappeared. "Twelve?"

He holds up all ten fingers then an additional three.

"Thirteen?"

Farrar nods, but doesn't speak. I guess living alone in the labyrinth for so long will make anyone shy.

"I can't believe it, we all thought you were dead." It hits me. "You went in the tower." A ball of dread knots up inside me. "You're stuck here."

Farrar's head droops.

"And that step you just took . . . "

He closes his eyes and nods.

"Hells." I can't fathom the pain he endured to get our attention. I guess not seeing another human being for six years would make anyone desperate.

"Zadie, we gotta go."

"Hang on." I glare at Dex over my shoulder.

Farrar gives a sad smile.

"Your Pa is gonna be so happy," I say. "He wanted to come in here looking for you, but the Leader forbade it. People left flowers outside the labyrinth entrance for months."

Farrar sniffles, wiping a tear from beneath his eye. Finally, he gives me the thumbs-up. I wish I could communicate with him a little better. Farrar definitely used to speak; they played clips of him cracking jokes and laughing on the Center Square screen for several cycles after his disappearance. So why is he so quiet now?

"I'm sorry if this is insensitive." I cringe. "But can you . . . talk?"

He shakes his head.

"Why not?"

He holds up his index finger, then disappears back into the tower. I peer after him, but can't see past the dark entryway. I can't believe he's survived like this for six years.

A selfish inkling tunnels into my mind. I'll be the one who brings Farrar back to Trinnea. If saving Landon and breaking the town's trance isn't enough to earn their respect, this will be. The Great Leader can't turn his nose up at saving this kid. I'm struck with the absurdity of it all—that it would take completing an impossible labyrinth and saving someone's life to prove I'm worth the same space in Trinnea that most people get just for being born.

Dex crosses his arms, impatience written all over his face.

"Come on," I say. "No one's seen this kid in six years. He sacrificed a year of his life to talk to us."

"He wasn't doing much talking."

"Fire hells! You can wait five minutes."

Dex rolls his eyes.

Farrar reemerges in the doorway, holding a dog-eared notebook and a pencil covered in teeth marks. He squeezes his eyes shut and steps back outside. His already pale cheeks grow pallid. But relief washes over his face when nothing happens. That first step must've already claimed its year debt.

He scribbles on the paper, then shoves it in my face.

It took my voice.

My blood turns to ice. "The labyrinth?"

Farrar nods, adding: *the monster.*

It's real. The monster is real. It isn't just the maze's magic entrancing people's brains; it's a person. Or a . . . something. Fear bubbles to life inside me, sending a wave of unease rippling through my body. My feet itch to run away, leaving Farrar and his problems in the dust. Selfish Zadie strikes again.

But Farrar's not like those people in the asylum. He's too expressive, too full of life. It's impossible. "The monster didn't scramble your brain though, right?"

Farrar shakes his head and writes.

Tried to attack me. Took my Skill and voice. I ran away. His handwriting is terrible. It reminds me of the uneducated Blanks in the bunks, scrawling out basic words.

"It didn't chase you?"

I hid here. It didn't come in.

"Because of the curse in the tower?"

Farrar nods with a sigh. I'm guessing the curse's existence was an unwelcome surprise for him.

"So it just left you here?"

Another nod.

I didn't know the tower would hurt me. There is a sign thing upstairs that says what happens. He keeps writing. *I thought it was a good place to hide. I was silly.*

"The labyrinth is tricky." If it weren't for Dex, I'd be in the same predicament. "You weren't silly. I'm so sorry that happened."

How is Trineea? How is Pa?

I don't have the heart to correct his spelling.

"Trinnea is . . . " I debate telling him about the Sirs, but he doesn't need that stress right now. "Fine." I almost tell him that his father got sick and had to close the confectionary that's been in the Jensen family for generations. Or that he's under a hypnotic daze with the rest of the town, controlled by a gang of sadistic strangers. But I can't bear to say it. "Your Pa's good, too."

Farrar relaxes, jotting down a quick message: *Praise the Leader.*

I return his smile, guilt burrowing through me. "How have you stayed alive? Don't you eat?"

His pencil dashes across the page. *Don't need to. Curse keeps me alive, but it hurts. I feel hungry and thirsty always.*

"That's terrible."

I wish I'd let the monster destroy me.

"Don't say that. You don't wanna be stuck in the asylum." I regret the words immediately. Honestly, I don't know which fate is worse.

I know the curse wants me to walk away, but I'm scared. The letters grow choppy from his shaking hand. *Message in the tower says it will hurt to die.*

I swallow hard. No one deserves that.

Dex leans against the red wall. Part of me doesn't want to know the answer. I want to believe in Dex, that his heart isn't made of darkness. He's saved my life in here more times than I can count.

But I need to know the truth. I touch the bulge in my boot, lowering my voice to a whisper. "Did Dex do this to you? Is he the monster?"

Farrar shakes his head. *Too tall,* he writes.

I breathe out a heavy sigh. After all this time worrying that I was sleeping beside the monster who destroyed Nadine, it's not him. Dex isn't the one scrambling people's minds. He's a killer, and a criminal, and a kidnapper—but he's not the monster. He's not responsible for all the people stuck living with permanent fear under the Labyrinth Stare.

"So what did the monster look like?"

He jots out an answer. *I didn't see its face.*

That's not good. The monster could be anyone or anything. "Is it the sand guardian?"

Maybe. The maze is evil, Farrar writes. *Sometimes I think the Leader hates us.*

My eyebrows scrunch together. That's random. "Why's that?" I'm not fond of the Leader, but I've never heard a Skilled say anything bad about him—on the rare occasion someone questions the Leader's decisions, they're exiled to the wastes, but it rarely happens. The Leader may hate Blanks, but the Skilled revere him. "The Leader keeps Trinnea alive. He protects us." Not that *us* includes people like me, but whatever. I laugh dryly. "Most people say the Leader *loves* us."

Farrar shrugs, scrawling out another note. *He built the maze. The maze hurts us.* He keeps writing. *You don't hurt the people you love.*

19

I don't know what to say. If the Leader doesn't care about Trinnea, then I'm dead. If the Leader won't help me, we're all screwed. "Don't . . . don't say that. Please." My hope dangles on a single thread. I need to believe the Leader will save Ma and Landon. He has to. Otherwise, this is all for nothing. "The Leader's protected us for hundreds of years. He has to care."

Dex materializes from a cloud of black smoke beside me. "Time to go."

"Not yet." I'm heavy. Weighted down. Like an anchor sits on my chest, crushing my lungs. I can't deal with this. With Dex and Farrar and the Leader and everything. It's too much.

"Come on."

"I need a minute."

"Zadie." He glares icicles at me. "We need to go."

I take a deep breath, then let it all out in a single gust. I have to keep moving. It's the only way. The sooner I find Landon, the sooner I can be rid of Dex forever. "Fine. Let's go."

Farrar tugs my sleeve. Fear reflects in his wide brown eyes as he holds up his notebook. *Don't leave me alone anymore!*

I sigh, pinching the bridge of my nose. "We can't leave him behind. Let's bring him with us."

"You know we can't do that." Dex's words drip with exasperation. "He'll be dead within ninety steps—probably fewer."

"There has to be a way."

"There isn't. Let's go."

I grab Dex's arm. "Carry him."

"It doesn't work like that." He twists out of my grip.

"There has to be a solution. I won't leave him behind."

"You're being unreasonable."

"You're asking me to leave a child here."

"We're not taking him with us. End of discussion."

Farrar pokes me in the arm. He holds up his notebook. *Kill me.*

"Stop that," I snap. "Be serious."

He points to the words.

"What? No way!" I rip the notebook from his hands and throw it to the ground. "We'll figure out a way to save you. Let me think for a minute."

Black smoke clouds around us. Great, now Dex is throwing a tantrum.

Farrar points to my rifle.

"Stop." I shove it behind me, out of his sight. "No way. I'm not gonna shoot you."

He picks up his notebook and brushes off the dirt. He points to the page again and adds the word *please*.

"Cut it out! I'm not gonna kill you, so stop."

He underlines it twice.

My mouth hangs open. I can't believe what he's asking of me. As long as Farrar Jensen exists, there's a piece of Trinnea that isn't broken, isn't cursed. Proof we can survive.

"Farrar." I press my hands to his cheeks. "Your Pa needs you. We're going to get help and come back for you. I promise."

His eyes gleam with sincerity. It hits me; he's been wishing for someone to come kill him for years. Dex and I happened to be the first who wandered by. I think about the poison knife in my boot, meant as my last resort for Dex. I can't kill a little kid.

Devil's Bell poison is horrible. I picture his childlike eyes bulging. His cheeks flushing purple. His breaths growing ragged until they cease. The thought makes my stomach roll. I can't. I can't do that to him.

More writing. *I don't want to stay here anymore. I just want to die.*

I read the words, but they're not in Farrar's voice—they're in Nadine's. I can still picture her blue dress fading into the night.

Death is better, Zadie. Her words echo in my head. *Let me go.*

"Please." My voice cracks. "Please don't make me do this." *Don't make me do this again.*

His throat visibly clenches as he swallows, then nods right at me.

"Come on. There's got to be another way."

Death is better.

Death is better.

Death is better than this.

"Look, Farrar . . ."

Farrar's eyes grow wide. He sputters, spraying blood from his mouth. His knees buckle.

"Farrar." I gasp as he collapses into me. "Farrar!"

The corner of his mouth twitches into the beginnings of a smile. Blood seeps warm and wet onto my fingers.

"Farrar." I shake him. "Come on!"

His body goes limp in my arms.

No. He couldn't die. He didn't take any steps. I didn't fire my rifle. My knife's still in my boot.

Dex materializes from the smoke, dislodging his blade from the boy's back. "There." He wipes his bloody hands on his pants. "Let's go."

I can't move a muscle. It's like I ate a whole bouquet of Ice Lilies and my body has frozen from the inside out, unable to move. Unable to think. My limbs react without thinking, stepping back to lower Farrar's corpse gently onto the gravel.

"You killed him." I've seen Dex kill before. I've seen him leave waves of death and destruction in his wake. But for some reason, none of that sunk in until now. "You're a murderer."

Dex sheathes his knife. "He was going to die anyway. He didn't feel any pain. Come on, we've gotta go."

Bile churns inside me.

Deep down, I understand. There was no other option. I almost pulled the trigger and did it myself. It was the kindest choice in a pool of terrible ones.

But none of that matters. Farrar being alive was a thread of hope that Trinnea wasn't lost. We could survive this. Things could get better.

And now he's dead.

A scream rockets from my mouth, draining my lungs. I scream until my lungs burn and then I shove Dex as hard as I can. "You killed him."

"He asked us to."

"He's a child." Tears sting my eyes. "You're a monster."

"I told you that a long time ago."

"You are!" I shove him again. "You're despicable."

"Someone had to do it, Zadie. He was suffering."

"I don't care! We could've saved him."

"That curse is designed to slowly torture you until you die. Is that what you wanted for him?"

I press the heels of my palms into my eyes. This mission is hopeless. I don't know the truth about the Leader. I don't know if Ma will ever snap out of it. I don't know how Landon really feels, or if he's even alive. I don't know what to believe anymore.

"You're a killer."

"Are you done?"

"You disgust me!" I shove him until my arms ache and tears blur my vision, streaking down my cheeks. When I can't fight anymore, I collapse against his chest and sob.

His muscles tense. But he doesn't push me away.

Tears pour from my eyes, soaking into his black shirt. My arms hang limply at my sides. This is useless. I'm going to die in this labyrinth and it will all have been for nothing. I survived the bunks. The mines. The beatings. Only to die right here in this maze.

Dex's arms hesitantly wrap around me. His heart beats against my chest. Steady. Calm. It hits me that the Devil of Trinnea has a heart.

We stand like that for hours that are only minutes. It's comforting, in a way.

Finally, I detangle myself from him. "We can leave." I sniffle. "I'm sorry."

He nods.

I want to bury Farrar. I hate seeing him out in the open, lying amongst the corpses and bones of his predecessors to rot. But in the end, we leave him there.

I wonder if I would have done it. If Dex hadn't killed Farrar, I wonder if I would have ended his life.

I'm grateful I didn't need to find out.

20

We wind through the maze until it's too dark to see. Dex stops halfway down a short, curved corridor. I don't need to ask to know this is our sleep spot.

I sink to the ground and wrap my arms around my knees. My eyes burn from crying. I don't even know what I'm crying about anymore. Landon? Nadine? Farrar? Ma? Chantry? Trinnea? It's all one giant, stewing heap.

Dex starts a fire between us. The flickering flames cast shadows across his face. We sit in silence for a few minutes, neither of us daring to look each other in the eye. He flicks his fingertips over his blade, making the metal warp and bend. "Can I ask you something?"

I'm not in the mood. I can barely get my brain to function properly right now. "I thought I was the one with all the questions."

His knife curls and warbles like ripples in water. "Why do you do that thing in your sleep?"

"What thing?"

"You do this thing with your hands."

I examine the leather gloves clinging to my skin. "What thing with my hands?"

"You make fists. You clench them really hard, sometimes you dig your knuckles into the ground. You mutter."

My face flushes. I'm not surprised; Ma has mentioned it before. "What do I say?"

"Last night you kept saying *No, please,* over and over. I almost woke you up."

"I was probably having a nightmare. I don't remember." It's a lie.

"I was curious. You don't strike me as someone who's afraid of the dark."

Clearly Dex has never lived in the bunks. "Why's that?"

"I guess you don't strike me as someone who gets afraid much, period."

I bark out a dry laugh. Me? Sometimes I wonder if I'm capable of feeling anything *besides* fear. I can't remember the last time I didn't jump when someone's shadow crept up behind me. "Good thing you didn't reveal that lie as a secret to the truth-couch, we would've sunk so fast."

The hint of a smile tugs at his mouth. "That's fair."

Dex's blade melts into a silver puddle in the gravel, then slowly reconstructs itself. I bite into an energy bar, but it tastes like ashes on my tongue.

I've tried to work around my issues. After Ma freed me, I forced myself to walk past the bunks every day on my way to the watchtower. I saw it as a challenge. I'd see if I could pass them without that dizzy, nauseous feeling in my stomach. I didn't tell Landon or Ma—I was too embarrassed.

A few painful attempts later, I ran into the Warden. She stood at the front door with her arms crossed, watching her sooty workers slog back inside for the day. She didn't talk to me, didn't approach. She just looked at me and smiled.

I couldn't breathe. I could barely remember where I was.

After that, I'd leave early and take the long way to work.

"The thing about . . . me," I muse, "is I'm pretty sure I'm broken. My mind doesn't work the way it's supposed to." I'm not sure why I'm telling this to Dex. He doesn't care. But for some reason, speaking it aloud to him comforts me.

"What do you mean?"

"I don't know how to describe it. It's tangible and invisible at the same time. Even when I'm home, with Ma, and I know deep down I'm safe, I don't really believe it. I'm still on alert. It's totally ridiculous and illogical and I can't *fix* it." I don't know where all this is coming from, but once it starts pouring out, I can't stop. "I could be sitting here, doing nothing, and the invasive thoughts would still creep in. They burrow themselves inside me and grow until they've taken over, dictating my every move. I can't shut it off. I'm always . . . *on*." My fingers drum against my thighs. "My eyes are always open, always looking. I'm always straining my ears for any little noise. It's like this constant buzzing I can't shut off." I swallow. The words hover on the tip of my tongue, before finally floating off, softer than a whisper. "I'm free of her, but I'll never be free of her."

Dex's gaze falls to the ground. "I understand."

I've heard those two words before. Every time I'm forced to regurgitate my experiences, there's always someone waiting to jump in and tell me they *understand*. But for some reason, I think Dex actually does.

I wait for him to elaborate, to tell me what happened to

his family or explain why he freaked out at the blood toll. But he doesn't.

"It's become a part of me, I guess." I shrug. "It's not something I can separate myself from. I have dark hair, I have burns on my palms, I'm a Blank, and I'm always scared. It's who I am—I'm weak."

"You don't have any Skills, Zadie." He snuffs out the fire with his hand, drowning us in darkness. "That's not the same as being weak."

Heat spreads across my cheeks, and I look down.

"Five hours," he says. "Then we go."

I can't sleep. A heavy pit has formed in my stomach. I can't tell if it's sadness for Farrar, or guilt about letting him die. But either way, it's not Farrar I'm ruminating about. I can't stop thinking of Nadine.

The teen and adult bunks were connected to the kids' room through the Warden's office in the middle. Some people made a big deal about moving up from one to the next. I didn't. I was moving from one hell to another, connected by the evil woman I despised. It was all the same—hopeless. I'd been working tirelessly for several years, but with the Warden's cut of my pay, I'd still only saved a few silvers. Not nearly enough to pay back even a quarter of my debt to the Warden. Every day I ate her food and slept under her roof, that little number ticked higher and higher. I'd be stuck there forever. Why celebrate anything? With Landon long gone to live with his new Skilled family, I'd never felt so alone.

I'd barely arrived at the teen bunks when the Warden made an announcement. The school's roof had rotted and its plumbing was a disaster. She'd made an agreement with some city officials, and a couple of us had the chance to spend the next few cycles working there instead of the mines. We'd even get paid a few extra silvers for the job.

Everyone's hands simultaneously shot up to volunteer.

I practically leapt up and down. I could spend time away from the caves. See my sister for the first time in years. Without the Warden breathing down my neck in the mines, maybe I could even talk to her.

The Warden didn't let us decide who should go. As far as she was concerned, as long as we owed her money for the years of food and shelter, we belonged to her and therefore didn't get autonomy. She scanned the room and picked two older teens. One was a lanky boy I'd never spoken to before. I recognized the girl, though. Her name was Nadine. She'd slept a couple rows down from me in the kids' bunks, a long time ago.

Resentment burrowed through me every morning. When I lumbered off to the mines, coal dust permanently clogging my throat, Nadine and the boy went to work at the school. They'd come back tired at night, but not coated in soot. Their limbs didn't dangle weakly after hours of chipping away at rock. I envied them. Terrible thoughts crossed my mind. If one of them grew ill, maybe the Warden would choose a replacement. After all, the Warden's workers got sick all the time. I forced the thought out of my head.

One night, Nadine approached me in the washroom. It was the first time we officially spoke.

"I met your sister, Chantry." Nadine smiled. "I'm fixing the leaks in her class's ceiling."

My heart jumped. "You did? How is she?"

"She's really good. She asked how you were doing."

"What's she like now?" I leaned in, desperate to soak up any details from home. "What's she studying? Is she healthy?"

Nadine unspooled her long indenture braid, freeing a swath of curly brown hair. "She's really into the sciences, said she's hoping to be a botanist. They grow these silver orchids in one of her science labs. And yes, she looks healthy. Very beautiful."

A lump choked in my throat. Chantry was happy. She was doing well. And I found out from somebody else. "Thank you for telling me."

I barely slept that night. I couldn't stop wondering about my sister. As much as I tried to suppress it, jealousy ate away at me. I wished I had that life. I wished I sat in a science classroom, learning how to grow silver orchids. It sounded magical.

The next day, I was washing my face over the sink when Nadine returned from the school.

"Another day of patching leaks. That roof is a mess." She rolled her eyes, but I could tell she was enjoying her break from the mines. "I've already saved up ten silvers against my debt. I'm hoping my Pa can help raise money for my pass, but he's slowed down a bit in his older years."

I knew it was super rude to change the subject, but I had to ask. "Did you see my sister?"

"I did. They had exams today. The tutor yelled at me for

hammering too loud. Not like it's possible to hammer quietly, but you know how it is."

"So you didn't get to talk to Chantry?"

"I did," Nadine said. "She finished her test last. Before she left, she came to see how I was doing. You know, since her tutor screamed at me in front of everyone."

"Aren't you forbidden to talk to the Skilled?"

"Technically. But no one else was in the room by then, so it didn't matter. She's really sweet."

"Yeah." Was she sweet? I didn't know. I hadn't seen her since I was a little kid.

Every night, Nadine whispered updates to me over the washroom sink. Chantry stayed after class a lot, saying she was keeping tabs on Nadine and observing her work; in reality, they'd become friends. Chantry helped Nadine complete her job early every day, so they could hang out. She brought extra cheese sandwiches and bowls of brown beans to school, for Nadine to have some real food. They shared stories and talked about their families. Chantry even snuck in a box of Battle Bones for them to play, once Nadine revealed it had been her favorite game.

I envied their friendship. Nadine hung out with Chantry every day, while I'd never see my sister again. But I clung to her as tightly as I could. I needed Nadine to tell me everything: how Chantry wore her hair, how she dressed, how she talked.

Several months passed. One night, Nadine came back to the bunks and went straight to bed. I waited in the washroom until the second before the Warden would've come prowling around looking to punish someone. Nadine never came.

I climbed into bed sulking. Nadine got to see my sister all the time. The least she could do was keep me informed.

Moonlight seeped through the window, casting a light glow over the rows of bunk beds. Snoring lumps filled most of them, their chests rising and falling with heavy, sleeping breaths.

But from across the room, I saw her. Nadine lay awake in her third-row slot, staring at the bottom of the bunk above her. She gently twisted the stem of a silver orchid between her fingers.

I don't remember falling asleep, but I wake up to a sharp pain stabbing into my abdomen. I grimace, clutching my stomach.

That's weird.

I pry my shirt up a couple inches and gag. A behemoth purple bruise stretches across my skin. My pulse races. This is it. The maze is killing me.

Stay calm. I probably banged into something and don't remember.

My head lolls as I push to my feet, like someone replaced my brain with a pile of feathers. I have to steady myself against the labyrinth wall.

"Dex?" I scan the empty corridor, trying not to panic. "Dex?"

"Zadie." He stumbles around the corner like a person leaving the Tap Room after inhaling a pitcher of grog. "Hourglass."

"What?" The word is heavy on my tongue, barely coherent as it leaves my lips.

Before he can respond, nausea rolls through my stomach and rockets up my esophagus. I bend over and vomit bright red all over the gravel.

It's blood.

21

"Hourglass," Dex repeats, urgency in his eyes.

I collect my rifle and stagger after him. I can barely walk. My pulse races. We must have triggered something, but we didn't do anything. We were sleeping. We didn't drink any potion.

My uneven steps falter and I careen into his side. He sways, struggling to regain footing.

Dex takes my arm and wraps it around his shoulders. Using each other for balance, we make our way around the corner.

A massive hourglass blocks the pathway, twenty feet ahead. Red liquid in the top half slowly oozes through the narrow neck, dripping into the bottom glass bulb. A thick layer of red has already settled over the bottom of the glass.

I cringe, rubbing my forehead. A searing headache pounds into my skull. It's like my body is slowly destroying itself from the inside.

"Blood," Dex forces out. "Our blood."

The liquid trickles quickly from one glass bulb to the other. The realization hits my blurry brain—the staggering, the bruises, it all makes sense. It happened to injured miners all the time. Terrors shoots through me. "Bleeding . . . internally. Gonna . . . bleed out."

A purple bruise stretches down Dex's neck, lengthening by the second.

His face blanches. "Hemorrhaging."

An unspoken question with an obvious answer hangs between us—*What happens when it all reaches the bottom?*

We look at each other for half a second before stumbling toward the massive hourglass. "Break . . . glass . . . " Dex mumbles.

My unsteady legs trip over each other as I force myself forward. I'll smash it with the butt of my rifle.

Dex stops short and curses, two paces ahead. He groans, pushing at the air in front of him.

That doesn't look good. My forehead creases. "What?"

I slam into the barrier before he can answer. My stomach drops. I press my clammy hands to the invisible grate blocking us from the hourglass. It reminds me of the transparent walls in the toll road. It's so solid, it might as well be made of steel.

I squeeze my fingers through the gaps in the invisible crisscrossing trellis. The openings are barely wide enough to fit three fingers at a time, let alone a whole hand. We're trapped.

"Skills." It's all I can force out. My head feels like I'm floating in a river.

Dex gets the hint. His body evaporates into black smoke, billowing toward the grate. The smoke violently rolls against it, but nothing happens. He can't get through.

My heart pounds. There has to be a way. From everything

I've learned about this labyrinth, there's always a way. No matter how impossible it seems.

The smoke morphs back into Dex. He waves his hand and fire roars to life, crackling against the trellis. The blaze suffocates me with a gust of heat. I lean against the barrier, throwing all my weight into it.

"Try . . . metal."

He's already ahead of me, flicking his finger at it. I press against the grate with all my might. It doesn't budge. He can't bend it. Whatever it's made out of, it's not metal.

Blood gushes downward, filling half of the bottom bulb, the level rising by the second.

Dex thrusts his hand toward the gate the way he threw me away from the tower. Nothing. He tries again and again, each strike draining energy from his arm.

"Six," I breathe out. "Six." I don't care what his sixth Skill is anymore—I just want to live. "Dex! Six!"

Dex shakes his head. "Won't . . . work."

"Try."

"You don't . . . understand."

"Please." Exasperation drips from my words. "We're . . . so . . . close."

"Won't . . . work."

It's hopeless.

Dex latches onto the grate's crevices and hoists himself up. Sweat beads across his forehead. I try to climb after him, but my arms are heavy as bricks. I watch with bated breath as he scales the invisible wall. Maybe he can reach the top. He'll save us.

Dex's body wavers and he misses a foothold. He slides down, slamming into the gravel.

Gritting his teeth, he lurches back at it with newfound vigor. He climbs until his head rocks back and forth.

"Dex!"

I see the dizziness cross his face before he seems to notice. His muscles go lax and he falls back to the earth. Dex kicks the wall, his eyes flashing with rage. But he's lost too much blood and loses his balance.

I help steady him, my vision swimming.

It's only when he's upright that I remember my rifle. My arms weak as straw, I position the barrel in one of the gaps in the invisible grate. I struggle to hold it steady in my shaking hands. The rifle mouth barely fits through the small opening. I un-click the safety. It's locked and loaded. The hourglass blurs in and out of focus when I try to aim.

Holding my breath, I squeeze the trigger. Sound explodes around us. The bullet strikes the labyrinth wall, missing the target by two feet.

Blood drips steadily through the unharmed hourglass. More fills the bottom than the top now.

"Again," Dex orders.

My sweaty fingers fumble with a fresh bullet. I load the magazine and slide the bolt. I can barely lift it. The grate doesn't support my rifle's weight; I'm holding it midair, like the grate's only solid when it wants to be. Dex puts his hands over mine, steadying my aim.

But his grip is as weak as mine. I pull the trigger right as the rifle dips.

The bullet ricochets off the ground.

I feel myself growing hazy. My knees buckle. Everything blurs around me.

Dex clings to the grate to keep himself upright. His body sags against the wall. Red fills the whites of his eyes.

I'm barely coherent enough to reach for a fresh bullet.

The top bulb is almost empty. Blood drains into the bottom like water through a sieve.

My fingers sloppily dig through my pocket, coming up with one final bullet. That's it. No more chances.

"Last . . . one."

The blood is almost gone, leaving the top glass shiny and clear. I watch as the final trickle of blood swirls toward the neck.

I'm fading. I load the rifle, barely registering my final bullet disappearing into the magazine.

My body is light, floating. Breaths come short and shallow, every gasp pressing against my swollen abdomen.

I point the rifle toward the glass, struggling to stay on my feet.

Dex wraps his hand around it. "Wait." He positions himself under my rifle, steadying the barrel on his shoulder. His face is slack, but he holds his body rigid. "Okay."

We only have seconds. The final drops of blood swirl into the neck.

I hesitate. His head is too close. "Gunshot . . . it'll . . . " It'll burst his eardrum and hurt like hell. His hearing might never return. But I can't force the words out. I can barely breathe.

I squint, forcing myself to focus on the hourglass.

"Zadie." Dex's tired eyes meet mine. "You can . . . do it."

My jaw clenches. Releasing my last gust of energy, I tug the trigger.

A sharp crack explodes around us. Dex grunts and doubles over, pressing his hands to his ears. The bottom glass shatters, spilling blood across the gravel.

I gasp for air. Deep breaths finally fill my lungs. It's like someone recharged my muscles, pumping life back into my body. I gape ahead, disbelieving.

Warmth floods through me. I lean against the barrier to catch my breath, but nearly topple over. The invisible grate is gone.

Sun reflects off the glass shards sprinkled over the earth. One by one, they disintegrate. The hourglass blood sinks into the ground as if the gravel is a sponge, absorbing it back into the maze.

I hike up my shirt a couple inches, but the swelling purple patch has faded into nothing. No sharp pain twinges inside me. We made it.

Dex grumbles behind me.

"Dex!" I rush toward him. "Let me help you."

A trickle of blood leaks from his right ear. He holds up his hand, turning his back to me.

I hesitantly touch his shoulder. "We did it," I whisper. "You saved us."

He doesn't respond. My heart sinks when I realize why.

"We did it." I raise my voice. "You saved us."

The bruise on his neck shrinks like water evaporating in

the sun, leaving his skin its normal color. "*You* aimed and pulled the trigger."

"We did it together."

A strange expression burns behind his eyes. "We should go."

"How's your ear?"

He grunts.

"How's your ear?" I repeat, a little louder.

"Like I'm holding a pillow over it and the pillow won't stop buzzing." He glowers at the ground. "It's late. We should keep moving."

Blood drips from his ear down his cheek. My heart sinks. I don't know how he always does this. He faces down the maze and then shakes it off and keeps going. I guess that would happen to anyone who's lived here long enough. I can't imagine going through this alone. I don't know Dex's end goal, but I hope it's worth everything he's lost.

"Wait." I tear a ragged corner off my shirt. It's sweaty and covered in dirt, but it's all I have. Uncapping my canteen, I dribble a few drops of lukewarm water into the cloth.

"Here." I gently dab it to his ear, bracing myself to get thrown across the hall again.

Dex's muscles tighten, but he doesn't push me away. I wipe off the blood, trailing from his ear, down the rough stubble on his cheek. I wish I had a proper bandage.

My fingers brush against his dark hair. It's not as coarse as I was expecting.

"Are you done?" he asks softly.

"Yes."

"We should go."

I nod. "Okay."

"We're only a day away from the Palace." He starts walking, his head tilted slightly to the right. "We'll get there tomorrow."

I'm not sure why, but his words fill me with dread. Reaching the Palace means facing the Leader and begging him to save my town.

Finding Landon and praying he's still alive.

Saying goodbye to Dex.

I'm taken aback by how much the thought bothers me.

A heavier realization drops in my chest like a rock.

We've almost reached the exit. Something tells me the labyrinth won't let us go without a fight.

22

For someone who nearly bled out an hour ago, I feel pretty good. Dex's ear stopped bleeding. He hasn't mentioned his injury since we left the hourglass, but I can see pain on his face. I stay on his left side so I can talk to him without shouting. I don't have the heart to ask about his ear. He's a smart guy; he doesn't need me to tell him he might not hear out of it again.

Dex tugs his earlobe, jerking his head to the right. I catch him glancing to the right every couple seconds, as if paranoid he'll miss a noise. His shoulders are tensed, braced for an attack.

I stay on my guard, straining my ears for any threat. At the slightest whisper, I whip my rifle out. At my lead, Dex jumps into position with his hands flexed. So far we've had four false alarms. I'm not as good at discerning innocuous sounds as Dex is—or, *was*. I don't mind. I'd rather be extra cautious.

He rips open an energy bar and takes a massive bite. My stomach gurgles, but I'm not sure I can force feed myself another sticky brick. I miss Ma's brown rice and beans.

Leader, if I make it home safely, I promise I'll never complain about the bland food you give us ever again.

"You hungry?" Dex fishes through his pockets, digging out a bar. "I've got plenty."

My nose wrinkles. "Honestly, I don't know how you eat these things for every meal."

"I don't eat them for *every* meal. Didn't you see my stockpiles?"

"I saw boxes of random stuff you stole from Trinnea. Not sure what you'd do with that and no electricity."

"When you live in the labyrinth for as long as I have, you get creative." He grins. "Hang on, stay here. I'll be right back."

Before I can protest, he's black smoke, drifting down the corridor and out of sight. My hands fidget. I hate being alone in here, and Dex could miss something without me. He's off his game. I sink to the ground, keep my hand close to my knife, and wait.

Ssszadie . . .

The whisper brushes through my hair.

"I was wondering when I'd see you again," I say as the sand guardian materializes. She sits cross-legged against the opposite wall. "Come to torture me? Trick me into lighting myself on fire or something?"

She's in that monstrous little girl's body, with pasty grayish white skin, dressed head to toe in black. Two gray horns protrude from the sides of her head. "I wanted to say hello." Her voice is sweet as honey and deadlier than the hive it came from.

"Fire hells that's a lie. What do you want? Just say it and get it over with. Are you here to kill me?"

"I can't kill you, silly girl." She smirks. "Not directly, anyway. It's against the rules."

"You're gonna tell me the shrub didn't try to kill me? The garden?"

"I led you to the shrub. You, my dear, chose to wear the necklace." She winks. "The garden wouldn't have harmed you if you'd stayed on the trail. I thought I had you both with the potion, though."

"Why?"

"I was certain you'd choose to stay in your dream world. Then you'd be unconscious forever, Dex would stay a rock, and I'd be one happy sand guardian." She sighs. "But you proved me wrong, Zadie. I guess you're full of surprises."

"Why turn him back, then? Why not keep him a stone, if that was your end goal?"

"My end goal is to keep you from completing the maze. But a deal's a deal, and since you drank the potion, I had to free him."

"How honorable," I say sarcastically.

"I see you haven't heeded my advice."

Like I'd trust any advice from her. "What advice?"

"Not to trust him."

"I already told you I don't trust him." I bristle. "Although frankly, I don't know why I should listen to you anyway. Every time you show up, something tries to kill me. So forgive me if I'm not tripping over myself to heed your every word." I take a swig from my canteen.

"No need to get defensive." Her mouth curves upward into a mischievous grin. "Dex is an interesting fellow. Did you know he killed his own mother?"

I nearly choke on my water. "Excuse me?" That doesn't sound like Dex. "I don't believe you."

She shrugs. "I'm just reporting the facts."

It can't be true. Dex's best memory was about his Ma, just like mine. He saw her when he drank the black potion. That doesn't sound like someone who would kill his mother with his bare hands.

"You're lying. He's not like that."

"Or maybe you don't know him as well as you think."

I can't let her mess with me. She's made of lies. "You must love seeing me so miserable in here."

"It pleases me, but I can hardly take credit. I didn't build the maze, I only serve it. I will accept the compliment on a job well done, though."

"Yeah, I know." I roll my eyes. "The Leader built it. Sometimes I think Farrar's right—he wants to watch us suffer."

"Oh, he didn't build this. The labyrinth has been around for centuries. The Leader merely uses it to his advantage."

"It wasn't built to protect him?"

She files her fingernails against the rough labyrinth wall. "It was built *for* protection, sure. They put it on this particular spot because of the magical properties in the soil. It allows for creatures like myself to form from the earth and enchant it. Magic has long since vanished from your world, but it remains unchecked here. What better place to build a labyrinth than around an area where magic runs free? They boxed it in, so to speak. That is why I cannot leave the labyrinth."

"You're stuck here?"

"Magic is confined in the maze, and I am made of magic, after all."

"So, you can't enter Trinnea? Or the Palace?"

"Trinnea, no. Palace, yes. The Palace is a continuation of the labyrinth, so to speak. I rarely go inside it, though. It's not nearly as exciting." She examines her nails. "I like the maze."

"So if the Leader didn't build the maze, who did?"

"Servants built the structure itself."

"Now I know you're lying." I snort. "Blanks don't have the Skills to build something this big. You'd need people with superior strength."

She grins. "I didn't say they were Blanks."

"Wait, what? *Skilled* servants?"

"I'll see you around, *ssszadie*." With a wink, she fades into the air and I'm staring at the labyrinth wall.

"Hey." Dex materializes from a cloud of black smoke beside me. I startle. "Anything happen while I was gone?"

I can't look at him without picturing him strangling his own mother to death. I shiver, forcing the thought away. "You missed the sand guardian."

"What'd she want?"

"To spew her nonsense, as usual."

"Well here, this might cheer you up." He holds out two fat brown potatoes and takes a seat. "I told you I don't always eat energy bars."

Food. Real, unprocessed food. "Do you eat them raw?"

"Here, I'll show you." He unfurls his blade, cutting thin slices into each one. They fan out, exposing little slits into the potatoes' white innards.

"It's like an accordion."

"Something like that." He pulls out a block of cheddar from his pocket and dices it into cubes, stuffing one into each slit. "Stand back."

I scooch backward until I'm flat against the labyrinth wall, cold and hard against my back. Dex flicks his hand and a fire roars to life between us. Skewering the potatoes on his blade, he sets them in the fire to roast. I inch closer to Dex, savoring the warmth radiating from the flames.

"That smells amazing." My stomach growls at the warm, cheesy aroma, practically eating my other organs.

"Better than energy bars." He makes the metal knife bend and twist, toasting the potatoes evenly on all sides.

I watch him with curiosity. "Can you use that metal Skill to make us more bullets?"

"The bullets you'd need are jacketed lead. I can conjure up the jacketed part, but unfortunately my Skills end there."

"Worth a shot."

"Pun intended?"

I grin. "Always." I'm not sure when I started feeling comfortable around him, but I notice I do. It's weird.

He removes the potatoes from the fire and pokes them. "Nice and soft. Here." He passes one to me, his bare skin brushing against my gloved fingertips. "Careful; it's hot."

Steam curls from the potato, dripping in melted cheesy goodness. I blow on it, but barely last five seconds before digging in. "So. Good."

He smiles.

"I'll have to teach Ma how to make these." I stuff more into my mouth. "We can never afford real cheese."

"I usually have pickled fruit for dessert with it—sprinkle some sugar on top, heat it until it caramelizes." It's the first time I've seen him genuinely happy. I can't help noticing he's got a nice smile, when he's not scowling.

"I had no idea you could cook."

"I'd hardly call this cooking."

"The fruit sounds good, too," I say between bites. "You'll have to teach me."

"Oh, it's easy. Prickly pear fry up nicely."

"Really? I always thought they were too seedy. They grow in this garden near my house, I'll have to tell Lan—" I stop myself short. Hells. Landon's name feels foreign on my tongue. I haven't thought of him once today. What's wrong with me?

Dex's smile sinks.

We finish eating our potatoes in silence. I shovel the rest of it in my mouth, but can't taste a thing.

A blanket of black night sky covers us, but Dex hasn't stopped to rest. The full moon illuminates our path. It's so bright, it feels like daylight.

We head straight for a while, our crunching footsteps the only sound breaking through the silence. I wrap my arms around my torso. Chantry's guard jacket doesn't offer much warmth, but it's all I have.

"Are we going to stop soon?"

Dex closes his eyes and takes a deep breath. "You need to speak up."

"Right. Sorry." I realize I'd been walking on his right and quickly dart to his left. "Are we going to stop soon?"

"We need to get farther if we want to reach the Palace by tomorrow." His voice is stern and cold. I haven't heard him talk that way in days.

"How's your ear?"

"Not good," he snaps. Irritation flashes across his face every time he misses something.

The potato sits in my stomach like a brick.

I'm so consumed, it takes a moment to realize I'm walking next to myself. Mirrors line the labyrinth walls around us. But instead of reflecting infinite images in the parallel walls, a single reflection walks on my left. Dex's reflection paces beside him on the right.

My reflection keeps pace with me, but she isn't sharing my curious gaze; she's scowling.

I tense, bracing myself for an attack. "What's this one?"

"Just keep walking." Dex looks straight ahead, refusing to acknowledge his sneering visage beside him. "It won't hurt you."

Curiosity gnaws through me. There has to be a reason for these mirrors.

I maintain Dex's brisk pace, but can't look away from my reflection. It's the first time I've seen myself since I left Trinnea. Grime coats my skin. Stringy tendrils frame my face, bursting from my messy ponytail. I frown, wishing I looked more presentable.

"*Worthless,*" my reflection says.

I stiffen. "Ex . . . excuse me?"

Other Zadie behind the glass grimaces. "*Weak.*"

"Ignore it," Dex mutters.

"*Unlovable.*" His reflection accosts him in that menacing Dex voice. "*Cruel.*"

"What's going on?"

"Ignore it," he repeats.

"*Vindictive,*" my reflection says.

"*Murderer,*" says Dex's, practically shouting so he'll hear it. "*Traitor.*"

"*Always needing to be rescued.*" I swallow hard as my reflection sneers at me. "*Can't take care of yourself.*"

"*Selfish,*" Dex's reflection says. "*Cold.*"

"*Ma would've been happier with a Skilled child.*"

The words punch me in the gut. It's only the labyrinth's tricks, but it still stings.

"*You can't save Shae. You couldn't even save your own mother.*"

A muscle tightens in Dex's jaw. I want to reach out to him, but his face is cold as ice.

"*Landon Everhart only hangs out with you because he pities you.*" My reflection purses her lips. "*He'll leave you for a better, prettier Skilled girl.*"

"*You could've saved your family if you weren't such a coward.*"

I quicken my pace to catch up to Dex.

"*It's your fault Chantry's miserable. Your fault Nadine's in the asylum.*"

"*You sacrificed an innocent child and it was all in vain.*"

"*You ruined your sister's life,*" Other Zadie says. "*You were too weak.*"

I squeeze my eyes shut, holding back the tears.

"*Make it slow. Make him hear it.*"

Dex cringes, his teeth clenched together. I don't understand what that means.

"*Make it slow.*" His reflection breaks into a run to match his counterpart's pace. "*Make him hear it.*"

"Dex!" I chase after him, my reflection jogging at my side.

"*The only thing you're good for is the Warden's work.*"

"Shut up, shut *up*!" I press my hands over my ears.

"*Make it slow. Make him hear it.*"

"*Trinnea would be better off if you never came back.*"

"*Make it slow. Make him hear it.*"

"*Ma lost everything because of you. She would be better off without you. Her life is so much easier now that you're gone.*"

"*Make it slow. Make him hear it.*"

"*It's your fault Nadine got hurt. She trusted you.*"

"*Make it slow. Make him hear it.*"

Dex seethes. He swings around and plows his fist into the glass beside him. A crack splinters through the mirror until the whole thing shatters. The glass shards glimmer in the gravel for a moment before fading away, leaving no trace of the mirror or its insults. Dex flexes his hand, his knuckles covered in blood.

My reflection winks at me before fading away, the mirror morphing back into red clay.

Dex leans against the wall with both hands, his back to me. I slump down, pressing the heels of my palms into my eyes. As far as the labyrinth goes, that wasn't so bad. But the words cling to me like the scent of sulfur after working in the mines all day. I can't get them out of my mind.

After an eternity, Dex starts a fire. He positions his right side against the wall, facing me at an awkward angle.

"Do you want to talk about it?" I ask, perching my chin on my knees.

Dex's silence answers for him.

"Whatever happened to your family," I whisper, not sure if he can hear me, "I doubt it was your fault."

I subconsciously tug at Chantry's jacket. Part of me wishes

Dex would repeat my words back to me, but it'd be a lie. What happened to Nadine was absolutely my fault.

I close my eyes and lean my head back until it rests against the wall.

Months had passed since that night I saw Nadine clutching the silver orchid in her bed. We kept up our routine of meeting at the washroom sink. Knowing I'd get an update at the end of my shift made the mines slightly more bearable.

Nadine rolled her eyes. "Another day, another burst pipe. I've become a master at patching these things."

"You see Chantry?" I asked, rinsing soot off my arms. "How's she doing?"

"She sends her love. She stayed after school with me today."

"To help patch the pipe?"

She blinked. "Yeah. To help patch the pipe."

Before I could dry my hands, she'd already left the bathroom.

The next day, I got back from the mines and went to wait by the sink. I dallied, scrubbing my hands until my fingers looked more like raisins. Nadine didn't come. I sulked, wondering if she'd gone to bed without updating me again.

Someone sniffled behind me. I startled; I'd thought I was alone. Two navy blue shoes were visible under the stall door. They weren't coated in coal dust.

"Nadine?"

"Go away," she snapped.

I cringed at the rejection. "Are you okay?"

Nadine stormed out of the stall and shoved past me. Her puffy cheeks were wet with tears.

"Hey, come back!"

"Leave me alone, Zadie."

I gaped at the washroom door as she slammed it in my face.

The next day, Ma bought out my debt and brought me back into Trinnea. I can't remember anything beyond the fact that it happened.

I got to Ma's house dripping in gratitude. Ma's hut was smaller than the one I'd been ripped out of eight years earlier, but it already felt like home. Landon came over, and I sobbed into his chest for an hour.

"Thank you." My voice came out scratchy and weak, but it was the best I'd felt in years. I squeezed Ma's hand. "Thank you for saving me."

"Don't thank me," she said. "I did what I could, but I'd never have raised the money without Lan and your sister contributing every dime they earned."

Chantry

I jumped up. "I gotta go see her."

"She might still be at school."

I hopped on Ma's rusty old airbike and weaved into town. The entire drive, I kept thinking of how to pay it forward. There were so many Blanks still indentured to the Warden—still dying in the wastes beyond Trinnea's borders—and I had to do something. I'd get a job. I'd raise the money and help as many as I could, starting with Nadine. The thought of my friend stuck in the bunks alone made my stomach ache. That moment, I made a vow to myself: I'd save her. I'd do it. She'd given me hope over the past few cycles, given me something to look forward to every night; I'd do the same for her. I wouldn't let her die there.

When I reached the giant rectangular building, I parked and rushed inside. School had ended for the day, but from Nadine's updates, I assumed Chantry would still be there. Maybe I could even see Nadine, too.

A long deserted hallway greeted me. I wrung my hands. I was technically allowed to be there, but I was still a Blank—and therefore a permanent target. Walking alone through a Skilled establishment felt like crawling into a snake pit.

I tiptoed down the hallway, peeking into any lit classroom. Other than a blonde tutor messaging on her communicator, every room was empty.

I was about to give up, when my ears pricked.

". . . Zadie will help, we'll do it together."

A door was cracked open, but I hadn't thought to check the dark room. I stepped back, squinting into the dimly lit lab.

Tears streaked down Nadine's cheeks. "I can't do it any- more. You promised you'd get me out."

"I will. I promise," Chantry said. "I'll work three jobs after class if I need to. Zadie will help, you said yourself she's your friend. We'll raise the money."

"It'll take ten years." I'd never seen Nadine so defeated.

"I don't care how long it takes. We got Zadie out of the bunks and back into Trinnea, we'll get you out." Chantry's forehead scrunched. "Hey. Don't cry. Please. I hate seeing you this way."

"You don't know what it's like there. Every day I come here, to this clean, happy place where people respect you and listen to you and give you food and opportunities." She sniffled. "And then every night I go back to the bunks."

"Nadine—"

"No. You wouldn't understand." Nadine rubbed her eyes with her palms. "You *can't* understand."

"I'm trying. Please. Help me understand."

"Your people—Skilled people—think I don't deserve to be here just because I was born with these . . . these . . . un-Skilled genes."

Chantry opened her mouth, then closed it. "I don't think that. I hope you know I don't think that."

"It doesn't matter. You still benefit from the system that does it." Nadine blinked hard, her eyes wet. I swallowed, watching from the shadows; I'd never seen Nadine break down like this before. "That woman—that horrible, awful Warden—thinks we *owe* her. She goes into those awful wastelands and preys upon children who get dumped there for being un-Skilled, and she bribes us with food and shelter and not dying in the wastes. And what do we do? We sign her awful contract, because we're ignorant little kids who just want a place to sleep at night. And then we're hers. Do you understand that, Chantry?" Her voice cracked. "This is my life. I'm indebted to her forever. I'll work in the mines until I die."

"You won't. I promise."

I promise, too, I thought, fighting the urge to burst in there and hug her.

Nadine's eyes soured. "You spent all your money buying *her* pass. You told me you'd rescue *me*."

Chantry gaped at her. "She's my sister."

It hit me. If Chantry hadn't put all her money toward saving me, Nadine could've been the one safe in Trinnea right now.

Nadine broke down in tears, her face in her hands. Pain flashed across Chantry's face. I could see in her eyes that she was hurting for Nadine, but she didn't understand. It was like Nadine said; only Blanks know what it's like. Only Blanks know about the horrible choices we were forced to make—to starve outside the gate, overrun with disease, or sign the Warden's contract and work for her forever. What kind of six-year-old should have to make that choice?

Skilled children got sent to this beautiful school to learn, while children like me and Nadine got dumped outside the city gates like garbage, just for having no Skills. We had to beg for scraps of pity from passing Skilled, living inside their cushy gated walls. Anger welled inside me. When the world tells you you're worthless—that your life isn't as valuable as the Skilled children—you start to believe it.

I started to believe it. Sometimes, I still believe it.

Nadine cried into Chantry's shoulder, muffling her sobs with the fabric of my sister's shirt.

Chantry reached out a hesitant hand, brushing a lock of hair behind Nadine's ear. There was something about the simple touch that hit me.

They weren't platonic friends. There was nothing platonic about the way they looked at each other.

Finally, Nadine pulled back, her eyes wet and her cheeks blotchy. "I wish . . . things were different."

"I promise you, Nadine. I will never stop fighting until you're free. We'll be together."

"I wish . . . " Nadine looked away. "I wish it were that simple."

Chantry scoffed. "Ma keeps pushing me to date Nina."

Nadine's face grew stony. "Maybe you should."

"No. I don't want to be with Nina." My sister took her hand. "I want to be with you."

I pressed my hand over my mouth. If the Warden found out about this, Nadine was screwed.

My pulse raced. The Warden forbade all her workers from intimate relationships, let alone her Blank workers having relations with the Skilled. Last year, a Blank man in the adult bunks was caught selling his body to Skilled women, while he was supposed to be out running errands for the Warden. He was saving the money to buy off his indenture and pay for a Trinnea pass. When the Warden found out, her lackeys flogged him in front of all of us until he died. The city guards just looked the other way.

If anyone learned about Nadine . . . I didn't want to think about it.

Bile churned inside me. Chantry was being unbelievably selfish. Skilled didn't understand what it was like for us. She could've easily been with any Skilled girl. How dare she risk Nadine like that? It wasn't fair. Chantry and Nadine deserved to be happy, and I hated that they couldn't be. As long as Trinnea put Skilled above Blanks—as long as Nadine wasn't an equal in the Leader's eyes—it wouldn't be fair. Chantry would never have to risk as much as Nadine. Meanwhile, Nadine had put everything on the line, just by standing there with a Skilled girl after working hours.

For the first time since my release, I let myself really feel it. *It wasn't fair.* It seemed like such a simple truth.

And in that moment, all the gratefulness I'd felt for my sister fizzled into anger. Rage simmered hot through my veins.

Maybe if I hadn't been standing there, everything would've been fine. But there I was in the hallway, drawing attention to that room.

The blonde tutor crept up behind me. Before I realized what was happening, she'd stormed into the lab. She yanked Nadine by her braid, calling her a thousand dirty names I'd only heard from the Warden and her lackeys' lips.

I slipped into an empty classroom and held my fist to my mouth, letting the shadows conceal me.

Chantry screamed and fought, but the tutor still ripped Nadine out of the room. Nadine's feet dragged against the tile, but she didn't fight back. Her skin was pale as flour.

I didn't dare make a sound. The woman hauled Nadine down the hallway. Chantry ran after them, tears streaming down her face, begging and shouting. It was the first I'd seen my sister in eight years, and I couldn't bring myself to let her see me.

I remember, in that moment, thinking it was the worst thing I'd ever seen. I hated myself. I was such a coward.

In retrospect, I was naïve. That wasn't the worst thing I'd do to Chantry and Nadine. Not even close.

I am so beyond tired, I can't feel it anymore. By the time

an orange sunrise breaks through the blackened sky, I'm still wide awake. Judging by Dex's unshifting stoic posture, I'm guessing he hasn't slept either.

He gets to his feet without words and cracks his knuckles.

A hawk makes lazy circles overhead. I squint, watching it fly over us. It's the first animal I've seen since leaving Trinnea.

"Time to go," Dex says.

I point to the bird. "What's that?" Another massive hawk joins, two black specks against the light morning sky.

"It means we're almost there." He sighs as two more birds show up. "It's the beginning of the end of the maze."

24

Seven hawks fly over us now, swooping in wide circles in the blue sky.

"Listen," Dex says. "We've made it this far. We're almost at the Palace."

I'm not liking the unease in his voice.

"The labyrinth is going to throw everything it has at us. Whatever happens, stay close to me, and don't stop. We can't stop until we reach the silver waterfall—no matter what. We cross under the silver waterfall, we reach the Palace." His knuckles grow white around the hilt of his knife. "Are you ready?"

This is the end. I'm either going to die here, or I'm going to reach the Palace, save Ma and Chantry, and get Landon back.

I swallow hard, clinging to my useless empty rifle. "I'm ready."

"Then let's go." He takes off running, me at his heels.

We've barely rounded the corner when a shrill screech fills the air. The first hawk dive-bombs us like a missile.

I swing my rifle like a bat. It cuts through the air, missing the bird.

The other hawks follow, falling from the sky, their sharp beaks pointed like daggers at our heads. Caws echo around us.

Dex pulls a metal rod from thin air and brandishes it like a sword. He smashes it into a bird. The creature snaps its beak menacingly at him, unscathed. A hawk swoops down and snatches the weapon from Dex's hand. Two more latch their talons around my rifle and wrench it from my grasp. I jump for it, but they've already thrown it over the wall. They're too smart.

Two more birds pluck the gloves from my hands. "No!" I watch helplessly as they fly away, taking my armor with them. The brands on my shaking palms are exposed for the world to see.

These are no ordinary birds.

Sssszadie . . .

"It's the sand guardian," I shout.

Dex plows his fist into a hawk's side; it doesn't flinch. "And she's got a lot of backup." He takes off down the path. "C'mon!"

I wrap my arms around my head and run. Beaks nip my sides, tearing my jacket. I wince as something sharp slices my skin, but I don't stop running. Blood trickles down my arm. The hawks swarm, blocking our path and forcing us back.

A bird comes at Dex from the right; he hears it a moment too late. Its beak digs into his shoulder, drawing blood.

"Zadie." Dex grabs my arm. Black smoke billows beneath us. I gasp as a familiar wind rips me off my feet.

Everything blurs. The edges of the red labyrinth walls blend with the blue sky into a solid purple mass. Dizziness sweeps through me. I cling to Dex, praying he won't let go.

When the smoke clears, I stumble over my feet. Gravel scrapes my knees as I hit the ground. "Where are the birds?"

"On our tail," Dex says. "Come on."

"Why didn't you smoke-transport us this whole time?"

"It doesn't last when I'm using energy to carry someone."

My cheeks grow hot. I remember Mirror-Zadie's words, telling me I always need to be saved. Squawks sound behind us, getting closer.

I follow Dex around the corner, our footsteps slamming against the ground.

The birds swoop in. I force myself to keep going, my lungs burning.

I peek over my shoulder. The birds stretch and transform, their bodies morphing into serpents.

"Dex!" I point.

Seven snakes slither toward us, their fangs bared. Dex throws a gust of fire at them. I'm helpless. I can't expose the blade in my boot—they stole my rifle too quick.

The snakes persist, nonplussed by Dex's flames.

Sssssszadie. . . come here, sssszadie. . .

"Leave me alone!"

The hissing whispers across my skin.

Dex positions himself between me and the serpents, squaring his shoulders. He flexes his hands, ready to fight.

"What can I do?" My heart hammers like a bass drum in my chest. "How can I help?"

"Don't die."

I gulp, wishing it were that easy.

All seven snake bodies twist together, creating a giant

cobra seven feet tall. It rears upward, towering over us. The scales around its face fan out into a hood.

We stand still as statues, watching. Waiting.

My hand darts to my boot. The cobra hisses, flashing its long fangs.

Dex conjures a massive ball of flames and throws it at the beast. Unfazed, the monster lurches at us. It slithers across the gravel.

"Run!" Dex takes off.

The cobra hisses, chasing after us.

I follow Dex down a straight corridor and bank a left. The labyrinth walls cut off. Dex jerks to a stop.

A wide, black river flows perpendicular to our path. The current runs steadily. Across the river, the labyrinth continues.

Dex hesitates.

"What's wrong?" I ask.

He opens his mouth, then shuts it.

The snake winds toward us.

"What'll it do?" I ask. "Torture us? Drown us?"

He doesn't respond.

My pulse races. I know this labyrinth—that's no ordinary river. But if I've learned anything in here, it'll be the only way. There's no going around. We have to cross.

The snake winds slowly toward us, a predator stalking its prey. It's not racing anymore; it's blocking our path back. Its motive is clear: force us to cross the river.

"I can't swim." Panic cuts my words. "I don't know how."

"It's shallow. Waist-high at most."

"Can I wade through?"

"This river's intent isn't to drown you." Dread creeps across his face. "Don't stop. No matter what you see, don't stop." He steps into the water. Like he predicted, it comes up to his waist.

Dex sucks in a sharp gasp. His eyes cloud over.

That doesn't look good.

Clenching my fists and praying I don't drown, I follow.

25

My boots hit the sludgy bottom. Cold, black water envelops my lower half, sloshing around my stomach.

My skin prickles.

The water vanishes and everything around me fades to black.

Ma tries shielding me, but the guards rip my six-year-old body away from her. My lungs heave for air that won't come.

The city official doesn't look up from her paperwork. "Say goodbye to your mother, Blank."

Ma is crying. I'm reaching out to her, but the door slams, separating us forever.

The vision flashes before my eyes as if it's happening now. I can smell that dank moldy odor of the woman's office. I'm barely aware of the current tugging me. My feet make slow, deliberate steps as if being pulled on strings.

The bunks are cold and quiet. I'm crying into my pillow, wishing I'd wake up. The past few hours had to be a nightmare—the lady pricking my finger, declaring me a Blank, stranding me outside the gate. Staring up at the city walls and realizing I'd never be allowed inside again. Meeting the Warden, agreeing to work in the mines for her forever—it couldn't be real.

The door flings open, flooding the room with light. I sob, wrapping my arms around myself.

The Warden clomps toward me. "Shut your hells-forsaken Blank mouth!" She grabs my hair and slams my head into the wall. Pain splinters through my skull. "I save you from the wastes and this is the thanks I get? Don't make me regret saving your life, Blank. If I have to come back out here, I'll kill you with my bare hands."

I can't see the river. All I can see are my worst memories, like they're playing on a screen I can't shut off. I force my legs to keep walking, the water chilling me to the core. I don't want to watch anymore. I need to reach the shore. Then it'll be over.

I'm seven-years-old. It's the middle of the night when a wailing siren shatters my sleep. The Warden flips the lights on and forces everyone out of bed.

Two burly Skilled men and a muscly Skilled woman have three of the Warden's workers pinned down. They tried to run away before their debt to the Warden was paid. The Warden sent her lackeys after them, and caught them trying to escape into the desert.

"Let this be a lesson to you all," she barked, before walking down the line with her serrated blade, slicing each of their necks in turn.

My insides turned to rock. I couldn't look away.

That was the moment it sunk in; I was going to die here. I never should have signed that contract. I'd made a huge mistake.

The dark water laps against me, slimy and cool against my skin.

I'm eight. My plastic dinner tray quivers in my shaking hands. The Warden makes the older adults in her service dole out food to the kids. They always take out their frustration on us—especially the Skilled workers. Even though we're all stuck under the same contract, they try to assert their dominance over Blanks any chance they get. I dread mealtime.

"What are you looking at?" An old Blank woman slaps a cup of glop onto my plate. She's missing her left eye. My mind jumps to all sorts of grotesque explanations for how that happened.

"N-nothing." I step back; one of the Skilled workers flicks her hand and the electrical cord on the floor snaps up. My foot tangles in the wire and I stumble, sending my tray toppling to the ground. Oatmeal

splatters all over the Warden's shiny black boots. The Skilled woman laughs.

But the Warden doesn't blame her for the spill. She seethes and grabs me by my collar. I can't move a muscle. I'm too paralyzed with fear.

The Warden drags me into her office and throws me to the ground. "I take you in off the street, and this is how you thank me?" She kicks me in the ribs, and pain shoots through my sides. "Blank scum. I should've left you to starve." I can smell the grog on her breath.

I cover my face, cowering. "I'm sorry."

"Not yet you're not." The Warden grabs her broom and smashes the handle into my back. I yelp, curling further into myself. The broomstick comes down again and again with a sharp crack.

I lose count of how many times she hits me before the office door swings open.

Landon stands framed in the doorway like the brightest star in the night sky. His face contorts into a fury I've never seen before.

It happens so fast. Landon throws himself at the Warden, attacking her with fire and lightning and Skills I didn't know he possessed.

Tears well in my eyes as I plug forward. The memories

suck the air from my lungs, suffocating me. Each step feels heavier. I can't see the shore. I can't see anything but the past.

I'm hugging Landon as tight as I can. Maybe if I squeeze hard enough, he'll stay.

Don't leave me here alone, I want to shout. But I can't. He never belonged here in the bunks with us. He deserves better than this. I need to let him go.

"I'll come back for you, Zadie," he whispers in my ear as I detangle my arms from his. "I promise."

I clamp my eyes shut, wishing I could believe him.

Valerie stands by the door with their new Skilled foster father. He's a heavyset man with a mustache and a perpetual smile. I hope he treats them well.

My best friend and his new family exit the bunks for the last time. Landon offers me a final smile before the door closes behind them.

The Warden hobbles up behind me. She hasn't walked straight since her altercation with Landon two weeks ago. Her hand rests on my shoulder, tightening like a vice. "Your friend won't be around to save you anymore."

My insides feel wobbly. I struggle against the current, doing its best to push me back and hold me here longer. I force myself to focus on wading. I need to reach the other side.

Beating after beating passes. The Warden doesn't grab any other kids out of bed anymore. Every night, she finds an excuse to punish me. Sometimes it's the broom. Sometimes it's a cord she uses as a whip. Sometimes it's her fists. I block it out, pretending I'm home with Ma. Somewhere else with Landon, far away. Every day, I wish I could go back and stop myself from signing that contract. I hate myself for signing it, even though I try to convince myself I did what I had to do to survive.

After a month, scars and gashes cover my back, from my shoulders down to my thighs. I examine my naked body in the bunks' bathroom mirror. The sight makes my stomach curdle.

It doesn't feel like my body anymore. Every part of me belongs to the Warden.

The cold water biting into me is the only reminder of where I am. My chest tightens. I know what's coming next. I don't want to face it again.

I'm fourteen. It's my first night as a free Trinnean, and I've spent it comforting Chantry as she cries and vomits. I can't stop blaming myself. I don't dare tell my sister it was my fault the tutor caught them.

"What'll they do to her?" Chantry asks between sobs.

I know the answer: The Warden will beat the crap out of Nadine. Break her bones. Torture her. But I can't bear to say it. "She'll be fine," I lie. "They'll . . . make her go to bed early and put her back in the mines."

Chantry nods, her face pale. My answer seems to placate her a little.

"You'll help me raise the money to release her from that hells-forsaken contract, won't you?"

"Of course. I'll do anything to help." I mean it. I haven't forgotten my vow to save her.

It's late by the time I get on my airbike to head back to Ma's. The night is eerily quiet, and I'm all too aware of the burns on my palms. I speed through the deserted city, praying to the Leader no one gives me a hard time.

A wailing alarm pierces my eardrums. I know what it is, even though I haven't heard it in years. It's the Warden's emergency call. One of her workers ran away without paying back their debt. I didn't think anyone else would have the nerve, after watching her murder those three men several years earlier.

Nausea percolates inside me. Whoever escaped will probably try to flee into the desert, but there's always the chance they'll come into town. Guards will be teeming in the streets in moments. I shouldn't be outside if they're looking for a Blank runaway, no matter what the Xs on my palms say.

I accelerate, taking a shortcut through Center Square.

That's when I see her.

A girl stands at the labyrinth threshold with her back to me, the moonlight illuminating her long braid. She shifts and I recognize the movement.

I pull over and cut the engine. "Nadine?"

When she turns around, my chest constricts.

Dried blood is caked across her face and in her hair. Her left eye is swollen shut, her right encircled with purple. She cradles her left arm to her chest. "Hi, Zadie."

I've faced the girl every night over the bathroom sink for a year now, but I barely recognize her beneath the blood and bruises.

"Nadine!" I jump off my bike and rush toward her. "How could you run away? You shouldn't have done that. They'll . . . they'll . . . " I can't say it. I go in to hug her, but stop when she slinks down in pain.

Her shoulders droop, but she doesn't respond. It hits me.

"Don't do it." I grab her arm, holding her back from the mouth of the labyrinth. *"Please. Don't go in there."*

Raised voices echo behind us. Rumbling airbike engines rip through the night silence, growing louder and closer.

"I can't do it anymore." Nadine's eyes crinkle at the sides.

"You have to. Please. Entering the labyrinth is suicide."

"Not necessarily." Determination flares across her face. *"Not if I can reach the end and find the Leader. Convince him to change the rules."*

"No one reaches the end."

"Not yet they haven't. But who's to say it can't be me? Why can't I be the first?"

I shake my head. "It's not worth it. Not even the Skilled make it through. The maze is a deathtrap. You can't risk your life like that."

"Some things are worth the risk, Zadie. Some things are worth fighting for. I'm doing this. I'm going to do it—for me, for you, for everyone who's ever been banished from Trinnea for not having Skills. For everyone who's starved outside the city walls. There's enough for everybody, right here in Trinnea."

"Just . . . wait." I hold my hands up. "Don't do anything rash. We're gonna get you out."

"No you won't. Not for years. And what about everyone else, huh? What about the others stuck in there?"

I don't have an answer. She's right; we'll never raise up the money to save everyone. But I can save her—I know I can. "It'll take a while, but I don't care. We'll do it. I promise. I can't let you go in there. What can I do to change your mind?"

"It's not my mind that needs to change. It's the Leader and his rules. It's this town. It's the Skilled."·

"Nadine—"

"Don't you see? They've designed a system that's nearly impossible to escape. That's what they want. They dangle the Trinnea pass in front of us like candy, so we believe if we work hard enough to get in, we will. But we won't." Venom drips from her words. She's like a soda bottle that's been shaken for years, finally ready to explode. "They want us to believe the ones who save up the money to buy the pass have earned the right to live there, but it's not true. What have the Skilled done to earn it? Nothing. We're fighting a rigged system from the start. The Skilled get to be there just because they're Skilled. They haven't earned it. We have to work twice as hard for the chance to get what they have for free. Every day my debt gets bigger and bigger, and that's the cycle. They don't intend for us to ever leave the wastes. The Skilled don't even want us here. They just want the coal we mine." Her chest heaves under ragged breaths. "I'm done, Zadie. I'm done following their rules. I'm getting out, one way or another. And if I make it to the Leader, I swear it, I won't let him get away with it anymore."

I blink at her. "Nadine—"

"You've seen the old Blanks in the bunks. They might as well be dead. We're all dying in there, slowly. I'm not giving them the satisfaction of killing me in there, of watching me work for years for a reward that I shouldn't have to earn in the first place."

I can't bear to admit she's right.

"And if I don't finish the maze?" She takes a deep breath. "Then I'd rather die than come back here. Death is better, Zadie. Death is better than this."

I should stop her. I should hold her down, offer to hide her, anything to keep her from entering the maze. But part of me wonders if she could do it. If she could reach the end, change things for the better.

"Let me go," she says. "Please."

Saving her from the labyrinth won't save her at all. It'll doom her to the Warden's whims. Life imprisonment for the crime of being born un-Skilled.

I know what it's like in the bunks.

This will destroy Chantry. But before I can talk myself out of it, I let my hand fall back to my side. "Reach the exit. I know you can do it."

Angry voices grow louder. Flashlight beams cascade over the buildings behind us.

"If I don't come back, tell Chantry . . ." Nadine's voice breaks. "Tell her I love her." She presses a dried orchid into my hands.

"Check the stage!" shouts a man.

Nadine shoves me toward my bike. "Don't let them see you."

I hide the flower in my pocket and jump on my bike. As I speed away, Nadine pulls the elastic out of her braid, freeing her hair. She steps into the maze, disappearing into a shroud of darkness. I hope it won't be the last time I'll ever see her. But deep down, I know this is goodbye.

I couldn't save her.

The water grows shallow. It sloshes against my stomach, then my knees, then my ankles. The world comes back into focus as I step on dry land, my pants soaking wet. My cheeks are damp with water, but it's not from the river.

Dex is waiting for me on the shore. His face is pallid. "Are you okay?"

I nod, forcing a smile. I don't feel okay.

The black river flows innocuously behind me. We amble back onto the path, leaving the river in our dust. I feel drained. The labyrinth has sucked every ounce of energy and courage from my limbs.

"We're almost there." Dex speaks in a monotone. I wonder if he's feeling the labyrinth's fatigue too.

Part of me wants to know what he saw in the river, but I don't dare ask.

We take a few steps when my ears prick. I hear it before Dex does.

Gravel crunches around the corner ahead—steady, even footsteps. Dex freezes, flexing his hands. I tense, waiting for another attack.

A woman rounds the corner and my stomach plunges.

It's the Warden.

I clench my fists. My fingernails dig half-moons into my palms.

No. It can't be.

She stands tall and broad, wearing her usual khakis and brown tunic. Her nose wrinkles when she sees me, like she smells something foul. "Blank scum."

My insides turn to gelatin. Just like that, I'm cowering in her office. She's standing over me, threatening me. I can feel her floor beneath me, cold and unwelcoming.

"Who are you?" Dex demands.

I try to answer, but the words won't come.

The Warden saunters toward me. "Zadie knows. She knows me well."

My heart slams against my ribs, on the verge of exploding in my chest. I'm a statue, my feet growing roots into the earth.

Dex positions himself in front of me. He subtly tilts his left side toward her. "Who are you?" he repeats.

"I'm here to collect what's mine."

Ragged breaths tear through me. Everything is closing in around me.

"Leave now," Dex snaps, "or I'll make you."

She can't be real. It's impossible. No. Ma already paid off my debt.

The Warden reaches behind her back, drawing a whip. "No one can help you, Zadie. You belong to me."

It's the labyrinth. It's messing with me. It's another trick.

"You're the Warden." Dex sneers. "Why don't you walk away while you still can?"

My pulse ticks like a bomb under my skin. Every organ in my body constricts, like I'm being shoved through a juicer.

I'm sick of this. I'm sick of feeling like I'm nothing. Like I'm two inches tall.

Dex waves his hand toward her, but she stays put. He's taken aback. She's immune to his Skills—the real Warden isn't.

She's not real.

She's not real.

She can't be real.

I step out from behind Dex. "I belong to no one."

The Warden's eyes flash yellow. She raises her knotted whip high over her head and swings it down. Dex flings his arm up to take the blow. It cuts his skin with a sharp crack, but he doesn't bleed.

It's not real.

Footsteps lightly patter against the earth. My senses spring to life. Not again.

A skinny man with a clipboard steps into the open. He's wearing a gray medical coat, like the doctors back in Trinnea. I've never seen him before.

"Hello, Subject Delta."

Dex inhales sharply. It's subtle, but I hear it. The color drains from his face.

The maze sent the Warden for me; whoever he is, this man came for Dex.

"Long time no see," he says to Dex. "You've grown. Still ungrateful though, I bet."

Dex steps back, his eyes wide.

"Who's that?" I whisper.

He doesn't respond. He doesn't even look like he heard me.

The Warden and the doctor slowly circle us. We rotate with them, not daring to take our eyes off them.

"Given the chance to live in the Stone Palace"—the doctor

shakes his head, jotting something on his clipboard—"and you threw it all away."

Dex lived in the Stone Palace. That's impossible. No one enters the Palace. That would only happen if . . .

"You were in the Selected Six," I say, more of a question than a statement.

Dex says nothing. He can't unglue his eyes from this man.

"What happened to you?" I ask. "What happened to the Selected Six?"

The doctor steps closer. "The results were inconclusive. I'll need to run another test. You'll cooperate this time." A smug grin stretches across his face. "Won't you?"

He's shaking. The Devil of Trinnea is shaking.

"After all, we both know what happened last time you . . . disobeyed."

I reach behind me and brush Dex's hand. I expect him to recoil, but his fingers latch onto mine, sending a zip of heat cascading through me. It gives me strength.

"Y-you need to leave," I stammer at the doctor, my eyes still flitting toward the Warden.

"Show us your Skills, Subject Delta. Go on. Show us your Skills." He unfurls a thin medical knife. "Let me take a look inside . . . unless, of course, you'd rather I take a look at Shae."

Something inside me snaps. "Leave him alone!"

"Shut up, Blank." The Warden slaps her whip against the earth. I stiffen.

The doctor doesn't flinch. "You got your own mother killed, Subject Delta. Would be a shame if you couldn't save your dear sister."

Dex lunges, grabbing the doctor by the throat. I press my hand to my mouth. I've always known Dex is violent, but seeing it again makes me tremble.

The doctor is unfazed. He winks at us before fading away, leaving Dex grasping at air.

Dex whirls around and sends a gust of fire into the wall. Then he fists his hands in his hair, throws his head back, and screams.

I tentatively step forward to comfort him, but the Warden's whip crashes down on my shoulder. I cower, but it doesn't bleed. It doesn't even hurt.

"You're not real!" I pick up a rock and launch it at her face. It's surprisingly satisfying, even when the rock sails straight through her body like it's air. With a gust of wind, the Warden fades away.

She's gone.

My knees buckle, as if the taut band holding me upright finally snapped. They knew my worst fear. They knew it, and they used it against me—and it didn't break me.

Dex rests his hand on my shoulder. Without thinking, I place my hand over his.

I want to know who that doctor was. I want to know what happened to Dex. I want to comfort him. But I'm too focused on what's directly down the path, fifty feet away.

The silver waterfall.

The silver waterfall glimmers in the distance, trickling over the edge of the labyrinth wall. It's the end. The Palace lies beyond it. All my concerns melt off me like mud in a rainstorm.

We're here. We're really here. We made it.

"Dex!" I throw my arms around him. "We did it!" He stiffens, and I awkwardly pull back, my face heating. "We finished the maze."

His face doesn't share my glee. "Zadie. Wait."

I don't want to wait. Waiting longer in the labyrinth sounds like a terrible idea.

I'm practically skipping. My pace quickens from walking, to jogging, to full-on running. Dex strides at my side. He glances at me out of the corner of his eye.

The silver waterfall gets closer. I've been running for days, but I don't feel the burn in my calves. After all this time, it doesn't seem real.

Sssszadie . . .

A whisper washes over me, prickling goosebumps down my skin.

With a flash, the sand guardian appears. I hear her and duck; Dex, with his bad ear, flinches a second too late.

She pounces. Teeth bared, the sand guardian tackles Dex to the ground. "You think you can get past me?" She growls a low hiss I've never heard before. Her yellow eyes sparkle with danger. "I'll destroy you."

Dex grunts, writhing and fighting in vain. He slashes his knife through her chest. She laughs as it rips through her without damage.

I go to punch her but she grabs my wrist. I barely slither out of her grip. The sand guardian reaches for me again but I scramble away. I'm closer to the waterfall than she is. She snarls, the realization settling in—she can't stop both of us.

Dex flounders, punching and kicking blows that don't stick. She's impenetrable. A manifestation of the unbeatable maze itself.

My mind races.

The sand guardian latches her skeletal hands around Dex's neck. He gasps for air.

"I'm not supposed to kill. But I swore I'd never let a Trinnean finish the maze," she hisses, "and if I have to break that oath at least I'll break you with it."

My eyes dart from the waterfall to Dex.

A simple blade can't kill her. Maybe a poison one can.

I rip open my boot buckle and unsheathe my knife.

I am brave. I am strong. And I am not afraid.

Clenching the hilt as tight as I can, I lunge at her. She releases Dex and turns on me, throwing me down and pinning me to the earth.

But I've already plunged the poison blade into her heart.

Her eyes widen in disbelief. A groan escapes her lips as black blood sprays from the wound. With a gentle breeze softer than her whisper, the sand guardian falls. Her body hits the gravel and evaporates in a cloud of ash.

Wisps of smoke curl from my blade. It disintegrates, leaving nothing but a gray dust that the wind carries away.

I'm still staring at the empty air. I did it. I killed her. I can't help it—I laugh. A Blank made it through the maze. A Blank slaughtered the labyrinth's guardian. No Skilled has ever done that.

I examine the circled Xs on my palms. They burned my hands to keep me down. But I have done something no Skilled person has ever achieved. I have a power no one else in Trinnea has ever possessed. I will wear that proudly.

Dex coughs, grasping his neck.

"Dex!" I rush toward him.

His brow furrows as he pushes to his feet. The movement looks painful, but he hides it.

"You saved my life." He's staring at me, almost in disbelief. "You saved me."

I gape at him. "Did you think I'd leave you behind?"

The look on his face betrays him; that's exactly what he thought I'd do.

"You shouldn't have saved me."

"Of course I should have. We're in this together."

"No. You shouldn't have. You should have left me there to die."

"Why would you say that? I'd never—"

"I'm not worth saving." He raises his voice. "Hells! How many times do I have to tell you? I'm not the hero. I'm a bad guy."

I shrink down.

"I know you want to believe in me or something, but you're wrong, okay?" He throws his head back. "You have no idea who I am. The terrible things I've done."

His shout reverberates between the labyrinth walls. We bathe in its echo.

"I've done terrible things, too," I whisper. I remember the look on Chantry's face when she arrived at school early and caught me leaving Nadine's flower on her chair. The betrayal. The pain. The shock when Nadine wandered out of the labyrinth a week later, but she wasn't the same. Because I could have stopped her, and I didn't. I could have saved her, and I didn't. And it was all my fault. "I've done terrible things to the people I love."

"I'm a killer, Zadie. A liar. A thief. A murderer."

"Maybe that's true. But that's not all you are." I swallow hard. "People are more than the worst things they've ever done."

The angry mask melts off Dex's face, leaving behind a veil of sadness. He deflates, like someone punctured him and let out all the air. "It's my fault. What happened to her."

His gray eyes meet mine. For the first time, it's like I'm looking inside him.

"My family was Selected. I was almost seven-years-old. The Leader picked us because I was a Six."

"How come nobody in Trinnea remembers you?"

"I went by a different name then. I was a little kid when I left. I didn't have these scars then. I don't know."

"You weren't always Dex?"

"Dex. Delta Experiment Subject. D-Ex. They wrote it on my files. It became me."

When people call you something long enough, you start to internalize it. It becomes ingrained into the very fabric of your being.

"The Selected Six was a trap," he continues. "They hurt us. All the Fours, Fives, and Sixes they took to the Palace. Kids. Fourteen children between the six Selected families. They experimented on us. Cut us open. Every day a new test. They'd make us use our Skills while they shocked us and cut us and bled us, trying to see how we worked. For years."

Dex was a prisoner. All those years I suffered in the bunks for being a Blank, he'd suffered at the Palace for being too Skilled. I can't believe the Leader allowed this.

"One day I refused. Said I wouldn't use my Skills. They told me to cooperate but I wouldn't. So they took my Ma into the next room and killed her. Slowly. They made me listen."

The mirror's words ring in my mind. *Make it slow. Make him hear it.*

"How did you escape?"

"The tests weren't working. They needed more. Almost all the Selected kids were dead. They . . . they were gonna take Shae and cut her open. Kill her. She was only nine."

I'm wracked with nausea. Why would anyone do this to kids? The irony isn't lost on me that I asked the same question every night in the bunks, after every beating.

All those years I spent envying the Selected Six, they were dying. Suffering.

"They kept her sedated in one of their rooms. Preparing her." He takes a deep, shaky breath. "She was all I had left."

I remember his darkest secret he gave to the toll road. "You sacrificed someone."

"I didn't want to do it. I think about it every day. I hate myself for what I did. But I had to save Shae. I couldn't lose her too, I just couldn't." He pinches his eyes shut.

I want to hate him for what he's done. But deep down, if it were Landon, or Ma, or Chantry's life on the line, I know I would've done the same. He was a kid, about to lose his only family. How can I judge him for doing anything he could to save her? Maybe we're all a little broken. We're all a little bit selfish and evil and good and dark and light.

"The girl was a Palace servant. Right height, right hair color. They never looked at their subjects too closely. I knocked her out and swapped them, swung Shae over my shoulder, and ran."

"Into the maze?"

"We didn't get far."

My stomach feels heavy, like I swallowed a rock. We barely survived the labyrinth now, working together and with several more years under our belts. I can't imagine entering as a child, with a younger kid on my back.

"A . . . monster came at me."

The labyrinth monster.

"I couldn't fight while holding Shae. I put her down. When I came back, she was gone. I searched everywhere. The sand guardian found me first."

"What did she do to you?"

"Nothing. She said the labyrinth took Shae to punish me. The Palace was holding her captive. I could get her back, but not alone . . . with help from a . . . a . . . "

It hits me. "That's why you need a Blank, why you need me. To help get Shae. They won't try to capture me, because I'm not Skilled."

He hesitates. "Yes."

A knot twists inside me as I realize. "Landon." The word barely leaves my lips. I squeeze the leaf pendant, pressing it over my heart. They're experimenting on people with the most Skills. That's why Landon's at the Palace. He's in danger. "I have to save him." I stop. "And Shae. We're going to save them both. Together. I'm going to break the spell on Trinnea. Get my Ma back."

"If I fail, they're gonna kill her." His voice cracks. "She's all I have left."

I take his hand in mine. His other hand brushes a lock of hair behind my ear. "We're not going to fail. We're going to get her back."

"Zadie . . . " He blinks hard.

I wait for him to finish his sentence. He starts walking toward the waterfall instead.

PART THREE
THE STONE PALACE

28

The waterfall is more beautiful in person. Up close, it's not water. Silver mist gently flows over the break in the wall, too opaque to see the other side. It sparkles as if glitter runs through it.

I run my hand under it. It's cool against my skin, rippling around my fingertips. I can't believe we're really here.

"You ready?" I ask.

He's looking straight through me. "Yes."

"Hey." I squeeze his shoulder. "We'll save her, okay?"

He nods.

I step through the waterfall. It envelops my body like a cloud of ice water.

I emerge in the sunlight on the other side. An elegant lavender gown clings to my body, replacing my dirty Trinnean clothes. The grime and sweat that's coated my skin for days is gone. My nose crinkles at the scent of flowers, then I realize it's coming from me. Waves of clean, brown hair cascade down my shoulders. I run my fingers through it. At least that quells my fear of meeting the Leader looking like a slob.

My hand frantically searches my neck. I relax when my

fingers meet Landon's leaf pendant. Hopefully I can give it back to him soon.

A crinkle in my bodice tells me I haven't lost Dex's maps either.

Dex emerges from the waterfall wearing a pressed black tuxedo. His messy dark hair is combed neatly to the side. My mouth runs dry. I'm not sure why I'm so surprised. He's always looked attractive. But for some reason, I'm taken aback.

From the look on his face, so is he. "You . . . clean up well." I look away. "You too."

The Stone Palace towers over my head. Gray bricks form the massive structure, from the ground all the way up to the turrets stretching into the sky. The spires I always admired from afar loom right over my head.

We stand at the beginning of a cobbled path. It leads straight out from the waterfall, a continuation of the labyrinth. Moss-covered sculptures line the walkway. They look like statues of people, but time has hidden their faces behind layers of green and brown.

My plan is so ill-conceived. I wanted to reach the Palace. I'm here. Now what? I guess I never believed I'd actually get here. I've never thought through the next step.

I expect to find guards, servants, Landon, anyone, but the courtyard is deserted. I squint up at the Palace, looking for doors. There are windows near the top, way out of reach. Maybe Dex could get there if he used his black smoke.

"We have to find the Leader. Where do we go?" The moment I say it, I second guess myself. The Leader allowed his doctor to torture Dex and the other kids. He could've been behind the experiments and cruelty that killed Dex's mother. Maybe Farrar was right. Hells. This is bad.

"This way." Dex strides past me, focusing straight ahead.

I bite my lip. I used to fantasize about meeting the Leader. I imagined screaming at him for what he's done to Blanks. He'd realize upon meeting me that he was wrong—Blanks should be treated like everyone else. Then he'd invite Ma and me to join the Selected Six. Maybe Chantry, too. Now, that old fantasy sends a shiver cascading over me.

A light scratching fills the air. Music plays from somewhere, swimming through my ears. Dex doesn't stop.

I'm going to find Landon, save Shae, and get someone to help free Trinnea. Then we're getting the hell out of here. Even with the sand guardian dead, I'm dreading reentering the maze. Maybe there's an easier route home.

A light *click* comes from above me. I scan the area for the source of the noise. "What was that?"

"I didn't hear anything."

Embedded in the nearest statue, a camera eye zooms in on me.

Click.

I'm simultaneously relieved and on edge. Someone knows we're here. They'll come looking for us.

We wind down the path. If nothing else, I'm glad I'm not alone. The hem of my long dress drags over the dirt. I hike it up, wishing I had something more convenient. This thing will be useless if I have to fight or run.

Dex leads me toward a marble archway, heading away from the Palace.

"Are you sure this is the right way?"

"Yes."

Brambles curl on the edges of the pathway. "Rubus Trilobus." I point at it. "That's what this is called. I love the white flowers."

"I'm sorry," he mumbles, not meeting my eyes. "I'm so sorry."

"For what?"

"For how I've treated you. For everything."

"Don't worry. We're here—none of that matters now."

I follow him under the arch, into a small stone-walled garden. It's better kept than the gardens in Trinnea, yet still looks rustic and overgrown. Vines trickle down the walls. A large rectangular granite slab sits in the center.

"What is this place?" I ask. "Is this where the Leader will see us?"

His eyes are hard, his mouth a tight line across his face.

"Should we wait here for him? I want him to see that you brought me here. You did what the sand guardian said. We'll get him to free Shae. How does it work, exactly? Will he send a guard or show up himself?" I cock my head. Dex's eyes are pinched shut. "Hey. What's wrong?"

"I'm so sorry. I really am. I didn't want any of this to happen."

"What are you—"

He waves his hand. An invisible force shoves me to my knees at the marble block. I can't move.

"I'm so sorry, Zadie." He grabs my hair and wrenches my head back. A cold blade presses against my neck. "I have to kill you."

I should have known Dex would betray me. But after everything we've been through together, it doesn't feel real. Even with the cold blade pressed to my skin, it hasn't sunken in. Dex is going to kill me. I am going to die. His betrayal spreads like poison through my veins.

"Is this why you brought me all this way? To murder me?"

His knife quivers against my throat. "I didn't have a choice."

"Why are you doing this?"

"I have to."

"You don't have to!"

"It's the only way." He forces the words through gritted teeth. "She's all I have. This is how I get her back."

"Killing me won't save her."

"I sacrificed an innocent life without getting blood on my hands. The labyrinth stole Shae as retribution." He sucks air through his teeth. "I have to feel the blood of taking a Blank life. It's the only way I get her back. The sand guardian said it herself."

Of course she did. She told me not to trust him. I was a fool not to listen.

"You lied to me!" Tears sting my eyes. "You really are the Devil of Trinnea. You're everything they say you are."

"I am who I am. I can't change that."

"You're a monster."

"I told you that from day one."

"I was just some Blank to you. A person to throw away. All you ever saw was my damn number like everyone else. You protected me this whole time so you could kill me yourself." My chest heaves. "I shouldn't have saved you. I should've let you die. I should've plowed that poison blade into your heart the way I'd planned."

I can feel him trembling. "Forgive me, Zadie."

Before I can choke it back, a pained moan escapes my lips. I beat the garden, the hourglass, the skeletons, everything—only to die at the hands of the person who got me through them.

"I have . . . always known my mission through the maze would someday end this way," Dex whispers. "But I . . . I . . . I have never let myself think about this moment. I don't want to do this. I don't want to hurt you, to hurt anybody. I hope you know that."

"I don't believe you!"

I should've stayed in Trinnea. I wish the Sirs had never come. Then I never would've met Dex. I wouldn't be dying in this hells-forsaken place.

My anger melts into pure fear. I don't want to cry. I don't want him to see how scared I am. But tears stream down my face anyway.

"Please." I pictured my death a thousand times—mostly by the Warden's hands. I never thought I'd go down begging. But right now, in this moment, all I can think is that I don't want to die. I know it's futile. He was always going to sacrifice me for Shae. Just like Landon always chose Valerie over me. There's nothing I can say to stop him and I'm so pathetic I try anyway. "Please don't do this."

Dex doesn't respond.

I can't fight back. I can't move. I can't even turn to see the look on my murderer's face. Dex's Skill holds me captive in place.

My pulse pounds in my ears. It's all over. It's really happening. There's no one here to save me. I am going to die.

"Go back for my Ma and sister. Please, save them. Do it for me."

He pauses. "I will."

I succumb to silent sobs wracking through me. My throat burns from crying. I remember how he killed Farrar—a painless death. "Make it quick, okay?"

I can hear Dex's breaths, heavy and hollow—or maybe they're mine.

"I promise."

Salty tears leak between my lips. I focus on the smell of the granite, cold and damp. The sound of the Leader's music, playing somewhere distant. The feel of the sweat under my dress, the rough skin on my burned palms, the gravel beneath me.

He's waiting. Why is he waiting?

Just do it. Do it and get it over with. Please.

I close my eyes and think of Ma. Sitting by the fire eating rice and beans. I imagine I'm back home in Trinnea, lying on the couch after a long day at the watch-post. Ma is safe and happy, humming while she knits. Chantry and Nadine sit beside us, hardly paying us any attention. Barton sends me a joke on my communicator and I laugh and laugh like there's not a thing wrong with the world. Landon's there, wearing his leaf pendant, his arm around my shoulders. There's no labyrinth, no asylum.

Everything is perfect.

I'm so caught up in forgetting, I barely register Dex's knife leaving my neck. The sound of it clashing against the granite. His scream ripping through the small space.

Free from his Skill, I get to my feet.

Dex rampages around the room. He curses the sand guardian. He curses himself. Fire and metal fly from his hands, slamming against the rock walls and fizzling into the air.

My mouth subconsciously hangs open.

He didn't kill me. I'm alive.

Dex fists his hands in his hair and throws his head back. "I'm sorry, Shae." He collapses to his knees, shaking under waves of sobs.

I touch my neck, disbelieving. He didn't kill me.

Why didn't he kill me?

Boots clomp against the stone.

Four armed men and women in gray uniforms flank the doorway. A fifth man stands behind them in regular clothes, crossing his arms. My hand instinctually drops to my boot, but the waterfall replaced my boots with silver flats. The poison blade is long gone anyway.

Dex jumps to his feet.

"You've gotten big." The plain-clothes man looks directly at him. "Bet you don't remember—it's me, Augustus."

I tense. This man could've tortured Dex. Killed his mother. Hurt Shae.

Dex flicks his hand at the man, but nothing happens. Panic shoots across his face.

"Yes, I can still mute your Skills." The man rolls his eyes. "C'mon, Subject Delta." He beckons with his arm. Dex is as defenseless as I am.

Two guards rush at Dex. He tries to fight them off, but one pulls out his nightstick and whacks him in the stomach. Dex grunts, doubling over. They escort him under the arch.

The other two guards come at me. I scramble backward until my hands brush the wall. My fingers wrap around a small pointed rock. I brandish it like a dagger. "Stay away from me."

The guards easily rip the weapon out of my hand and grab me by the elbows. I writhe and fight but can't shake their grip.

"Careful!" Augustus snaps. "Don't hurt her!"

I struggle, dragging my feet in the dirt. "Who are you?"

"Zadie Kalvers, we're under orders to bring you to the Ruler."

I blink. "The . . . the Leader?"

They exchange glances. "You need to come with us."

This is why I came here. I need to speak with the Leader. I need to save my family.

"Okay." I stop fighting. "Take me to him."

The guards tell me I'm not a prisoner, but they don't relinquish their grip on my arms. All seven of us make our way toward the Palace. Dex and his two guards walk in front, with Augustus in the middle. My guards escort me last, considerably gentler than Dex's.

I need an escape strategy in case this goes south. I wish I could talk to Dex privately. I need to know if he's on my side. Can I still trust him? Why didn't he kill me?

We reach a massive door. As if triggering a sensor, the door cranks itself open, revealing a stone-walled entryway. A chandelier dripping in cobwebs hangs from the ceiling. Dusty chairs and benches line the walls, but they look like no one's sat in them for a decade. It's not as glamorous as I expected for the Leader's home.

One of my escorts releases me, joining Dex's guards instead. I'm a little offended; Dex requires three armed guards plus Augustus, while one person is deemed enough to handle me.

"This way." My single escort guides me toward a wooden door.

Dex strains against his captors, but they yank him back.

"Not you," a guard snaps. "Just the girl."

This is bad. "No." I make myself deadweight. "We stay together or I don't go." I recognize the irony of demanding to stay with the boy who tried to kill me five minutes ago, but being alone with these strangers sounds like a terrible idea.

"I'm sorry, we're under strict orders." Augustus gives me a sympathetic smile. "We're to escort you upstairs to see the Ruler, Ms. Kalvers."

I eye him suspiciously at the word *ruler*.

Dex thrashes, but their grip is too strong. "Don't go with them!"

I can't trust anyone. But I came all this way to see the Leader. I can't chicken out now.

"We'll wait for you here." Augustus nudges Dex with his elbow. "Don't worry, this one's not going anywhere."

Before I can protest, my guard ushers me through the doorway. A stone staircase winds upward at our feet. I peek over my shoulder, meeting Dex's eyes one last time before the door shuts behind us. My heart beats faster the moment we're alone.

A million possibilities flash through my mind. What if they're taking me to that evil doctor? What if they try to cut me open?

Stop freaking out! You're not Skilled. The Leader doesn't want you.

We slog up three flights of stairs and enter a hallway. A frayed crimson rug stretches the entire length of the floor. Music plays from somewhere, getting louder.

"In here." The guard holds a door open for me.

I wrinkle my nose at the smell of mothballs. Dusty

bookshelves, an old desk, and a cracked coffee table fill the room. A record player on the desk churns out scratchy music. Sunlight pours in through a tiny window.

I cautiously step inside, surveying the musty office. "What is this place?"

"Wait here. The Ruler will be with you shortly." He slams the door in my face, leaving me alone in the room.

I press my ear to the door and wait until his footsteps fade before jiggling the handle. Of course, it's locked.

I am brave. I am strong. And I am not afraid.

Okay. I can do this.

I peruse the room, running through my script for the Leader. First priority: talking him into freeing Landon, followed by Shae. Next will be Ma, Chantry, and the rest of Trinnea. He has to listen to me. I'll make him.

I scan the bookshelves, running my finger across the faded and tattered spines. I don't recognize any of the titles.

A figure-eight-shaped lamp sits on the desktop. I pull the cord to turn it on, illuminating pens and scrap paper scattered across the desk. The Leader is awfully disorganized.

I open the top drawer and find a long, pointy letter opener. Perfect. I slip it into the bodice hem of my dress. Just in case.

I slide open the bottom drawer. A thick book sits inside, taking up the entire space.

I shouldn't be snooping. The Leader could walk in and catch me at any moment. This could be some sort of morality test. I think back to Barton's rambling, trying to remember if he mentioned anything like that.

My mouth scrunches to the side. They left me in this room alone. It would be absurd not to use that to my advantage.

I open the book, paging through lists of Trinnean names. Each one is marked with a number.

Skills.

I've always wondered about this. When city officials take our blood at age six, they test to see if we have the Skilled gene. All the Skilled samples are sent to the Leader, and I never knew what happened after that. Everyone learns their number as their Skills develop naturally. But apparently, the Leader had it all written down the whole time.

I flip to the Ks and find my name.

There's nothing new, but my heart still sinks at the blank space where a number would be. I sigh. I'm the only Blank on the whole page, and there are at least a hundred names on it.

I find Chantry, and can't help the surge of jealousy when I see her *1*.

I wonder . . .

I'm not sure what compels me to do it, but I flip to the Es. What quantifies Limitless? I don't think Landon even knows how many Skills he has—but the Leader might.

Everhart, Landon—2

I do a double-take. That can't be right. I check again, thinking I misread, but the number stays the same. Landon hasn't had only two Skills since he was a little kid. It must be a mistake. Perhaps the Leader hasn't updated this in years.

I stow the book safely back in the drawer. My fingers fidget against my dress. The Leader sure is taking his time. How long is he going to leave me in here?

I go stand by the window. Maybe I can see Trinnea from here.

But all I see is blue. A giant mass of blue. Like looking at the desert sand, only rich cerulean instead of red. Ribbons of white ripple through the blue. It's . . . moving?

I squint. Before the blue, there's a strip of brown. I've never seen anything like it.

To the left, wisps of smoke curl from the roofs of circular stone huts. Cobbled roads wind between them. If I didn't know better, I'd say those were people ambling up and down the streets.

My forehead wrinkles. That's not Trinnea.

But that's not possible. There's nothing beyond the Palace.

"Enjoying the view?"

I jump at the deep voice.

But it's not the Leader standing behind me.

It's Landon.

31

"**Fire hells!**" I nearly tackle him to the ground.

"Zadie. I missed you." He wraps his arms around me. I inhale that familiar Landon scent that always meant safety. It's him.

"I missed you too," I mumble into his chest. My tears leak into his blue jacket. I don't want to let him go. "You're here. You're really here."

"*You're* here. Did not see that coming." He winks. "But I'm glad you are."

"I thought the Leader captured you. I thought he was experimenting on you, hurting you. I thought . . . I thought . . . " I don't know what I thought. But seeing him here, safe, makes all those bad thoughts fade away. "I'm just so glad to see you. Oh!" I unclasp the leaf pendant from my neck and press it into his palm. "This is yours."

"I was wondering what happened to this." He puts it on, admiring the leaf. "I've felt naked without it."

"Wouldn't want you to be naked. I mean—not that it's bad for you to be naked. I mean, not that I've thought about it." My face gets hotter than the Trinnean sun. I mentally slap my forehead. "That's not what I meant." Why do I turn into such a fool around him? "Forget I said anything."

He grins. "Did you come all the way through the maze to find me?"

"Of course. I'd go anywhere to find you." I blush. It sounds corny, but I mean it. If I could survive the labyrinth, I could survive anything.

"I hope you know I'd do the same for you." He rakes his hand through his hair. "Hells, I'd do anything for you."

We share an awkward grin before quickly looking away. I can't forget I have a job to do.

"That's not the only reason I came," I say. "I need to see the Leader."

"Why's that?"

"Trinnea's in trouble. My Ma, Barton, Chantry, Valerie, they're all in danger, we need to—"

He presses his hand to my cheek and the warmth makes my chest all fluttery. "Don't worry about that right now. They're safe."

This feels a bit off for some reason. "How do you know?"

"I'll show you."

He puts his hand on my lower back and leads me into the hallway. We go through several empty corridors before we stop and he pulls out a giant keyring big enough to fit around my wrist.

I raise my brows. "Where did you get those?"

He thumbs through several brass keys before settling on a tiny one with a sapphire encrusted in the side. "Took them off the Leader's belt when I incapacitated him."

"Wait, you did *what*?"

He unlocks the door. "After you."

I duck under his arm to enter the room.

Digital screens make up the entire wall. I recognize the silver waterfall on one screen and the statues on another. I shiver at the sight of the marble slab where I almost died.

"What is this place?"

"The control room." He presses a couple buttons on a keypad and the screens change. Center Square fills the biggest screen, with a great view of the stage. I see the Tap Room, the asylum, the bunks, all of Trinnea. People mill about, minding their daily business. "See? Everyone's fine. Look!" He points at the screen. "There's Nina."

Chantry's friend walks past the Tap Room, an empty smile on her face. She doesn't look fine. At least the Sirs haven't killed everyone yet.

"This is how the Leader watches us?" I don't know why I'm so surprised. A surveillance system is logical. But if the Leader is omnipotent, he shouldn't need screens. "Where is he now?"

Landon presses more buttons. The top screen cuts to a small, dingy room surrounded by glass. A dirty-looking man with a shaggy beard and stringy hair sits against the back wall. "Here he is."

I give Landon a befuddled look. The Leader's twice this guy's age—probably more—with gray hair and a kind smile. "That's not the Leader."

"You mean, that's not the guy in the projection screen over the stage."

"Well, yeah. The Leader. What are you saying?"

"The man in the screen died over a hundred years ago. This guy's name is Alfred. He's been calling the shots, projecting the Leader's image for a few years. There was a woman before him. And I don't know who else before that."

I can't comprehend this. "The Leader we know in the screen . . . *died*?"

"I wouldn't call him a leader. More like a power-hungry Vonnish fraud."

"Vonnish?"

"Vonn, the town." He thrusts his thumb over his shoulder. "You probably saw it out the window. I can't wait to take you there, you'll love it."

My mouth hangs open. "There's another town? I wasn't imagining it?"

"There're lots of other towns. Straight past Vonn is Azonali. And those watchtowers you work at? Keep walking far enough, you'll reach Kern."

"I've worked there for years. There isn't anything beyond the watchtowers. Just sand."

"There's sand, yeah." He shrugs. "And a town, if you go that far. They don't want us to find it. The Kerns put up barbed wire around their entire town to keep Trinneans out, so I wouldn't try going there."

This isn't possible. But suddenly, I remember something. That flash of red fabric in the desert. Maybe it wasn't a ghost, or a mirage. Maybe it was a person. A person from Kern.

I'm gawking at him now. "How did they keep this from us?"

"Decades upon decades of lies. I bet you don't know how Trinnea came about."

"I mean, I know a little bit. After drought and disease killed everyone else, the Leader—"

"Nope. That's what they taught us, but it's not the truth. Scientists created Skilled genes in a lab, several centuries ago. They got scared of the people they created—called them dangerous, called Skills abominations of nature—so they built Trinnea to quarantine them. The so-called *Leader* was hired to make sure Trinneans didn't starve out there alone."

"Skilled people are only in Trinnea? So that means . . . "

"Yes." He smiles. "Most people are Blanks, like you." I can't comprehend it; Blanks are the majority. Are they banished to the wastes in other towns? Or are they . . . equals? "The scientists destroyed all their research so others couldn't repeat their mistakes. This *Leader* tried to duplicate the research. If you ask me, he wanted to get some Skills for himself. But it didn't work."

"The Selected Six," I whisper.

"I have so much to fill you in on. The Leader lied to us, Zadie. All the fake Leaders operating his screens are nothing but frauds." Landon laughs. "Alfred? He's a Blank. They're all Blanks. The Vonnish, the Azonalis, everyone. Which is ironic, considering old Alfred's serving time in his own dungeon for crimes against Blanks. I thought he'd put up more of a fight, but then again, I was expecting him to have Skills to fight me with."

"*You* threw him in the dungeon? Why?"

"You never believed me, Zadie." He brushes my arm. "I told you I'd do anything for you. I meant it."

I open my mouth, then close it again. "I don't understand. You locked up the Leader . . . for me?"

"He was hurting you." Landon takes my hand, tracing his thumb over my burns. "Every day I saw those marks on your palms, I wanted to kill him. Every day you had that scared look in your eyes passing the bunks, I wanted him to share your fear." He takes a deep breath. "There's . . . there's something you should know about me. About my parents."

This is what he was trying to tell me in the Tap Room. It was only a week ago, but it feels like an eternity.

"They were Blanks, Zadie."

I realize I'm gaping and snap my mouth shut. That's the last thing I expected him to say. "How? That's not possible. Two Blanks can't produce a Skilled child."

He laughs, but there's no amusement in his voice. "The scum who paid for my Ma's Trinnean Pass to use her twice a week for six years afterward? Who wanted nothing to do with Valerie or me because we were half Blank? That man's my blood, but he's not my father. My Pa was a Blank man named Thomas Everhart. He married my Ma—loved my Ma. Loved us, even though we weren't his." He twirls a lock of my hair around his finger. "You remind me of her. I've felt that way since the moment I saw you."

Our faces are only inches apart. "What happened?"

He looks away. "They were murdered. In cold blood. A hate crime by a bunch of drunk criminals who just wanted to hurt Blanks. For fun."

I remember that conversation in the bunks so long ago. The tears in Landon's eyes.

"Landon." I hug him as tight as I can. "I'm so sorry." I hate that this happened to him. I want to take all his pain away. "I never knew that happened to you."

"As if abusing my mother for years wasn't enough, the

bastard couldn't let her be happy with her new husband. He had to get his drunk friends and kill them both." He snorts. "You probably know the scum, everyone does. James the botanist."

I remember James. Now that I know his dirty secret, I'll tell Ma never to buy cactilixer from him again. But . . .

"James walked into the bubble wall." The realization hits me, cold as ice. "The Sirs killed him."

"His justice was long overdue."

I blink. Landon doesn't look surprised. "*You* killed him . . . didn't you?"

His sheepish smile answers for him.

It's impossible. Landon couldn't have killed James. He was in the Palace. The Sirs made the announcement. I rip my hand out of his grasp. "How?"

"I hired some Vonnish Blanks to maintain order in my absence. I mean, I needed to be here, locking up the Leader. But that doesn't mean I couldn't . . . intervene."

No. Landon couldn't be behind it. "*You* put everyone under a trance? Made them subservient, complacent zombies? Hired the Sirs to terrorize us?"

"Hang on." His brow furrows. "You're not happy? No one bullies you anymore. You have more freedom than anyone in Trinnea."

"Happy? How could I be happy? My Ma is a mindless shell. So is my sister. You left without telling me. No one could re-member you—I was terrified."

He sighs. "Sorry about that. I didn't mean to scare you, I was always going to come back for you and Val. I just . . . I wanted to get everything settled here. I couldn't bring you two to the Palace until I incapacitated the Leader and took over his castle. I wanted to introduce myself as a new ruler for the people—*all* the people. Not just Skilled." His eyes light up. "I have *huge* plans for Trinnea. I can't wait to show you. We're going to do so much good, you'll see. I've been finalizing my plans and thinking over how to put them into action. Trinnea will finally be the paradise it always should've been."

Landon. Ruling Trinnea. Humble, modest, kind Landon. It doesn't fit. "You want to be the new Leader?"

"Not the Leader, exactly. That name has too much poison behind it. I want to be Trinnea's . . . king." He kisses the back of my hand. "And I want you to be my queen."

I blink at him. *What?* It strikes me as weird that I'm not jumping up and down at this. It's *Landon. My* Landon. But somehow, I can't muster up the excitement.

"No. What? That's not . . . no."

He looks stung. "You're offended by the idea of being with me?"

"No! I mean. We know the truth now. Shouldn't we tell everyone? Free the Trinneans to live how they want?"

"They had their chance, Zadie. And look what they did to you—to all Blanks."

I have no words. There's a part of me that wants to go with it. Rule Trinnea. Accept everything Landon told me without question. "I don't know what to say."

"Come here." Landon grins, tugging me toward the screens. "I have a gift for you."

He pulls up a shot of the Trinnean stage, where the whole town is assembled.

"I don't understand."

"You will. One second." He zooms in until we can see the pink bubble wall. "Here. See this wall?"

I cross my arms and nod.

"They built this force-field bubble when they built Trinnea," he says. "It was meant to enforce the quarantine, but the Leader disabled it once he realized we wouldn't leave. Watch."

Landon presses a button; the pink bubble fizzles away. He presses it again and the bubble returns. "Understand? Now, here's my gift to you, Zadie." He takes my hand and places it over the button. "Control."

I don't know what he means. Landon concentrates on the screen, focusing on the assembled Trinneans. The lethal pink wall holds them in.

He raises his hand.

Within seconds, the Warden steps out of the crowd. She drifts toward the edge, walking in a trance.

My jaw clenches as I catch on.

The Warden steps without thinking, one foot after the other, inching toward the bubble. Her eyes are glazed over.

I see it in slow motion, unfeeling. The mirror's word repeats over and over in my mind—*vindictive*.

I should push it. I can save her. I can be the better person. I want to prove I'm not a monster like she is. After all those years she tortured me, abused me, made me wish I were dead; now I'm in control. Her life is in my hands.

I hold my breath as she gets closer and closer. My fingers twitch over the button.

I don't press down.

32

Black ash floats across the screen, all that remains of the Warden. The dazed crowd stands still as statues, unconcerned with her death.

Landon claps my shoulder. "I'm proud of you. That was a just decision."

I stare at the screen. She's gone. She's really gone. The permanent knot in my chest slowly untangles, loosening its grip on my lungs.

I killed her. I'll never see her again.

She'll always be a ghost, tainting my mind and haunting my dreams, but she won't be lurking in Trinnea anymore. I can go to a festival without worrying she'll be there. I can try to move on.

That one word repeats over and over in my head: *vindictive, vindictive, vindictive*. Discomfort weasels through me. I don't feel guilty. I should feel guilty. But all I feel is an overbearing sense of relief.

"How are you feeling?" Landon asks.

I hesitate. I don't want to say how I'm feeling, because I just killed someone and I'm feeling fine. That's so screwed up.

"Come on." Landon takes my hand. "I've got so much more to show you."

I let him lead me through the door, down the stairs, and into a large square room.

"It's . . . extravagant," I say.

"Isn't it?"

I soak in the gold ceiling, the elegant furniture, the marble floor. I recognize it immediately, although it's far more luxurious in person. The Leader used to broadcast from this room. It feels so fake now. A room full of lies.

Two intricate silver chairs with red cushions sit at the far end of the room.

Landon points to the one on the right. "That will be my throne." He gives me a half-smile. "And I'm hoping the other one will be yours."

I don't answer him. It feels wrong to be standing here talking about ruling Trinnea when Ma and the others are still trapped. Yet I'm intrigued by his offer.

I've become selfish. I'm everything my reflection said I am.

"What about the Blanks beyond the gate? The ones without passes?"

Landon shrugs. "We'll demolish the gate. Keep the Skilled in their trance for a while, let the Blanks come back into Trinnea and take control of the city. Let 'em have the upper hand. Give the Skilled a taste of their own medicine for once."

"Not you, though."

"What do you mean?"

I fidget. "I mean, the Blanks would run the city, lording over a bunch of dazed Skilled, but really you're in charge, ruling from out here—right? They'd still all be under your spell—your control?"

He shrugs again, but doesn't respond.

Another set of screens faces the chairs. A camera is perched on the biggest one. I imagine the fake Leader, settling into his fancy chair and lying into the lens. Distorting his image so we'd believe him and keep living in his own personal dollhouse.

I snort. "I really hate the guy."

"I do too." Landon takes my hand. "But he's gone now. He can never hurt you again."

"What about the rest of Trinnea? Will they keep hurting?"

Landon doesn't reply.

One screen broadcasts the entryway where they escorted us into the Palace. Dex sits on a bench with his arms crossed. All three guards flank him, with Augustus glaring over him. Dex's piercing stare doesn't falter.

Landon shakes his head. "I can't believe you lasted over a week with that monster."

The word strikes me as odd. I've called Dex a monster before. He's never shied away from the title, and he's not a civilized person. I wouldn't even call him a good guy.

But a monster wouldn't have hesitated. A monster would have slit that blade through my neck and slept soundly afterward. Dex didn't.

"He's not a monster."

Landon raises his eyebrows. "He's the Devil of Trinnea."

"You don't even know him."

"I know enough."

"I'd never have found my way through the labyrinth without

him. I mean, he wouldn't have survived without me either. But I needed his sense of direction."

"He would have killed you if my guards hadn't intervened."

No. Dex threw his knife down long before the guards showed up. He screamed obscenities at himself for five minutes. The more I think about it, the clearer it is: Dex chose not to kill me. He wouldn't have done it even without the interference.

I shrug, picking at a thread on my dress.

Landon's brows pinch together. "What? Is there something going on with you two?"

"No! Of course not." My face heats. "We're friends." I think.

We watch the screen in silence. I fidget my fingers, tracing the burns on my palms. I don't know what I expected to feel upon seeing Landon again, but this is awkward.

"I still can't believe you went through the whole maze." Landon laughs. "I assumed you'd be hiding under your covers the moment my Vonnish friends showed up."

His words slap me in the face. I spent the last week hiking through hell to save him, and he's not even grateful. He's shocked I wasn't cowering in fear the whole time. "You expected me to be a coward?"

"Of course not. It's just . . . you're you. I figured you'd stay away from the danger."

"Why? Because I'm a Blank?" I bristle. "Or because I'm weak?"

"Zadie. That's not what I meant. You've always been afraid of the maze. That's all."

"Everyone's afraid of the maze. Of course I was afraid of

it, but I went in anyway to save you," I snap. "Meanwhile, you were sitting here in the Palace enjoying yourself."

"Don't be mad at me. I'm sorry, okay? I didn't mean anything by it. I'm just used to . . . helping you out. That's all."

"You mean saving me."

Landon leans his head back and groans. "Can we forget I said anything? You were very brave. I was foolish to underestimate you."

The condescension in his voice irks me.

Always needing to be rescued, my reflection says in my mind. *Can't take care of yourself.*

Maybe last week I would have agreed. Last week I would have been grateful he wanted to help me. Now I realize—Landon always saw me as a damsel in one of his stories, needing to be rescued. A weak Blank who can't do anything for herself. He's not alone; everyone in Trinnea saw me as helpless. *I* saw me as helpless.

Now I know—I've never been weak. A weak person wouldn't have survived what I have. This world has been trying to kill me for years.

But I'm still here.

Landon always liked saving me, swooping in to rescue me. Being my *hero.* I always loved it. I always thought it was a privilege having him in my corner. But now, thinking it over, I'm unsettled. He always convinced me to go to the Tap Room—a place he *knew* made me uncomfortable, where the city guards would be waiting to mock me—and for what? So he could come save me from them? It's like I was some prop, a damsel waiting to fuel his ego.

"Hey. I hate seeing you frown," he says.

I force myself to smile. It doesn't reach my eyes.

"That's more like it." He winks. "Here, let me show you around the Palace. There's a beautiful sunroom you'll love."

I follow him toward the hallway, but something snags my gaze. "What's that?"

In a darkened corner of the room, pink light seeps under a cracked-open door. I hadn't noticed it before.

"Oh, it's just a storage closet, don't worry about—"

I'm already yanking it open. A large glass orb is perched on a wooden podium. Pink light glows inside it, swirling and billowing like clouds of fog.

"Wow." I circle the podium. "What is this thing?"

Landon shuffles his feet in the doorway. "It's probably nothing. We should go. I want to show you the courtyard and—"

"Wait." I bend to see the sphere at eye-level.

Something whirls inside the glass. It's only there for half a second before fading. "I swear I saw a . . . a . . . " A face whooshes inside the orb; it hits the glass and evaporates. I gasp, jumping back. "Was that a person?"

"You're seeing things. Come on, let's go."

"There it is again!"

"It's your imagination." Landon's looking at my forehead. He's hiding something.

"You know," I say. "I can see it in your face."

Landon pinches the bridge of his nose.

My eyes narrow. "Tell me what I saw."

"Zadie."

"Don't be like the Leader. Don't lie to me."

Landon sighs. "It's the Trinneans. It's the part of their consciousness they can't access right now. I'm holding them here for safe keeping."

"So it's the trance? This is what's keeping them under the Sirs'—your—spell?"

"Yes."

I scrub a hand down my face. This is too much. I can't absorb any more secrets today. "You're literally holding all of Trinnea hostage in this . . . this . . . *ball*."

"It doesn't have to be permanent. Just for now. Until I figure out how to keep them under control."

Under control. Like how the Warden kept me. Like how the Leader prefers his Blanks. My stomach roils. I feel sick.

His smile sinks. "I'm sorry. I didn't want you to find out like this. I thought I'd locked this door."

"Free my Ma. Right now."

"I can't do that, Zadie. They're all in there together. I can't pull out an individual consciousness, otherwise I would've freed Val days ago."

Another face rushes through the pink mist. I know those eyes. That hair. But I don't want to believe it. I press my hand to the sphere right as Nadine's face evaporates against the cold glass.

Every vein in my body hardens into ice. The realization sinks into my skin like poison.

Slowly, I turn around. "Why is Nadine in there?"

He doesn't reply.

"Tell me the truth. What else have you done?"

Please explain it. Please have a logical explanation for this. Please tell me I'm wrong.

Tell me my best friend isn't behind it.

"No more lies, Landon. Just tell me."

He gives me a guilty look. "I'm not Limitless. I was born a Two."

The book was right. I should have seen that coming.

"My first Skill that developed was useless. I had above-average hand-eye coordination. I could throw without aiming and hit my target. Nothing that couldn't be done by anyone with a little practice. My second Skill was a bit more complicated. I could steal other people's numbers."

I don't move a muscle. "Numbers?"

"Everyone thinks the blood test determines a person's Skills. It's not true. It determines a person's *capacity* for Skills. A One has the capacity to develop one Skill, and so on. I can steal that capacity. If I steal from a Two, they lose their capacity for two Skills and I develop two new ones of my own—not the same specific Skills they had, just the amount.

"The first time I stole a number, it was by accident. I was playing tag with this kid Brandon from my class—a One. He fell, and when I grabbed his hand to help him up, something happened. I felt the charge run through my fingers like electricity. Suddenly, he couldn't use his levitation Skill; it was gone."

I'm numb. I can't believe what I'm hearing.

"I tried to talk to him, but he wouldn't listen. He freaked out and ran to get the tutor. I was scared I'd get in trouble. I didn't know what to do. I chucked a rock and hit him in the head, knocked him out."

"The . . . the brain scrambling? The Labyrinth Stare?"

"That was the Skill I developed from him. Brandon woke up after a couple minutes. I reached for him, not knowing what I was doing. A little pink wisp curled out of him—the bit of his consciousness. I tried to catch it, but it floated back into him. The life settled back in his eyes, so I tried again. This time, when the pink wisp came out, I trapped it in a soda bottle. I left Brandon wandering by the maze, and he was discovered there later that day. Everyone assumed the labyrinth did it. That he'd wandered inside." His voice is calm. "After a while, I realized what I could become. I could stop the dangerous ones, people who didn't deserve their Skills. The labyrinth was the perfect scapegoat."

It's like I'm looking at my best friend and seeing someone else. I don't recognize the person standing in front of me.

"I took their numbers and wiped their minds so they couldn't remember. I hid their consciousness in a fishbowl I kept buried in the sand. I couldn't release the pink wisps without them returning to their rightful bodies and ratting me out."

I can't believe it. All those patients in the asylum, showing up with their eyes glassy and their Skills gone—everyone assumed their Skills got stolen by the maze monster; but all this time, the monster was Landon. The hero. *My* hero. Stealing others' capacity for Skills so he could keep all the Skills to himself. A glut of Skills. I had zero Skills, and his two weren't enough for him. He just kept taking more and more and more, not caring what happened to the people he stole them from.

"The Leader caught on. He had too many cameras for anything to go unnoticed in Trinnea for too long. He told me I could keep doing it if I agreed to keep up the labyrinth's reputation to protect him. I had to agree to scramble anyone who went inside—even Blanks."

As if Blanks didn't have it hard enough. "But . . . Nadine." A tear drips down my face.

"I'm so sorry, Zadie. The Leader made me promise. I didn't have a choice."

"There's always a choice! You're as bad as the Warden."

"Calm down."

"You're doing to them what they did to me. You've made all of Trinnea your slaves."

"It's not the same."

"It is the same! I don't know you anymore."

Silence hangs heavy in the wake of my shout. Landon swallows, his Adam's apple bobbing up and down. "I haven't changed. I'm the same guy I always was."

I open my mouth, then close it. This isn't my Landon. My Landon is a hero. My sun, shining in a dark night sky. My Landon is the boy who hid my stolen apple to save me from the Warden's wrath. This power-hungry dictator isn't my Landon. I don't know who he is anymore.

Maybe I never did.

I don't know what to believe. I wish I didn't love him. I wish I could bleed the love for Landon out of my heart like the infection it is. I've spent ten years building him a shrine inside me; its walls are too thick to break with a single blow.

But I'm not the same girl I was when I fell in love with him.

I'll never be that girl again. He can't change what he's done. He can't take back the things he told me, and I can't un-hear them. I'll never look at him without seeing Nadine, vacant and empty, staring back at me behind the asylum window.

Maybe Landon was always this way, and I was too smitten to see it. Maybe he hasn't changed—but I have.

Landon's face softens. "I'm so sorry, Zadie. I never meant to hurt you. I only ever wanted to help you, to make things better for you." He brushes a lock of hair behind my ear. "I love you."

My heart explodes and the dam breaks, flooding my face with tears. I want to tell him I love him too. I want to forget any of this happened. I want to go back to a week ago and stop myself from leaving Trinnea.

But I can't.

"Don't cry." He wraps his arms around me. I let him.

We stand like this for a while, my face buried in his chest. I know I have to pull away. I have to leave him behind.

"I thought you'd agree with me," he says. "I really did. I thought you'd want to rule Trinnea with me, be my queen. Keep everyone safe and happy, living in the glass sphere. I didn't know you'd be so upset."

I look into his honey eyes and see the little boy who comforted me in the bunks. I wish he could be that little boy again. Carefree. Kind. "I can't agree with that, Landon. Not after everything they did to me. It's wrong."

"So . . . you're never going to want that?" Landon gives me a sad smile. "Okay."

Before I can respond, he presses his lips to mine. My insides turn to jelly. I know I shouldn't, but I'm kissing him back. I am so weak. I hate myself for allowing this, but I don't want him to stop. I've wanted this for so long. I twine my fingers in his light hair, savoring the softness.

He puts his hands on my waist, pulling me closer to deepen the kiss. I close my eyes and open myself up to him. Everything inside me flutters.

There's a pull in my stomach. It works its way through my body, tugging up my chest.

Something's wrong.

My throat tingles. What's happening?

I try to pull back, but Landon holds me firmly in place. His mouth is cemented to mine. The more I struggle, the tighter he holds me, pinning my arms to my sides.

Right as he lets go, I jerk my knee into his groin.

Landon doubles over in pain.

Back off! I shout the words, but silence comes out instead. Panic jolts through me. I try to talk, but nothing happens. Not a croak. Not even a rasp. I press my hands over my mouth.

Landon straightens up. "I'm sorry, Zadie. I'll give your voice back when I can be sure you won't try to stop me."

I clutch my throat, feeling for a vibration in my vocal chords. There's nothing.

"Please try and understand."

I jump back, holding my hands up. Fear pulses through me.

"Don't worry. I'll keep you safe. I'll keep Trinnea safe. I know you're struggling to come to terms with it, but it's for the best. You shouldn't compare me to the Warden, though. It's not like that. I'm not beating them, not hurting them." He shrugs. "That's not me. I'm not a monster."

I have no voice. No way to call for help. My best friend did this to me. He was the monster all along.

That familiar knot twists inside me, sucking the air from my lungs. I am a captive again. A prisoner to a different type of Warden.

"Now, Zadie, I hope we can get past this."

I glower at him. There's no getting past this.

Give me my voice, I mouth.

"In time, I will. All you need to do is be amenable."

A fire lights inside me, burning me from within. He has freed me from one prison and thrown me into another.

Shouts erupt from the screens, jerking our attention. Dex knocks out Augustus with a quick elbow to the face.

Landon frowns. "What is going on down there?"

The three guards are no match for Dex's Skills, and within moments, they're sprawled across the floor. One of them twitches, releasing a pained moan.

"Zadie!" Dex calls, punching the twitching man in the face and knocking him out cold. "Shae!"

I stomp my feet as loud as I can. *Dex! I'm up here!* I shout, even though the words make no sound.

"Well we can't have this." Landon cracks his knuckles. "I'm going to go take care of him."

Not if I can help it. I pounce on Landon from behind, jumping onto his back. He yelps, struggling against me.

I loop my arm around his neck.

Dex! Dex! Find me!

Landon snaps his fingers. My body goes rigid. I slide off him and fall to the ground, hitting a cushion that appeared out of nowhere.

"I never thought I'd see the day you tried to hurt me, Zadie. I thought we could trust each other." Landon adjusts his shirt. "I need to go deal with Dex. I'll be right back." He darts out of the room.

The moment he's gone, I throw myself at the door. I jiggle it, kick it, slam my body against it, but it doesn't budge.

There has to be a way out.

Ssssszadie . . .

The hair on my neck pricks up. The sand guardian can't be here. I killed her.

"Hello, Zadie."

I whip out my letter opener.

The sand guardian sits cross-legged on Landon's throne. I recognize her new form from the tea party. She's that tall, spindly figure with the bird's nest growing flowers on her head.

"Oh, put that thing away." She rolls her eyes at my weapon. "I know *that* one's not dripping in venom. Can't hurt me, girl."

Help me, I mouth. *Please.*

"Well, I wish I could. Sincerely." She doesn't sound sincere. "But I can't. Against the rules, you know. Plus, I'm the type to hold a grudge, and you did drive a poison blade into my chest. If you recall."

I sink to the floor, burying my face in my arms. It's hopeless.

"You destroyed my body. This one will have to do, for now. But it doesn't fit me quite right." She sighs. "I miss my horns. Ah, well. It appears you're the one in the predicament after all. So I've done my job."

I'm not in the mood. She can be smug somewhere else.

"Oh, don't give me that look. It's not my fault you're stuck here. Tsk tsk. I told you not to trust him. Guess you didn't listen."

My jaw slowly drops. She wasn't warning me about Dex; she was warning me about Landon.

"You didn't actually think I meant the dark haired boy, did you?"

I press my lips together. She was purposely coy and she knows it. I wish I had another poison knife; I'd fling it through her head.

"No, I like Dex," she says. "I almost feel bad about what I did to him. Almost."

My eyes narrow. *What did you do?* I mouth at her.

"I'm a liar. It's who I am. Sometimes I lie. Sometimes I tell the truth." She shrugs.

What was the lie? I mouth.

The sand guardian examines her fingernails. "It's fascinating. The ones so quick to dive onto a fleeting speck of hope are always the ones who have nothing left to lose. They're so gullible. It's almost too easy."

What was the lie? I get to my feet. *Tell me!*

"Find a person dripping in desperation? They'll believe anything, really. Even nonsense you write on a mirror."

I stomp toward her. *What did you do?*

"I did my job, Zadie. I keep people in the labyrinth by any means necessary. Never let them leave. The only time I failed my job was with you." She smirks. "But it all worked out. You're trapped in a different type of labyrinth now."

I close my eyes, forcing back the tears.

"Oh, don't cry, silly girl. You have everything you wanted. Power over those who harmed you. The boy you love. It's your perfect world. Aren't you happy? Is it everything you dreamed?"

No. It isn't. If I could go back and slap that silly dream out of the old Zadie, I'd do it in a heartbeat.

I am held hostage by this perfect world. Smothered by it.

What did you do? I mouth again, wishing I had a voice behind it. *What lie did you tell him?*

Dex races down a hallway on the screen. His shouts echo through the speakers. "Zadie! Shae! Where are you?"

"You'll know soon enough," the sand guardian says. "You can watch as it all plays out." She winks at me before vanishing into the air.

Dread boils inside me. I grip the screen with both hands, wishing Dex could see me through it. *Come on. Find me.*

"Shae!" he shouts, fire blazing in his hands. "Zadie!"

To my horror, a girl's voice responds. "Dex! I'm here!"

I know that voice. It's *my* voice.

No.

"Zadie!" Dex turns on his heel and charges down another corridor.

Stop. Don't go that way.

"Dex! Help me!"

"I'm coming!"

Turn around. It's a trap.

Don't do this, Landon.

"Down here!" My voice cries out. "They locked me up!"

No. Stop.

I follow him to the next screen. Dex rips open the wooden door. He becomes black smoke, billowing down the stairs at top speed.

It strikes me that he could've escaped the Palace, fled back into the maze. He could have left me behind—found his sister and ran. But he didn't.

The smoke transforms back into Dex at the bottom of the stairs. He flares his hands out, scanning the empty room. "Where are you?"

My heart thuds when I recognize the stone walls. It's the dungeon. *Don't fall for it. Get out of there.*

"I'm in here! Hurry!"

I see what's going to happen before it does. Dex storms into the open cell. Before he realizes it's empty, thick glass spreads itself over his exit, blocking him in.

Fire flies from his palms. The gust hits the wall and fizzles out. He creates a metal anvil out of thin air and chucks it at the glass; it doesn't crack.

Come on. Break.

A figure steps out of the shadows.

"Help me, Dex." It's my voice again. But it's coming from Landon's mouth. "Save me."

Dex seethes at the realization. He slams his fists against the glass.

My throat burns. I'm helpless. All I can do is watch.

Landon flicks a lightning bolt between his fingers. "Hello, Dex," he says in his normal voice. "Long time no see."

"If you hurt them, I'll kill you with my bare hands."

"Hard to do that when you're in my dungeon. But never fear, I'm not hurting anyone. *I'm* not the Devil of Trinnea."

Dex's jaw clenches. "Where are they?"

"Where's Zadie? She's Trinnea's beautiful new Blank queen. Which brings me to why I'm here." He stretches the electricity in his hands. Dex's muscles tense. It makes me uneasy. Landon might know about Dex's past. Maybe he's using it to mess with him. "You threatened our queen in the garden earlier. That's treason."

Dex and Landon square off on either side of the glass, neither one daring to blink.

"In case you weren't aware of our laws—I don't know what all that time in the maze has done to your basic reasoning—the penalty for treason is death."

Dex doesn't falter. His face doesn't twinge with anything except rage.

"As king, I'm required to carry out your sentence myself."

"If you try to kill me I'll take you down with me."

Landon shakes his head. "Your mental-blocking Skill only gets you so far. I'm afraid it won't save you from the gallows. Or the firing squad. Or . . . something else. I haven't decided which method best atones for your many crimes."

Mental blocking. That's how he's avoided Landon's Labyrinth Stare all these years. That's his sixth Skill.

"I vowed the first time I met you that I would destroy you," Dex says. "I haven't forgotten what you've done."

"Why? Because I blocked you in the maze? Stopped you and your fugitive sister from fleeing the Palace like a couple of cowards?"

My mouth tightens.

Dex flicks a wave of metal at the glass, aimed directly at Landon's face. His eyes are lethal. "I will kill you."

"You can try. I'm going upstairs now." Landon yawns. "My queen is waiting for me."

Dex pounds the glass. "Zadie's not your prisoner!" I've never heard him shout so loud. "Where's Shae? Where's my sister, you scum?"

Landon walks straight up the stairs as if he can't hear him. His coldness freezes me to my core.

Dex's Skills rain down on the glass long after Landon disappears from view. He shouts my name, shouts Shae's.

A gruff, scratchy laughter fills the air. "Shae. I remember Shae."

I click some buttons to pan out the camera. The phony old Leader leans against the wall of his adjacent cell, separated from Dex by a thick layer of rock.

Dex's lip curls back. I can tell he recognizes the voice. "Where is she?"

"Shae. Subject Gamma. Tiny girl, jet-black hair. You ran away with her, into the maze. I sent my guards after you. I remember it well."

"Where is she?" Dex repeats, raising his voice. "Answer me you murderous traitor, or I'll rip your throat out."

The Leader smirks. "They brought her back to the Palace. We finished our tests. She's been dead for years."

Dex's face pales. I press my shaking hand over my mouth, disbelieving.

That poor little girl.

I can't take my eyes off the screen. After all those years suffering in the maze, kidnapping Blanks and leading me to the Palace, it was all for nothing. The sand guardian sent him on a wild goose chase, just to distract him and prevent him from completing the maze. How disgusting that she'd force him to target and kill a Blank as part of her little game, like we're just people to throw away. People like Dex, and me, and all the Blanks and the Selected Six, we were never even seen as people. Just pawns.

Landon could walk in at this moment and drive a stake through Dex's chest. I don't even think he'd feel it.

Dex slides to the floor like a rag doll. My heart cracks. I touch the screen, wishing he knew I was here.

Footsteps patter in the hallway, getting closer.

My sweaty fingers tighten around the heavy letter opener. I savor its weight in my hand. I am not powerless anymore.

"I'm back." Landon waltzes through the door. I quickly hide my weapon behind my back. "Sorry about that." His eyes coast over the screens, still showing Dex in his cell. "Were you . . . watching that?"

I give a terse nod, clenching my weapon.

"Ah, well. It is your kingdom too, after all. Are you hungry? You must be starving."

Give me my voice, I mouth again.

"We've been over this already. I'm happy to give it back to you, as soon as I can trust you."

Trust? You want to talk about trust?

He says he loves me, but this is not love. This is power. And he has taken all of my power away.

Venom runs through my veins. They have taken everything from me. My mother. My voice. My freedom. This is Landon's fault. The Leader's fault. They were in it together for so long, I don't know where one's culpability ends and the other's begins.

"We should take a walk through the garden," Landon says. "I bet you'll recognize all the plants. I couldn't identify any of them." He laughs.

I can't feel anything anymore. All I know is rage.

"Then I'll show you your new room. You're welcome to share mine, of course, but I figured you would want your own. For now."

There is still a part of me that doesn't want to hurt him. But I must shut that part off. I must force myself to stay numb.

"How does that sound?"

No. He has not taken everything from me. I am brave. I am strong. And I am *not* powerless.

My anger boils over. I know what I must do. Before I can stop myself, I plunge the letter opener at his neck.

It hits an invisible barrier six inches from his skin, unable to break through. My breath catches. I stab the air again; it feels like hitting brick.

Bile churns inside me. I can't kill him. He can't be stopped. It's impossible.

Landon sighs. "You can't hurt me. I'm too powerful. I wish you'd stop trying." He holds out his hand. "Give me the letter opener."

It's useless. I am his prisoner.

Determination flares up inside me like fire.

But I can stop him from imprisoning everyone else.

I pivot and hurl the heavy spike across the room. It strikes the pink orb, shattering it into a million pieces. Glass showers the floor. Direct hit.

"No." Landon's jaw drops. "No!" He races toward the obliterated sphere, but it's too late.

A deafening whoosh fills the air. Pink wisps fly around us like tiny sparrows on a mission. They bounce against the walls and ceiling for a moment before zipping out the open door.

I may have lost. But he has not won. There is hope.

The last wisp zings past me, brushing my skin. Goosebumps prickle on my arm where it touched. Maybe it's my Ma. Maybe it's Nadine. Maybe it's a stranger. Still, I take comfort in the brief contact. It makes me feel less alone.

Landon's face burns red. "Sit. Down."

At his words, my legs push me forward. I'm walking toward the throne like a puppet on strings. My butt plops onto the red cushion against my will. My hands perch themselves on the armrests. I try to twitch my fingers, but they won't move. It's like they're glued to the chair.

Raised voices erupt from the screen speakers. One by one, Trinneans blink to life. They stagger up and down streets, getting their bearings. Some hug each other. Others desperately plow toward the stage, seeking loved ones. A few test their Skills, crying with joy. I imagine how strange it must have been, living with power their whole life only to lose it all within minutes. Maybe that's where Blanks are strong. We have a different kind of power, one they can't take away.

Landon watches as his plan disintegrates. Sure, he could enchant them again, but it would take time. Trinneans will fight back. He's got his bubble wall, but as I've seen, there are ways around it.

I grin as a woman tackles one of the Sirs to the ground. Two more Trinneans use their re-obtained Skills to stop another Sir in his tracks. Soon, there's a mob of Skilled, taking down the people who held them hostage in their own bodies.

The remaining Sirs rush to their tri-bikes, speeding into the desert as fast as they can. They plow straight through the gate, demolishing it. Blanks in the wastes jump back to avoid getting run over, then peek hesitantly through the gap in the wall that kept them out for so long. A couple of them hesitantly step over the threshold.

If Landon is taking over, everyone's going to know about it. He can no longer sweep in and assume power while everyone's hypnotized into complying. It will not be peaceful. I hope they give him hell, fight him tooth and nail. I will do the same.

Landon says he wants to protect Blanks, but it's clear all

he wants is power over them—over everybody. He's looking for a cowering little Blank girl he can control? I will fight him every step of the way. A cage of ice forms around my heart. He wants a queen? I'll give him one. A brutal, vindictive queen bent on burning her king's reign to the ground. I will trick Landon into returning my voice. I will play him the way he played me. And I will show him how *weak* I really am.

Landon smiles a calm, steady grin, but I know it's contrived. "It's okay," he says. "I'll work with this. Trinneans are free now—free to accept their new ruler."

I roll my eyes.

"You watch, Zadie. They'll love us. We'll be worshipped more than the Leader ever dreamed."

Someone does wheelies on a tri-bike, shouting obscenities about the Sir she stole it from.

In the crowd, I find Barton's face. He's grinning, as always. I wonder where he spent the past week—probably doing his job, hanging with his boyfriend, staying low. I miss our talks at the watch-post.

A wave of sand carries my Ma onto the stage. Shading her eyes from the sun, she frantically scans the crowd. A stone drops into my chest; she's looking for me.

Everyone floods toward Center Square seeking answers. When collective gasps and cheers fill the screen, my ears prick.

People in green medical robes wander through the sand. The asylum's former patients grin and laugh, full of life. Regardless of their previous statuses, they're all Blanks now. I recognize Jenny, bounding through the crowd. She latches onto an older man in a Blank indenture uniform who must be her father.

Another girl with curly brown hair sweeps through the throng of people–*Nadine.* She cups her hand to her mouth and calls out in the crowd, her voice lost in the soup of Trinneans.

My sister dances on the stage in one of the Sirs' jackets. I wouldn't want to be the Sir who faced her wrath. It's good seeing her eyes back to their natural shade of brown.

"I'm going to address the crowd," Landon says. Sweat beads across his brow. He runs his hand down his body; his clothes morph into regal crimson robes. A spiky gold crown forms on his head. Most people would assume he's dressing for his new role, but I know better. He's about to demand respect from thousands of people he wronged. This could go very badly, and he knows it. If Trinneans don't realize he hired the Sirs and enchanted them, the asylum's patients will speak the truth about what he's done. His little secret about the identity of the monster in the maze won't be a secret for much longer.

"You should look the part, too." Landon draws a circle in the air. A silver crown weaves itself out of nothing. Tiny silver flowers adorn a silver vine that wraps itself around the head-piece. "I thought the leaves suited you."

Leaves from Landon would've meant something to me, once. Our garden was my safe place, but he violated that sanc-tity. I suppose the flowery tiara would be beautiful in a different context; now, it looks like a necklace from the sand guardian's death shrub. With a flick of his hand, the crown floats through the air and lands gently on my head. It's cold against my scalp.

"Do you like it?" he asks.

I don't let my face falter.

On screen, Chantry's gaze coasts over the square and she freezes. She leaps off the stage and elbows through the mass of people, nearly bowling them over. Within seconds, she throws her arms around Nadine, whose eyes are filled with life. Tears flood down their cheeks as they hold each other, not daring to let go. Chantry touches Nadine's face, as if not believing she's real.

I can't stop the bittersweet smile from exploding across my face. The Skilled–Blank divide isn't over—not when there is still so much hate in the hearts of so many Skilled—but seeing my sister and Nadine smile means everything in the world to me right now. There is still some good in the world. There is still love. There is still something to fight for.

"Good afternoon, Trinneans," Landon addresses the camera. He takes a seat in the other throne, puffing out his chest.

The crowd noise dims to silence. I sit still as Landon weaves an intricate tale—how the Leader forced him to attack Trinneans in the labyrinth all these years. How Landon boldly defeated the corrupt Leader and apprehended the criminal Dex. How he took control with a mission of peace.

Murmurs float through the crowd. Some people nod along with Landon. Others eye him with suspicion. Chantry shields Nadine, her hands balling into fists.

"In our new society, there will be no rankings," Landon announces. "As of today, all Blanks are free to live as they please. I will set a decree in place to destroy the bunks and demolish the wall that separated us for too long. Also, we need to begin a diplomatic relationship with the neighboring towns, and that doesn't happen by locking ourselves away."

I fight back a laugh; count on a Skilled to assume all Skilled will magically start treating Blanks like human beings, just because he said there are no more rankings. I'll believe it when I see it.

"From now on, *everyone* will share Trinnea's resources. Blank children will receive an education alongside their Skilled peers. From this day forward, Blanks and Skilled will live harmoniously—as equals. Anyone currently indentured to the deceased Warden or anyone else is hereby released from their contract."

The news should thrill me. I should be excited at the prospect of Blank equality. But I am not an equal in Landon's new world. I am still at the whim of somebody with more power than me. Saying inequality is over doesn't make it so. A few simple words can't erase what they've done to us for centuries. People's minds won't change just because he demands it. He is not our savior; he is another captor, set on ruling us. He is the next iteration of the Leader.

I have Dex's maps. If I can get a communicator, somehow, I can send them to someone in Trinnea. My eyes immediately find Chantry in the crowd. My sister is there. With the fire in her heart, she could complete the maze. Maybe, together, we could overthrow him. I will get the maps to her. Somehow.

"To celebrate the unity of Blanks and Skilled, I am appointing myself your Skilled king. The lovely Zadie Kalvers beside me will be your Blank queen."

I will not rest until I have my voice. Until Landon pays for what he's done.

I am brave.

Landon thumps his fist to his shoulder. "All hail the new Trinnea!"

I am strong.

The entire population of Trinnea mimics his gesture. "Hail!"

And I am not afraid.

ACKNOWLEDGMENTS

First of all I would like to thank the brilliant team at Flux and North Star Editions, who saw potential in my weird murder-maze story. Mari Kesselring, thank you for believing in this story enough to acquire it and for all your support. Ashley Wyrick, I'm so thankful I had an editor who really "got" the story (and tolerated all my annoying emails!). Carlisa Cramer—I first connected with Flux because you requested my #Pitmad pitch—thank you for all your support! And shout out to the design team, because my jaw dropped when I first got this gorgeous cover in my inbox. Finally, thank you to everyone else at Flux/ North Star who helped *Red Labyrinth* get to where it is.

To my super agent, Sarah Landis, I know you didn't technically represent this book, but your endless support for my books and career has been instrumental in *Red Labyrinth's* success, and I'm so lucky to have you on my team!

Jamie Howard, as always, thank you for being such an amazing CP and friend! *Red Labyrinth* wouldn't have gotten this far without you. Thanks for instilling in me your love of villains (you're clearly a terrible influence). I am forever so thankful you responded to my #CPMatch tweet back in 2014.

Jennifer Stolzer, as always, thank you for your amazing support, friendship, and CPing over the years. You're an epic plot whisperer and I'm so grateful I was able to talk through all plot holes and snags in *Red Labyrinth* with you—your notes made it infinitely better!

Thank you to Amanda Heger and Marie Meyer—I'm so

lucky to have such wonderfully supportive and talented author friends on my side.

My fabulous beta readers: Julie Abe, Kirsten Cowan, Monica Craver, Diana Gardin, Charlotte Gruber, Amanda Heger, Shannon Knight, Jamie Krakover, Marie Meyer, Annika Sharma, Ron Walters, Ara Grigorian, Marnee Blake, Tegan Wren, Diana Pinguicha, Sophia Henry and everyone else: whether you read the beginning, a few chapters, or the whole book, your feedback and support helped Zadie's story get to where it is—thank you for everything! Also, thank you to fabulous authors Joanna Ruth Meyer, Amy Hilliges, Erin Callahan, Kate L Mary, Jess Ruddick, Zoulfa Katouh, and Laura Steven for all your support.

A big thank you to all my Twitter writing buddies who are some of the best and most supportive people in the world—I'm so thrilled we are all in this publishing community together!

To #TeamLandis—Elisabeth, Erin, Jennie, Jess, Julie, Ron, and Shelby—I'm so grateful for all your support and so thankful to know such talented writers!

Shout out to everyone in the St. Louis Writer's Guild, Electric Eighteens, the NAC, and the Write Pack for being such amazing writers I am lucky to call friends.

Thank you to all the agents and industry professionals who have ever given me feedback on this book. It was all appreciated, taken into consideration, and used to improve the manuscript.

Vincent, you're the best husband in the world, and I could never have gotten this far without your love and support over the years. Thank you for everything. I love you.

Dad, thank you for all your love and support and for everything you've done for me and my books. I love you!

Thank you to my in-laws, the Servellos, Murrays, Bombardiers, and Pions, for all your support!

Thank you to all of the Tates, Rosses, Siegels, and everyone else in my family.

To all my incredible family and friends—Caitlin Clark, Kirsten Cowan, Kristina Rieger, Bekah Mar-Tang, Caitlin Stevenson, Sarah Winters, Corey Landsman, Joanna Wolbert, Caity Bean, Alexis Carr, Audrey Desbiens, Katie Levesque, Brett Roell, Monica Craver, Ashley Taylor Ward, Katie Gill, Jill Schaffer, Brendan Bly, Eric and Amy Lousararian, Molly Hyant, Amy Debevoise, Paige Donaldson, the Dizzy Dames, Robin and Larry Corson, and everyone else—you know who you are—thank you for being so supportive and staying friends with me even though I'm a weirdo who writes about mazes that kill people. You're the best friends in the world and I'm incredibly lucky to have all of you in my life.

And finally, I could not have gotten this far without my amazing mother, Jessica Ross Tate, whom I will always carry in my heart.

ABOUT THE AUTHOR

Meredith Tate grew up in Concord, New Hampshire, where she fell in love with the many worlds of science fiction and fantasy. Pursuing her love of travel, Meredith spent a semester in London and then backpacked in Europe for a month before earning her master's degree in social work from the University of New Hampshire. After graduation, Meredith worked in the field in Boston for a few years before deciding to pursue her dream of telling stories. Meredith and her husband spent three wonderful years in St. Louis, Missouri. They recently moved to Zurich, Switzerland as expats. Meredith spends her days eating cheese and chocolate by the lake, and writing about characters much braver than she is.